firefly

AIM TO MISBEHAVE

ALSO AVAILABLE FROM TITAN BOOKS

firefly

Big Damn Hero by James Lovegrove (original concept by Nancy Holder)

The Magnificent Nine by James Lovegrove

The Ghost Machine by James Lovegrove

Generations by Tim Lebbon

Life Signs by James Lovegrove

Carnival by Una McCormack

What Makes Us Mighty by M. K. England

Coup de Grâce by Una McCormack

AIM TO MISBEHAVE

firefly

BY ROSIEE THOR

TITAN BOOKS

Firefly: Aim to Misbehave
Hardback edition ISBN: 9781789098396
E-book edition ISBN: 9781789098433

Published by Titan Books
A division of Titan Publishing Group Ltd
144 Southwark Street, London SE1 0UP
www.titanbooks.com

First edition: November 2024
10 9 8 7 6 5 4 3 2 1

This is a work of fiction. All of the characters, organizations, and events portrayed in this novel are either products of the author's imagination or are used fictitiously. Any resemblance to actual persons, living or dead (except for satirical purposes), is entirely coincidental.

A CIP catalogue record for this title is available from the British Library.

Printed and bound by CPI (UK) Ltd, Croydon, CR0 4YY.

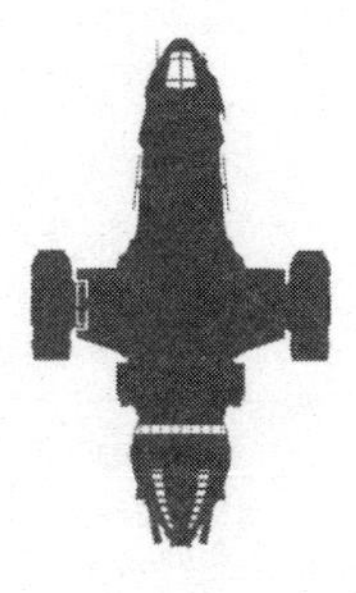

For fallen friends and those still flying.

1

Henry Evans didn't like God. It wasn't that he didn't believe, just that he didn't have much proof that God liked him either. All these years, and the big man upstairs hadn't done much to make his life better. Despite his imagined mutual disdain, every so often Henry got the distinct feeling he was being watched, and not by the raccoons patrolling the dark back alleys of Patrick, capital city of the planet Valentine.

"You're late," he said into the night.

"How do you do that?"

"Do what?" Henry turned to face the direction of the voice just as the familiar figure of Lyle Horne stepped into the dim light of the alley behind Scatter Shot, the once bustling but now derelict tavern where they'd made their hideaway.

"Know exactly when I'm coming." Lyle was not a tall man, but what he lacked in height he made up for in sheer magnetism. A sly smile twisted his lips and a flicker of gold caught in the hazel of his eyes. "It's like you're some kind of oracle."

"I'm just observant," Henry said, and uncrossed his arms, the tension in his muscles unspooling at the sight of his partner. Truth was, he'd mistaken some native possum-type creature for Lyle just a few minutes earlier, but he wasn't about to tell him that. Let him think Henry was impressive once in a while. "So, what kept you?"

"I don't know if I like the path this narrative's takin'. *You're late, what kept you…* You know I don't keep a schedule, Hevans."

"Your relationship with time is rather fluid, yes."

"All my relationships are."

"You gonna tell me what you got or keep me guessing?" It'd been a week since their last job and Henry was getting a tad nervous. They didn't sit and wait, he and Lyle. That wasn't their way. It was much harder to hit a moving target, and Henry and Lyle hadn't stopped moving since they'd started up together a few months back. When the next job hadn't lined up, Henry had thought it might be a welcome break from all the action, but that was six days ago and he wasn't breathing any easier.

Henry motioned Lyle inside the abandoned tavern. Splintered wood stuck up from the floorboards, and a large ceiling beam had split the counter in two—a safety hazard if Henry had ever seen one. It was better this way, though. No one would come looking for a couple of lowlifes in a dried-up watering hole.

"Got us a job," Lyle said, his grin as wide as his big-brimmed hat. "Well, got us some loot."

"And you got us a buyer, I hope?"

"Surely do." Lyle drew out one of the more stable chairs and plopped down. "A potential buyer, anyway. We just gotta track 'em down."

"Why do I get the feeling this isn't so much a job as a hunch?" Henry had picked up most of Lyle's tells, but it didn't take much to know when Lyle was hedging. He was always hedging. That was Lyle's way, and most of the time it worked in Henry's favor, even if it had taken him by surprise the first few times. Maybe *surprise* wasn't strong enough a word for it. It took him by outrage, or by horror, the cavalier way Lyle carved a path through life, leaving bodies in his wake—sometimes enemies, sometimes friends. Henry didn't plan to be one of them. By now, he knew better than to ask questions. With Lyle, you either followed or you didn't, and Henry wasn't about to get left behind.

"Do you trust me?" Lyle asked, throwing Henry a wounded look.

They were the same words he'd asked that first night when they'd met, when Henry had been double-crossed by his own crew, left bruised and bleeding and primed to take the blame for their misdeeds. "Do you trust me?" Lyle had asked without preamble. Henry hadn't even known Lyle's name yet, but he had a kind smile and a gun, and Henry found he needed both desperately, so he'd said yes.

He'd kept on saying yes, and it had kept on working for him, so he rolled his eyes, drew up a chair, and said it again. "Yes, fine, I trust you. Now, what have you got?"

Lyle's face quieted and he placed a small data card on the table between them. "Took this off a uniform at the Crooked Rose."

Henry's stomach dropped. There had been rumblings for months. At first, Henry had thought it was all talk—the Allied planets were so numerous, it seemed impossible that they'd all come together and actually agree on a course of action—but then the soldiers had come, and war was officially in motion. An independent movement had sprung up quickly, and no matter how hard the Alliance tried to eradicate them, they kept popping back up like weeds. Henry didn't like to think about it if he could help it. War didn't make work like his any easier, and the longer it went on, the more likely it was to sweep him and Lyle up in its current.

"Alliance? Lyle, what do you think you're doing, messing with them? I thought we agreed—no war," Henry said.

"War's coming for us all, Hevans. I ain't of a mind to wait around for it to get me."

"So, you went to an upscale bar and pickpocketed an Alliance soldier?"

"Officer, at least. Might've been ranked higher. Wasn't really paying attention to his medals. I was busy swiping this." Lyle tapped the data card, a light-gray chip with nothing more than a faded Blue Sun logo on its top side.

"And what if he noticed your hands in his pockets, Lyle?"

"Oh, he noticed." Lyle's eyes danced with mirth. "I reckon we got a few hours' peace before he realizes it's gone, and by then we'll be rid of it anyhow. Independents will be pleased as punch to get their hands on this kind of intel."

"I don't like this. Not at all."

"That would have more weight if you liked much of anything."

That wasn't really fair, or true. Henry liked things. He liked clean socks and the scent of rosemary. He liked watching the sunrise and the sound of a city asleep. He liked fruit when he could get it, and he liked soup. And loath though he was to admit it, he liked Lyle Horne as well. He wouldn't say so, of course—the man would be even more insufferable than he already was if he ever got wind of anything more substantial than a begrudging agreement to a mutually beneficial partnership coming from Henry. And Henry wasn't all that keen to alert Lyle to any fondness that his partner might find a way to weaponize against him, should their luck turn.

In truth, though Henry's time working with Lyle Horne had been brief, from the moment Lyle had swooped to Henry's rescue, they'd been a real team. Life hadn't been easy since Henry left home—it hadn't been easy before, either—but these past few months working with Lyle had at least been fun.

"All right, say I'm in. What then?" Henry asked warily.

"What then? We get ourselves a drink to celebrate."

"To celebrate what?"

"Henry Evans, getting off his high horse." Lyle punched him

playfully on the arm. "That's the fastest you've ever agreed to a job, I think. Bring out the fireworks, folks, we've gotta commemorate this." Lyle gestured around as if to invite a nonexistent crowd in on their private joke.

"Very funny. You buying?"

Lyle chuckled, one hand braced on the table as he tipped his chair to balance on its back legs. The chair, as it turned out, had other plans. The wood splintered under his weight, sending Lyle crashing to the ground.

"Lyle!" Henry reached for him, their hands meeting just before Lyle hit the floor.

Laughter bubbled up from the man on the ground. "You pay," he said weakly. "This chair ain't the only one around here who's broke."

Before Henry had a chance to argue, there was a sound like a gunshot and the world around him went sideways as Lyle kicked Henry's feet out from under him and pulled him down.

"What happened to a few hours?"

"Guess my estimations were off," Lyle whispered. "*Run.*"

Henry didn't need telling twice. He scrambled forward on his hands and knees, catching a glint of shiny metal out of the corner of his eye before he dove for one of the broken windows. Splinters of wood and glass scraped his arms, but otherwise he was unscathed when he rolled to a stop outside.

Brushing himself off, Henry ducked behind a trash can in the alley as the sound of gunfire filled the air. "I told you this was a bad idea," he began, but Lyle wasn't beside him. Henry cast about for any flashes of movement, and there, illuminated by a small spotlight sweeping the tavern, was Lyle, darting back toward the table. He was visible for only a moment, as his fingers closed around the data card, before he bolted toward the alley.

"I told you to run!" he yelled, grabbing Henry's elbow and pulling.

As Henry let the momentum carry him forward, he caught a glimpse of their pursuer. An Alliance officer, it was not. Instead, a steel, angular drone exited the Scatter Shot tavern, a low hum reverberating through the space as it speared a bright pillar of light directly at them.

Henry dipped toward another alley, slinking deep into the shadows. He knew the streets of Patrick about as well as he knew Lyle—which was to say, by instinct alone—so he let himself be guided only by the soft patter of Lyle's boots on the concrete and the thunder in his veins.

"Lyle," he whisper-shouted as concrete bled into a dirt path. They were in outer ring of the city now. It was darker here, and the architecture had gone from ramshackle to almost nonexistent. Encampments of unhoused people spread out to the northeast, punctuated by the occasional street lamp. Henry couldn't hear the drone anymore, so he slowed to a jog. "What was that thing?"

"Some kind of Alliance drone, I guess." Lyle put his hands on his knees, panting. "Too bad. I was kind of hoping that *shuài* young officer would come looking for me himself."

Henry rolled his eyes. "You know we almost died, right?"

"*Almost* being the operative word."

Despite himself, Henry smiled. It was a good thing it was dark. He didn't need Lyle seeing that. "Now, about that buyer of yours—"

Lyle held up a hand.

Henry heard it before he saw it: a motor softer than a cat's purr. The spotlight came into view, shining down on them both. There was a moment of quiet as Henry stared wide-eyed, stunned into silence by the blinding light, but at the first sound of gunfire, Henry tackled Lyle into a large bush. They rolled out of the spotlight and back into the shadows.

"How in the hell did it follow us?" Lyle asked, his whisper a furnace in Henry's ear.

They laid still, not daring to move a muscle as the drone proceeded toward them. Moonlight illuminated the stamp on its metal plating—a blue semicircle with letters in English and Chinese above and below. *Blue Sun*. Henry had his answer.

"I think it's tracking the data card."

"Well, shit." Lyle tried to push himself up, but his arm buckled. Henry reached out to brace him and something dark and warm trickled down from his compatriot's bicep between Henry's fingers.

"You're bleeding."

"I'm fine. Just grazed me."

"Yeah, but you're *bleeding*."

"Doesn't matter," Lyle hissed, keeping low to the ground. "We'd best find our buyer, and quick. Then it won't be our problem anymore."

"It's our problem *now*," Henry said, but he needn't have bothered. Lyle was already gone into the night, and the drone wasn't far behind.

They ran until Henry's breath was as ragged as the slums they passed through. After several minutes, they finally shook the city. Here, at the edge of town, where Patrick nestled up against a steep drop-off, light pollution made way for dust and sky. They could see the stars, now—a wide sea of them, hosts to worlds unknown. Henry had left his own home planet behind, a thing he had never thought he'd do. Maybe someday Valentine would just be another place he'd lived once upon a time.

"It's no use," Henry panted. "They'll keep on following no matter what."

"That just means we've got something valuable." Lyle held up the data card, a glint of mischief in his eyes.

Henry just stared at the chaotic churn in Lyle's gaze, the endless depths of the unknown, not unlike the stars above. He'd seen that expression before. Nothing good ever came after.

There was danger in a look like that. But there was promise, too. It would be easy to follow Lyle anywhere he went. It would probably get them both killed.

Henry deliberated for a split second, then he grabbed the data card and bolted.

"*Hún dàn!*" Lyle called after him. "You owe me fifty percent!"

Henry didn't need to be a genius to know fifty percent of zero was better than dead. With all the strength he had left, he hurtled toward the cliff's edge, weaving back and forth as he went. The whirring of the drone and the pounding of Lyle's footsteps followed in his wake.

"Hevans, you son of a bitch, slow down!"

Henry did as he was told, not because Lyle asked but because the lip of the canyon was coming up mighty fast. He skidded to a halt in the loose dry dirt, kicking up a cloud of dust, and held the data card high in the air.

"Track this!" he shouted, then threw the card as far as he could into the abyss below.

Almost as if the world had slowed down around him, Henry watched the data card sail into the air, flying end over end, and the drone dive after it. The card could have meant a lot of money. It could have changed the tides of war. It could have been a whole lot of nothing. Now it was just a story of one wild night he'd had on Valentine.

"*Zāo gāo!*" Lyle shouted, hands outstretched.

The card was too far away. There was barely a sliver of a chance he'd catch it.

Lyle jumped anyway.

His shoulder bumped Henry's, and time—and gravity—caught up with them both. Henry's balance slipped, his foot catching on a protruding rock, and he went down. The ground caught him, once on his knee, then on his hip. Pain rocketed through his left side as he felt more than heard something snap. He rolled until he was flat on his back, staring up at the sky. His vision blurred, tears pricking his eyes.

"Hevans?" came the gruff voice of Lyle, muffled as though from far away. "Hevans, a little help?"

Henry twisted toward the sound and dragged himself on his hands back toward the edge.

There, hanging by his fingertips, was a red-faced Lyle.

Relief unspooled from Henry's shoulders, and he scrambled forward. "Take my hand."

Lyle shook his head. "Can't," he said.

"What do you mean, can't?" But his question was answered with a mere glance. Blood dripped down Lyle's other arm as it hung limp at his side, fingers closed in a fist. "Wasn't just a graze, was it?"

Lyle grimaced. "It was a good arm, too."

"And it will be again." Henry's knowledge of medicine wasn't precise, but he knew if he could just reach Lyle, he should be all right. "Just… stay there. I'll try to get closer."

Henry pushed himself forward, leaning out over the edge with his right foot hooked around a large rock. From there, he could just brush Lyle's knuckles with his fingertips.

"You're gonna have to grab me," he said, straining. "On three?"

Lyle bit down on his lip, eyes narrowed in pain, but he nodded.

"One… two… three!"

With a heave, Lyle pushed off the cliffside, and his hand grasped Henry's.

"There we are." Henry gripped Lyle's hand as hard as he could. "I won't let go," he said. It was more a promise to himself than to Lyle. "Now, slow and steady, all right?" He tried to pull Lyle up, but his strength wasn't with him. Between the pain in his leg and the awkward angle, he couldn't get the leverage he needed. "We'll just have to keep trying. Maybe if we—"

"Hevans," Lyle cut in, catching Henry's gaze with his. There was a focus there that went beyond pain, beyond desperation. "I need you to listen."

"What is it?" Henry asked.

A low whir of a motor answered.

The drone was back.

Henry's gaze darted around, searching for the data card. Maybe he hadn't thrown it as far as he'd thought. Then his eyes fell on Lyle's closed fist, and his heart sank.

"You stupid man," he murmured, words lost on the wind.

"Do you trust me?" Lyle asked.

His reply came like a Pavlovian response, even though it couldn't have been less true. "Yes."

It was the last thing Henry Evans ever said to Lyle Horne.

The drone didn't fire a single shot before Lyle's hand slipped from Henry's. One moment he was there, hanging on to the cliff through sheer force of will. Then he wasn't.

Henry lay there at the edge of the cliff for a long time, staring at the place where Lyle had been. He watched the dust clear. He watched the drone fly away, down into the canyon. He watched the first pink and yellow rays peek over the horizon as White Sun rose in the sky.

Henry retreated from the light as it illuminated the cliff's edge, and he looked up at the sky. In the months, the years, the decades that followed, he would think about this moment and wonder. Was his grip not strong enough? Or was it his faith? Maybe it was neither. Maybe it was all chance, or maybe it was God's plan.

He'd left his home, he'd lost his way, and Lyle… was gone. Henry Evans was utterly alone in the 'verse. And still, somehow, he felt watched.

And so, for the first time in his life, Henry Evans got to his knees and prayed.

"I'm gonna need you to tell me what I'm lookin' at, little Kaylee," Captain Malcolm Reynolds said as he eyed the obstruction in the cargo bay—a row of shipping containers, a few chairs from the dining area, and the Mule, all lined up to form a ramshackle blockade.

"That'd be a flock of geese, Cap'n." Kaylee pulled at a loose thread on the waist of her jumpsuit, unraveling the petals of a blue embroidered flower she wore. "Nine of 'em, to be precise about it."

"Isn't that nice? One for each of us." Hoban Washburne, *Serenity*'s pilot, said as he descended the last few rungs of the ladder with a hop and flashed Mal a winning smile. "I'll take the one with the spot on its nose. Maybe grow back my mustache so we match. What about you, Jayne?"

"I ain't goin' nowhere near them birds." Jayne Cobb, their hired-muscle-slash-public-relations-officer wasn't difficult to spot, hiding inexpertly behind the weight rack in the corner of the bay. "I don't do geese, Mal."

Mal shook his head to clear it. He'd stumbled across plenty of *niú fèn* on his boat over the years—literally, in the case of their job transporting cattle for Sir Warwick Harrow—but a flock of pearl-white geese sure was a surprise. They toddled back and forth across the cargo bay, long curly feathers swaying.

"I'm less concerned about the what than the why," Mal said, taking a tentative step toward the birds. One of them let out an almighty honk and Mal raised his hands instinctively. The blockade his crew had built suddenly seemed a lot more necessary than it had before.

"Arvin dropped them off 'bout an hour ago." Kaylee said, a quaver in her voice. "Thought you had an understanding."

"I ain't in the business of takin' on new jobs 'fore I get paid for the last one." Mal turned toward the cargo-bay door and the dusty open planes of Brome, where Arvin Helios's Knorr-class cargo freighter was stationed in the distance.

They'd only been docked a few hours, but Mal didn't relish staying any longer than they had to. A remote moon of the planet Whittier in the Kalidasa system, Brome didn't have much to offer besides a meager market, a fuel refinery, and a good stretch of barren land on which to conduct his business without prying eyes. The plan was to drop the cargo, get paid, and move on. He wasn't interested in deviations. They needed coin. Badly. Without it, they couldn't keep *Serenity* in the sky, let alone feed her crew or keep them paid. If Arvin Helios was trying to pull one over on them, he had another thing coming.

"Payment, actually," said Wash. "Arvin said something about these being a valuable… variety? Species? Breed?"

"Sebastopol."

They all looked up to see River dangling her arms over the railing above the cargo bay. She wore a white dress and her hair fell across her face, swaying just like the goose feathers below.

"Don't go naming them just yet. We ain't keepin' them." Mal had come to respect the unpredictability of their youngest passenger in recent months. She and her brother, Simon, had earned their keep and then some with the job they'd pulled on Ariel, and though the money had finally run out, he wasn't likely to forget Simon's doctoring ways had saved his ear after their recent run-in with Adelai Niska. The fugitive siblings might have been trouble, but Mal was beginning to believe they'd prove their worth. Still, he didn't much think it wise to go mixing River's brand of peculiarity with potentially violent poultry.

"Sebastopol geese," River continued. "First documented on Earth-That-Was in the nineteenth century. A luxury bird. Very rare."

"How rare?" asked Jayne, leaning out from behind the weights rack.

"Didn't we agree, no more livestock after the cows?" Mal muttered as the rest of the crew joined them. Zoë Alleyne Washburne, Mal's first mate and perhaps the only person he'd truly trust his life with, led the group, followed by Shepherd Book and Inara, laden with a thick layer of dust and nothing much else. They'd gone with the intention of restocking *Serenity*'s meager kitchen, but to no avail, it seemed.

"Do they lay eggs?" asked the Shepherd. "Would be nice to cook with something other than artificial protein for a change. The market was a little sparse for my liking."

"I wouldn't say no to an omelet," Zoë said wistfully, leaning in to kiss her husband on the cheek.

Wash melted into the touch, eyes glazing over. "I wouldn't say no to watching you eat that omelet."

"Sebastopol geese lay on average only thirty eggs per year. Their plumage is quite valuable, though," River said.

"How valuable?" Jayne, extracted himself from his hiding place to join them on the far side of the barrier, a light in his eyes that could mean only one thing. "Changed my mind, Mal. Maybe I want one after all."

The geese appeared unperturbed by Jayne's declaration.

"Well, I certainly don't." Inara smiled, composure intact as always.

Mal tried not to admire her poise too overtly. Of all *Serenity*'s passengers, none embodied the ship's name so expertly as Inara. As much as she and Mal needled one another from time to time, she rarely lost her temper. Sometimes, he wished she would.

"Can I have hers, then?" Jayne asked.

Mal heaved a sigh. Of all the things his crew might get rowdy over, geese hadn't been on his mental list of possibilities when he'd woken that morning.

"Nobody's keeping the geese. We're giving them back, *dǒng ma*?" Mal turned to Kaylee, whose nervous fidgeting had resulted in a pile of blue thread at her feet. "You get them herded up while I track down Arvin and get us paid right and proper."

Kaylee looked into the enclosure with an expression of great trepidation. "I don't know, Cap'n. I'm not so good with animals. Their wings are so… flappy."

"I'll do it!" Jayne vaulted over the Mule and into the enclosure.

"This ain't a petting zoo," Mal muttered, but it was too late. Jayne landed on the other side of the barricade with a thump, and the volume of the geese's warbling increased tenfold. Their wings beat with tremendous force and they honked with furious abandon. Flappy, indeed.

"What's going on out here?" Simon Tam slid open the door to the infirmary, eyes wide and mouth agape as he took in the scene before him. "River?"

"They are full of honks and have teeth on their tongues." River leaned away from the railing. "I'm staying put."

"You heard your sister, Doc. You're not needed here." Jayne circled, center of gravity low as he closed in on his prey.

Mal checked his holster for his trusty pistol. The smooth grip of his Liberty Hammer was a comfort to him, even after all the bloodshed it had seen him through. There weren't many he could trust after the war, but his gun had never misfired. Well, rarely.

"You expecting a fight?" Zoë asked. She extracted herself from Wash's embrace and gestured toward the stairs.

Mal didn't need her to say it to know she was offering backup. Zoë was a better shot than him. Hell, she was a better *soldier* than him, no matter that the war was over. He'd take a bullet for her, and she him. Hopefully, it wouldn't come to that.

"Guess that depends on Arvin," Mal said.

Before he could stomp off in the direction of the scheming lowlife who'd somehow mistaken birds for platinum, there came an almighty yell from the enclosure. With a flurry of feathers and garbled honking, Jayne tumbled into the barricade, knocking several containers over as he fell, landing flat on his back, hands clasped over his face.

"My eye! The gorram goose got my eye!"

Kaylee and Wash scrambled to reform the wall around the geese while Shepherd Book knelt beside Jayne, prying the man's fingers away from his face to reveal a bloody gash.

"Well, you're wrong on two points, son," Shepherd Book said with a sigh, rocking back on his heels and hailing Simon over. "First, you haven't lost your eye—not yet."

"Don't feel like it." As soon as Book released him, Jayne's hands flew back up to cover his wound. "What's the second thing?"

"The doctor's services will be needed, after all."

Simon darted through the geese, who mostly ignored him. They'd either already satisfied their bloodlust thanks to Jayne or didn't perceive the doctor as much of a threat.

With Jayne attended to and the geese properly corralled once more, Mal nodded to Zoë and patted his Liberty Hammer. "Best get your gear."

"Mal?" Wash's voice took on a rising lilt, as it so often did when the captain took his wife on potentially dangerous missions. Since their run-in with Niska a few months back, Wash hadn't complained about the treacherous nature of Zoë's job—well, not much. Still, Mal wasn't about to leave her behind, not when Jayne was out of commission.

"I ain't lookin' to argue. Zoë and me are going to have a chat with Arvin and that's final."

"No, she isn't." Wash, pointed out at the horizon. "Neither of you is."

In the distance, Arvin Helios's Knorr freighter retreated in a cloud of dust. Its engines burned hazy against the bright summer sky as it sailed up, up, up… and then, it was gone.

3

Things never did go smoothly for the crew of *Serenity*. It was a marvel Mal still managed to be surprised by it.

It was supposed to be a simple job, but then weren't they all? The simpler they seemed, the worse the derailment. They'd picked up cargo on Beaumonde—a few crates of computer parts from one of the factories. Their contacts, Fanty and Mingo, a set of crime-curating twins, had assured them the goods weren't tagged—they were rejects from one of the factories with only a few aesthetic defects, they'd work fine for anyone looking for a discount who didn't mind a few scratches. The crates had been scheduled for recycling, and technically that's exactly what Mal and his crew had done with them. For a price.

As it turned out, that price was nine fully grown geese—not exactly the figure he and Arvin had agreed upon. He should've known better than to get involved with Arvin, who'd shorted Mal on a job some three years back. A misunderstanding, Arvin had said. Now, Mal wasn't so sure misunderstandings weren't a key part of Arvin's business model.

"We in any shape to go after him?" Mal asked, but he knew the answer already. He'd only agreed to sell to Arvin on account of *Serenity* being out of fuel and out of funds. They weren't equipped to make it much further than Whittier, and they'd no other contacts in range. It had been Arvin or starve.

"I could try a full burn, maybe divert some of the power from the drive feed to the engines," Wash began, but his tone was subdued. Usually when Mal asked Wash for some superhuman piloting, he'd spring to life, like adrenaline was a power source. This time, he just looked tired. "Could be enough to catch up."

"No way," Kaylee said. "*Serenity* ain't up for that."

Mal knew better than to argue with Kaylee when it came to *Serenity*. Sometimes, he thought she knew his ship better than he did. They had some kind of silent communication he'd never quite understood. She had a gift with machines. He'd be a fool to ignore it.

"Then we'd best make course for somewhere with a taste for goose." He wiped his hands on his trousers and turned back to survey his crew, sweeping his eyes over them and finding their numbers one short. "All accounted for?"

Zoë nodded. "River's hiding in the galley."

"Doc?" Mal called over the din of honking. "How's our patient?"

"He'll live," Simon said coolly.

"And my eye?" Jayne asked. "You can save my eye?"

The doctor, with the Shepherd's help, half-carried half-dragged Jayne through the infirmary doors.

"He'll do his best, son." Shepherd Book patted Jayne's bicep.

Wash's face split into a grin. "One might say he'll… take a gander."

"One might refrain from pun-based humor while a man is in pain," the Shepherd shot back.

Undeterred, Wash turned to Zoë and said, "It's too bad we got geese instead of ducks."

"Dare I ask why?" Zoë gave her husband an appraising

look, though her hand snaked around his shoulders to give an affectionate squeeze.

"Because then I could say Simon was tending to Jayne's mallardy."

Zoë scoffed and hoisted herself up the ladder.

"It's a good thing he's not a quack!" Wash called after her.

"Wash, get on the Cortex and see where else we can get to that might have a market for expensive geese," Mal said.

"Hang on, I've almost got something about birds of a feather—"

"I don't pay you to make jokes, Wash. Bridge, now!"

Wash popped a salute and followed his wife up the ladder, leaving Mal to survey nine angry birds.

"Cap'n," Kaylee murmured, sidling up beside him with an apprehensive expression. "*Serenity* don't have enough fuel to get anywhere. She barely had enough to land."

Mal nodded gravely. It was as he'd suspected. Not far off Beaumonde, Kaylee had discovered a leaky pipe. She'd patched it up, but the damage had been done. The mechanic had done all she could to extend *Serenity*'s fuel supply, but in the end Brome was as far as they could get. Even the planet below was out of range with their current fuel levels.

"Sorry, Cap'n." Kaylee's face was contorted in a frown, her eyes watery.

"Hey, no need for apologies. This ain't your fault."

"I know." Kaylee's fingers danced up the steel plating around the cargo-bay door, eyes traveling around *Serenity* like she could see the ship's nervous system. "I just don't like it when she's not her best. Feels like I failed."

Mal braced his hands on Kaylee's shoulders and caught her gaze. "Everybody gets sick now and again. No helpin' what's already happened."

Kaylee nodded, swallowing.

"Now, put that brilliant brain of yours to work thinkin' about how we can fix it." Mal let go, turning back to face the inside of his ship. He didn't have Kaylee's mind for machinery or Wash's quick instincts, but it didn't take an expert to know what came next. "Right, so we need to fuel up."

Inara slipped out of the shadows. How a woman like her managed to hide in plain sight was beyond Mal. She wore a dusty rose robe with velvet trim. Even in one of her more understated articles of clothing, she still looked strangely opulent on board *Serenity*, like a polished gemstone in a box of rocks. "Can we afford to do that?"

Mal tried not to react to her use of the word *we*. It had been cropping up in her vocabulary more and more these past weeks. He knew it had been some time since she'd been able to conduct business, what with their work taking them to the Rim, but he'd get her back to her world soon enough. Still, his skin warmed at the thought of Inara conspiring with him. He'd long stopped thinking of her as only a passenger. She was part of his crew, even if he wouldn't say it out loud.

Mal jammed his hands into his pockets and shrugged. "Might be the folks out here could use a flock of geese. Get us a payday, refuel, and get to somewhere less…"

"Remote?" Inara angled her gaze up at him, unblinking. "You didn't see the market, Mal. No one there can afford a single one of your geese, let alone the whole flock."

"Thought that might be the case," Mal said with a sigh. Brome was a perfect location for off-color dealings, on account of it being out of the way, sparsely populated, and economically fragile. It also made it less-than-ideal for their current predicament.

"There's a refinery here, if I'm not mistaken." Shepherd Book exited the infirmary to join them. Judging by the quiet, Jayne had been given a sedative or elsewise passed out from the pain.

"You suggestin' we relieve them of some of their burden? Didn't think a Shepherd would approve of thieving." Mal raised his eyebrows.

He'd long wondered about the Shepherd's history with crime. It was obvious he had one, based on his breadth of knowledge of the subject. He was useful in a fight as well, adept at martial arts, and a fair shot. He had to be an ex-smuggler at the very least. But just when Mal thought he had the preacher figured out, Shepherd Book had proven to have even more secrets. Back on Jiangyin, when he'd taken a bullet to the chest, the Alliance of all people had come to their aid. What kind of man could get such a warm reception by the people Mal most hated and still want to fly with outlaws? It boggled the mind.

"I'm suggesting nothing of the sort." The Shepherd clasped his hands behind his back. He nodded to the still-open cargo-bay door. "Simply pointing out that there is an established center of commerce on this moon, and that we might consider participating in their economy in exchange for what we need."

"I could see if anyone in town got somethin' needs fixing," Kaylee said with a shrug.

"Now, that's an idea, little Kaylee." Mal straightened. "Could be we all find work in town. Just enough to get us somewhere there's a bit more civilization."

Kaylee brightened. "Simon could help. There's always folks need a doctor."

"We'll see how Jayne's faring," Mal said tentatively. "Don't want to see a repeat of the last time we let the doc loose planetside."

"The boy does seem to always find trouble," the Shepherd agreed, giving a meaningful nod to Kaylee. "Best he doesn't go alone."

Simon Tam was indeed a magnet for misfortune. The last few times they'd let him wander on his own on a border world, he'd ended up being either kidnapped or taken hostage. Even their job on Ariel had almost resulted in the Alliance apprehending him and his fugitive sister, though none of that was Simon's fault, and Mal wasn't one to lay blame where it wasn't due. After all, his line of work didn't exactly invite the most trustworthy of folk into their orbit, but Simon sure had a knack for ending up where he didn't belong. Same with that sister of his. The Tams were trouble. But then, so was Mal. Maybe Wash's birds-of-a-feather quip was apt, after all.

Wash's head appeared up above, just past the door to the dining area. "Cortex keeps shorting out. Signal's scrambled."

"That's no good," said Mal.

"I know! Prefer it over-easy, myself. I like a runny yolk."

Mal groaned. "Kaylee?"

"Hard-boiled, for me," Kaylee said, eyes wide and innocent even as her lip twitched. "I like peelin' the shell. It's nice. Cathartic."

"I swear—" Mal began, but Inara cut him off.

"You can try my shuttle. If I can connect, I can pay you next month's rent as an advance."

Mal's body stiffened. Inara's generosity might get them out of a bind, but he didn't like the idea of owing her. Still, he couldn't very well decline because of his own pride. He had his crew to think of.

Before Mal had a chance to decide what to do precisely, Wash joined them below, a glum expression on his face—a rarity for the pilot. In the years Mal had known Wash, he could count on his hands the number of times he'd seen the man without a smile or some joke or other.

"Won't make a difference. There's some kind of interference. Brome was only terraformed recently, so it's possible signals just can't reach here." Wash gave a shrug, looking from Mal to Inara. "Can access any data that's already downloaded, but nothing new. No long-distance waves unless we head back into orbit. Can make whatever local calls you like, though not sure there'd be anyone to answer."

"Still, I'd like to try." Inara swept up the ladder toward her shuttle.

"Well, that narrows our options," Mal grunted, trying not to watch Inara go. "S'pose we'll have to take our chances with Brome after all."

From the way his crew reacted, Mal might as well have told them there'd been a sudden windfall or one of them had a birthday to celebrate.

"I do so love to mingle with the locals," Wash said, unfastening the top button of his tropical shirt. He headed for the Mule to begin extracting it from the makeshift barrier, but seemed to think better of it once the geese started flapping their wings in response to his approach.

Kaylee clapped her hands in a flurry, bouncing on her toes. "I'll go get Simon!" The light was back in her eyes and a smile played at the corner of her mouth.

Mal watched as the mechanic practically skipped from one end of the cargo bay to the other, carefully maneuvering around the goose enclosure to reach the infirmary. Everyone was too gorram happy about this.

"What's got you smilin' there, preacher?" Mal asked when it was just him and Shepherd Book left. "Eerie sight, a man of God grinnin' at you."

"Oh, just the thought of us all engaging in some simple, honest work," Shepherd Book said, a slippery quality to his tone.

Mal narrowed his eyes. There was that word, *simple*.

"Makes for a nice change, don't you think?" asked the Shepherd.

"Well, just don't go countin' on it being permanent," Mal said, breaking eye contact. "Once a scoundrel, always a scoundrel."

"Oh, I don't know about that." Book eyed him carefully, his gaze so sharp Mal felt for a moment the Shepherd could see right through him to his core. "We can all find redemption in the eyes of the Lord. The word of God will set all sinners free."

"Yeah, but I ain't lookin' to God for my freedom." Mal patted *Serenity*'s frame affectionately. "Already found it right here."

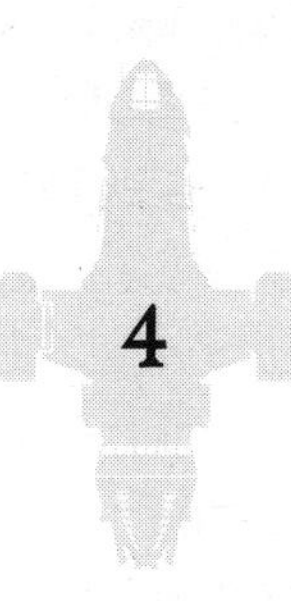

4

There was something intoxicating about a new world. Kaylee loved her life in the sky, and wouldn't trade flying around on *Serenity* for anything, but there was novelty to the feeling of her boots on the ground and sun on her skin, a little slice of the unknown waiting for her on the horizon.

In the case of Brome, that horizon was obscured by tall grass, framing the small market ahead of town. They'd passed through a heavy thicket on their way, the long blades tickling their arms and legs as they went, leaving them covered in a dusting of seeds by the time they reached their destination.

"Excitin', don't you think?" Kaylee's eyes flicked to Zoë on her left and Simon on her right. "A new place to learn about?"

"If you like breathing in dust and pollen, sure." Zoë wrapped an amber-colored cloth around her nose and mouth.

"Oh, come on, I'm sure there's more to recommend this place." Wash gestured them toward a market stall with a muted blue awning and a sign that boasted *Fresh Brome Beef*. "See? A local delicacy!"

An eager stallholder stood to greet them, a young woman with a red scarf braided into her brown hair like a crown around her head. “Best meatless alternative you’ll find this side of Red Sun.”

The enthusiasm drained from Wash’s expression.

“Having second thoughts, dear?” Zoë asked, taking his arm.

“Not at all.” Wash’s voice had gone rigid. “My passion for new cuisine remains as ardent as ever. I just remembered we don’t have any money to spend.”

“How unfortunate?” Simon glanced from Wash to Zoë to Kaylee and back again, brow furrowed in concentration as he tried to follow the subtext of the conversation.

“It is very, very sad for me,” Wash said to the woman behind the cart. “You wouldn’t happen to know where folks might find work around here? What we lack in cash, I promise we make up for in work ethic.”

Kaylee let her eyes wander as Wash and Zoë conversed with the Brome beef merchant. The market space was large, but there weren’t many stalls—a dozen at most. Most sold food and drink, but a few peddled metalwork pendants or woven-grass baskets. The vendors stood behind their stalls with eyes downcast. Some crouched to keep their faces and necks out of the sun while a few wore wide-brimmed hats that looked like they’d been made by the basket weaver. The crowded markets of Kaylee’s childhood had all been tightly packed, the vendors squeezed together, but here there were large spaces between carts, like maybe there were some missing. As Kaylee’s gaze skated over them, something in her chest constricted. She didn’t know why, but she felt like crying.

“Lot of grass-related products,” Simon observed as he followed her toward the other stalls. “Is this like that moon with all the mud? If Jayne’s a hero on Brome, too, I think that might actually be too much for me.”

“You know, they said nothin’ would grow here? Soil’s too rocky, or something. Alliance didn’t even want to terraform it. But look at all this!” Kaylee gestured at the grass that surrounded them.

"They were probably hoping for more life-sustaining crops, I imagine."

"Nice to see something green, though, right?"

Simon gave her a dubious look.

"Okay, maybe not so green. But it's alive, ain't it?" Kaylee nudged him with her elbow. "Come on, relax a little!"

"One of the few things I'm notably bad at." Simon sighed, eyes traveling up toward the cloudless blue sky. "I've never liked field trips."

"Why's that? I bet you used to get to go to all sorts of incredible places!" Kaylee took the moment to look at him properly. With smooth skin and shiny hair, Simon appeared as out of place here as he did on *Serenity*. Every day she hoped maybe he'd learn to blend in a little better, really embrace his new life with the rest of them. Sometimes, she saw slivers of it—Simon living his life instead of running from it—but it was fleeting, never there for more than a few minutes. "Guess this doesn't really compare, does it?"

"What? No." Simon's gaze snapped to hers. "It's just difficult to focus on what's in front of me when part of me is always thinking about what might be going on back on the ship."

"You're worried about River."

Kaylee could hardly imagine how Simon felt. Family was one of the most important things Kaylee could think of. She loved her folks something fierce, but in the end she'd found her true family among the stars. Inara was the older sister she'd always craved, Wash the lovable uncle, and Jayne the slightly less lovable uncle. Family was about love, not blood, and *Serenity* was the glue that held them together. River and Simon had something special, though. Didn't take a genius to see there wasn't anything Simon wouldn't do for his sister. Kaylee wished sometimes he felt that way about the rest of them, too.

"She's got Inara lookin' after her. She'll be all right."

Simon just shrugged, a few grass seeds falling with the motion.

Kaylee cracked a smile. "You're a bit of a mess, ain't ya? Let me help." It was damn near electrifying, being this close to him. She knew her brain didn't have wires or nothing, but it felt like every time she touched him, her nervous system short-circuited. "Still got some in your hair."

Kaylee and Simon both reached at the same time, their fingers colliding in his hair. She had just enough time to register that it was fine and soft before snatching her hand back and averting her gaze.

"Sorry. Didn't mean to—" Simon began.

Kaylee ran right over his apology. "It's okay. Nothin' to be sorry about. Shouldn't have… Don't need to be… You can take care of yourself, of course."

Simon nodded and straightened up, running a hand roughly through his hair.

"Still, maybe it's nice? You know, to have someone lookin' after you for a change?" Kaylee couldn't keep the hope from her voice. She and Simon had danced around this for months, neither one of them all that gracefully. She wanted something more with him, even if she didn't know exactly what, but she just couldn't make heads or tails of Simon's feelings. Sometimes he blew hot, other times cold, and she was left fiddling with the thermostat, trying to keep things steady. These days, the best she could do was leave the door open and see if he walked over the threshold.

Simon looked at her, his blue eyes stormy with confusion. "What do you mean?"

Kaylee let her gaze travel over to Wash and Zoë. The first mate was bent in conversation with a gray-haired woman behind one of the stalls. Wash stood just behind his wife, his eyes trained on her like they didn't know how to look anywhere else. His fingers hovered near the small of her back, tracing light circles into her leathers.

Now there was a pair. Other folks might not always have understood Wash and Zoë, but Kaylee did. Zoë was smart and capable, not to mention beautiful, and Wash—he knew what it was to love someone precious. What she wouldn't give to have Simon look at her the way Wash looked at his wife. And it wasn't just the love—she knew that sort of thing didn't blossom overnight; it was the enthusiasm. Wash never hesitated to show Zoë how he felt. Simon could learn something from him.

"Like them," Kaylee said, pointing out the other two. "Must be nice, don't you think?"

"What must be nice?" Simon barely glanced up, still removing grass seeds from his clothes.

"Oh, you know." She looked from Simon to Wash and Zoë and back again. "They always know they've got each other. It's a comfort. Reassuring." Kaylee shot Simon a sidelong look. "Don't you think so?"

Simon shrugged. "I suppose."

"You ever wanna be married?"

"Me? Married?" Simon's face split into a grin. "Can you even imagine? Me with a wife? I've got way too much on my plate, taking care of River, patching up this *jìng cháng méi yòng de* crew. Oh, and not to mention I'm a fugitive. No self-respecting girl would want that kind of life."

Kaylee's heart sank. Her hands felt clammy and her throat dry. "You better finish cleaning yourself up."

"Huh?"

"You've still got seeds in your hair." That wasn't strictly true, not that Kaylee could see, but she wanted to make him feel silly. Make him feel how he'd made her feel. A cold front blew in on her voice, and she said, "Have a little self-respect."

Leave it to the doctor to ruin a perfectly good moment.

Kaylee cast her gaze about and it snagged on something

she did know how to fix. One of the carts had a loose axle, with splintered wood at the joint poking out dangerously.

"Mind if I take a look?" Kaylee asked, pointing to the broken cart.

The cart minder, a young man around River's age, started, jumping back a foot. "I, uh… It's been like that for months. Wheel sticks, but it moves okay."

"Just means she's a stubborn ol' girl." Kaylee lowered herself to her knees to get a better look. A thread of braided bromegrass had been wrapped through the wheel spokes and around the end of the axle to hold it in place. Not a bad solution, though if the splintering of the wood was anything to go by, it wouldn't last. "Ah, there's your trouble." She pointed to the place where the axle met the wheel. "Parts don't fit. This here is too big for this kind of wheel. When you move it over rough ground, it jostles, causes too much friction." She reached for the braid of grass, untying it and rewrapping it around the axle like a makeshift washer. "There. That'll absorb some of the shock, keep her goin' longer."

The vendor gave the cart an experimental shove. The wheel held.

"Wow, you know your stuff!" His eyes lit up, and he ran the cart forward and back a few more times. Each turn of the wheel was as smooth as the last. "I can't pay you, though."

"Oh." Kaylee had almost forgotten their purpose in coming to town. It felt so good to listen to machinery, even a simple wooden cart, and cure its ills. She couldn't help *Serenity* get where she was going, but she could help this vendor. "That's okay. Nothin' too troublesome there, anyhow." Her eyes skated over the wares—woven baskets, hats, and other such crafts. "You make all these?"

The vendor nodded. "Harvested, dried, and woven."

"They're beautiful…" Kaylee's fingers danced over the intricate workmanship.

"It's just grass?" Simon asked, appearing at her elbow.

His question was innocent enough, but it irked her anyway. Maybe he didn't mean anything by it, but a defensive chord struck somewhere inside her. "Nothin's *just* grass, Simon. Don't you see all the colors? And these pretty knots." She pointed to a hat with little rosettes around the brim. "Must be hard on your hands," she said to the vendor.

At that, the vendor quickly snatched his hands off the cart and hid them behind his back. "Not so bad."

Simon leaned forward, eyes narrowed in focus. "You're injured."

Kaylee knew better than to ask how he knew. Simon was with people the way she was with machines. Bodies just talked to him like that. If only he bothered listening to hers once in a while.

"No, I'm not," the vendor said, shifting away from Simon.

From her vantage point at the side of the cart, Kaylee could see behind his back. Strips of cloth were wrapped around his fingers as makeshift bandages. Kaylee knew there were all sorts of reasons to hide an injury. Maybe he was worried they'd devalue his craft or try to steal from him. For all he knew, they were thieves looking for an easy mark. He'd only be half right, but still Kaylee wanted to put him at ease.

She laid her right hand face up on the cart and pointed to a small burn mark on her palm she'd sustained years ago. "Accidentally put my hand on the compression block before the cooling drive was done cycling. Couldn't hold a wrench for near a week after." She grimaced, then pointed to Simon. "Lucky for you, this one's a doctor. Could take a look if you want."

Simon stepped forward, hand outstretched. "Please, I'd like to help."

"Ain't nothin' to be done about it. Got hurt. Now I can't work in the refinery no more, so this is how I make my way." The boy's eyes darted to Simon, but then he shook his head. "Course, it ain't much of a way. I don't got coin for a doctor, neither."

"Oh, I, um..." Simon glanced at Kaylee, an unspoken question in his eyes.

Kaylee liked that Simon was generous with his skills. Doctoring, in her mind, ought to be available to everyone who needed it, no matter the size of their purse, but that wasn't the world they lived in. Besides, she'd already fixed his cart for free, and Mal wouldn't like it if they came back empty handed. Maybe what the captain didn't know wouldn't hurt him. But before Kaylee could communicate anything of the sort, another vendor sidled up to the cart, an older woman who looked to be in her mid-sixties. She loomed out at them, arms crossed and wearing a scowl.

"They botherin' you, Zane?" asked the woman, eyes narrowed, exaggerating her already prominent wrinkles.

The boy, Zane, lowered his gaze. "Nah, just visitors. A doctor."

"A medicine man, eh?" asked the woman.

"Yes, uh, you wouldn't happen to know anyone who might need my services, would you? I can set bones, suture cuts and wounds, whatever you need."

The woman laughed. "Ain't a matter of need."

"I don't follow," Simon said.

But Kaylee did. Her stomach sank.

"You could be hockin' honest-to-God miracles, but not a one of us could afford to pay you," the woman said with a deep frown. "If it's coin you're after, you've come to the wrong moon."

5

Brome's central tavern was quiet. With walls made from some kind of clay mixture and a thatched-grass roof, it wasn't much to look at, but then none of the best watering holes were. Zoë didn't trust a place that was too clean or too flashy. Even when she could afford the drinks, they weren't worth the trouble that came with them.

"*Wěi*," Zoë hailed the barkeep, a middle-aged woman with a stained apron and big circles under her eyes.

"What'll it be?"

Zoë knew better than to ask for help before ordering a drink. Her purse was feather-light, but she knew the cost of doing business. Sliding a few coins across the counter, she held up four fingers and the barkeep busied herself behind the counter, filling four ceramic mugs.

Zoë swept the room with her gaze, mentally noting the exits and headcount in case something went awry. There were only six people in the bar besides her, Wash, Simon, and Kaylee—two men in the corner, a trio of youthful looking townsfolk bent low over a table, and an elderly woman nursing an unlit pipe beside the door. Only two of them had weapons that Zoë could see, and not a single gun between them.

Wash slid onto the stool next to her, his hands making a detour along her waist before he folded them atop the counter. Kaylee took the seat beside him, leaving Simon to stand awkwardly by the door.

"Everything all right?" Zoë asked in a low voice.

Kaylee gave a noncommittal shrug.

"Of course it is, honey," Wash said, squeezing Zoë's knee beneath the bar. "The doctor always looks like a startled amphibian with a death wish."

Zoë generally liked the Tams. Simon had more than earned his keep since he'd been flying with them. Still, she couldn't help but think they would have been better off leaving him behind on *Serenity*. He reminded her of too many wide-eyed soldiers she'd buried, too caught up in watching the war to remember they were supposed to be fighting it.

"As long as he doesn't start eating flies…" Zoë turned her attention back to the barkeep, who'd returned with their drinks.

"What brings you to Brome?" the barkeep asked. "Don't get many visitors this far out."

"Just stopping to fuel up." Zoë found the truth was usually a good place to start, though she didn't want to linger on it too long. Brome wasn't well tended by the Alliance, but all the same, she'd rather avoid running into any local trouble. "Looking for work in the meantime. Short term only. Not planning to stay long."

The barkeep gave Zoë a once-over. Zoë knew what people saw. Her muscles told people she was capable, her posture told them she was confident, and her eyes told them she didn't suffer fools.

"We can run short-range transport. We've got a doctor, a mechanic, and all of us are good for some physical labor if you've got a need."

Wash held up a finger as he chimed in, "I also make a mean martini."

"I ain't hiring." The barkeep shifted her gaze to Wash, eyes narrowing. "Nobody is."

"Well, *somebody* is," Simon said.

The doctor had wandered to the other side of the room with his drink. From the looks of it, he'd poured about half of the contents into a vase full of dried flowers covered in cobwebs. Beside him was a notice board with a few tattered bits of paper pinned to the wall, and in his hand was a crisp flyer.

"'Refinery machine operator shift workers urgently needed,'" Simon read aloud. "'Competitive pay, overtime available. Inquire with manager at large.'"

A silence fell around the bar. The woman by the door gripped her pipe with white knuckles and the men in the corner watched with interest. Even the three young-looking folks stopped their whispering.

"The foreman ain't nobody worth workin' for," said one of the men in the corner. "Least, not if you know what's good for you."

"Gary," the barkeep said, a warning in her tone. "Don't go telling folks what to do in my bar."

"Why not?" asked the man called Gary. "I recall you tellin' me what to do in my house just this mornin'."

"And I recall you liking that well enough."

Zoë caught Simon's eye, then glanced at the door. Now was as good a time as any to make a quick exit. Better to leave now before anyone had a chance to pick a fight. Even without Mal or Jayne present, Zoë didn't like to linger too long where alcohol was flowing and emotions were running high.

"Let's get out of here," she murmured to Kaylee, pulling Wash to his feet.

"Thank you!" Wash called over his shoulder, pointing to his still mostly full cup. "Very good... whatever that was supposed to be."

"What *was* that supposed to be?" Simon asked when they'd stepped out into the hot and dusty Brome air. "It tasted like... mold."

Wash shrugged. "Fermented grass water, is my guess."

"As thrilling a mystery as this is, best we make haste. The captain will want to hear about those refinery jobs." Zoë plucked the flyer from Simon's grip, folded it, and tucked it safely into a pocket. "I mean it. No detours."

"Right," Wash spread his arms wide as he walked backwards up the street. "Because it's so likely we'd wander off to take part in the robust slate of entertainment Brome has to offer."

A smile bit onto Zoë's lips as she watched him go, carefree as the wind that carried the tails of his tropical shirt out behind him like a sail.

Zoë hadn't been looking for a husband when she'd met Wash. Truth be told, she'd never once in her life been looking for a husband at all. She'd found one just the same. She was a woman who always carried a gun, but he had a way of disarming her anyway. After the war, she'd struggled to move past her identity as a soldier, but Wash made it easy to laugh again. She'd done her level best to keep him at a distance until one day she woke up to her life out in the black and discovered he'd brought more light into it than all the suns combined. Zoë had always been a master of stealth, but love was the rare beast that actually got the drop on her.

"*Āiya*!" Kaylee shouted beside her. "Watch out!"

Zoë's gaze snapped into focus, but it was too late.

A blurry form knocked into Wash from behind, sending them both toppling to the ground.

"*Tā mā de!*" Wash grunted, rolling and pushing himself up on his knees. "Sorry about that."

Beside him, the other form got to their feet. From Zoë's position near the tavern, they looked short of stature, with dark clothes covered in a thin layer of dirt from the fall. They wore a hood, but a strand of curly ginger hair peeked out from beneath.

Wash got to his feet and brushed dust from his pants. "You all right?" he asked.

But the stranger bolted, disappearing down a side street.

"That was… odd," Simon said, walking over to Wash. Kaylee and Zoë followed suit.

"You still got everything? Your money?" Kaylee asked. "Are you hurt?"

"What money?" Wash patted himself down anyway, then shrugged. "Nothing wounded but my pride."

Zoë reached for his collar, smoothing out the lapels, never mind they'd been wrinkled from the start. Wash was hardy enough, as he'd well and truly proven back on Niska's space station not long ago, but she could take care of herself in ways he couldn't, and she didn't like to think of him in any pain.

"Are you sure you're not injured?" Simon asked.

"Takes more than a fall to ruffle my man," Zoë whispered, letting go at long last.

"No ruffles to see here. Not a ruffle in sight. Wouldn't dream of being ruffled."

As her husband rambled on, Zoë's attention slipped to the ground where the stranger had fallen. There, obscured by a thin layer of dirt, was a roughly cut wooden placard attached to a handle by two rusted nails. She flipped it over and her heart sank.

"Guess we know why they didn't want us taking those refinery jobs," she said, pointing to the words on the sign:

WE'RE DONE WITH BLUE SUN.

6

After fifteen years as a registered Companion of House Madrassa and a while on *Serenity*, there wasn't much in Allied space that could surprise Inara Serra. River Tam was the rare exception.

"Do you have any pants?" River asked from beneath a heaping pile of fine fabrics.

"Pants?" Inara couldn't help but laugh. "Let me take a look."

She crossed to the closet from the other side of her shuttle, pushing aside a heap of dresses. Inara didn't wear trousers often. She found them constricting and not particularly useful. She knew, of course, the history of women's rights through fashion. The right to wear trousers at all was a hard-won fight, one that continued in some corners of the galaxy to this day, but Inara knew the true power of liberation was choice, and she would choose a dress every time.

"I don't know that I do, *mèi mèi*," she said after a quick foray to the back of her closet.

River had become a fixture in Inara's shuttle over the past few months. At first, the girl had come only when directed by her brother, but once she'd learned to trust that the shuttle was safe, she'd begun visiting whenever the desire struck her. Though she was the doctor's sister by blood, out in the black they were all of them siblings of a sort, and Inara relished her time with River, whatever version of the girl she got.

"Do you want to try this on instead?" Inara asked, holding up a gown of burgundy velvet. She hadn't had occasion to wear it of late, but it was one of her favorites.

Serenity had lingered on the Rim a bit too long for Inara's liking. She hated to think it was Mal's way of poorly communicating his distaste for her profession. Rather, she hoped it was a consequence of his line of work. Still, keeping *Serenity* this far out in the black meant a distinct reduction in her employability. The last planet they'd been to with any sort of respectable society was Beaumonde, and they'd not stayed long enough for her to engage a single client.

River shrank away from the velvet gown and shuddered. "No, no, no. Like too many spiders on my skin."

Inara promptly put the dress away. She knew better than to argue with River by now. Though she'd never met anyone precisely like the younger Tam, she'd known a girl back on Sihnon who was sensitive to textures, light, and sound. No matter how odd River could be, Inara knew from experience it wouldn't help to try to force her to be different. She was who she was. If she didn't like velvet, well, that was all right with Inara.

"What about this?" Inara pulled another dress from the closet, this one made of aquamarine silk with slits on either side. "It's not exactly pants, but—"

River sighed heavily and took the dress in hand. "I'll make it work," she said with the air of a beleaguered seamstress looking at a suboptimal sample of cloth.

It was a strange ritual, one Inara didn't yet fully understand. River had been denied so much of her childhood, perhaps it was a latent exploration of the years she'd lost, a game of dress-up.

River was just playing. But Inara's strength was in her ability to read others—their emotions, their desires, their innermost instincts—and something told her it was more complex than that. River wasn't just putting on a costume to pretend to be someone she wasn't; she was dressing to express who she was. And every time River stepped over the threshold of Inara's shuttle, it was a surprise to discover who exactly that might be.

Assured that River would be well occupied for at least a little while, Inara returned to the screens on the far side of the shuttle. She had the Cortex open, but no signal was going in or out, just as Wash had said. She tried to refresh the connection one more time before giving up. Instead, she opened the existing entry for Brome, barely glancing at the meager paragraphs of text describing the moon's origins and terraforming. She wasn't interested in how it came to be, only in who it was for.

She flicked past another page of uninteresting text about the Blue Sun Corporation's investment in Brome's economy, landing finally on a short article dated a few months back about a philanthropic venture, headed by one Jenessa Leon, seeking donations. She blinked, sure she must have navigated to a different topic by mistake. The piece detailed Ms. Leon's previous charitable causes—an orphanage on Oberon, desalination technology on New Melbourne, and even a high-speed train on Meridian, all in partnership with the Blue Sun Corporation. It wasn't until she reached the very end that everything became clear. Ms. Leon had made Brome the beneficiary of her next undertaking, whatever that might be.

"She is not who she appears to be," River said into Inara's ear.

Inara jumped. She hadn't noticed River sneaking up on her.

"Fancy lady, with her fine dresses." River swished the skirt of the aquamarine gown back and forth, eyes trained on the ripple of fabric. "You think she's one thing, but she is many."

Letting the cloth fall back down across the display, Inara turned back to River. The Tams came from money, Inara knew, and standing before her was a version of River who might have existed had the Alliance left her alone. Glamor suited her. She was a vision, with silk draped like liquid across her skin. If she'd let Inara rake a comb through her hair, River would be indistinguishable from the upper crust of the society they'd both left behind.

"Blue is certainly your color," Inara said. "Do you like it?"

River nodded emphatically, then her face fell. "Don't tell Simon. Only make him sad."

"Of course, *mèi mèi.*" Inara stood, wrinkles falling seamlessly out of her own pink ensemble. "Whatever you want."

"Dance with me." River gestured to the open space at the foot of Inara's bed, and began to move her arms in graceful patterns, teasing the shape of a port de bras.

Inara had trained in dance at House Madrassa—years of it—but even she couldn't harness the pure freedom of movement that River could. Simon said his sister loved dance, but Inara wasn't so sure it wasn't the other way around.

"There's no music," Inara said, though she joined River anyway, mimicking her fluid movements. Their arms twisted and wound through the space as they twirled together, legs sweeping the floor.

"It's better when it's quiet," River said.

Inara laughed. "I suppose you're right." It had been a long day of various goose-related noise, and it was no surprise that River preferred the silence of the shuttle to the honking in the cargo bay.

"Shh." River pressed her finger to her lips, suddenly growing still. She reached for Inara's arm, her grip so tight the Companion nearly yelped. Her eyes found Inara's and held her gaze, unblinking. "If you listen, you'll know when they're about to strike."

Inara leaned in closer, the beat of her own heart the only sound punctuating the silence in the wake of River's words. "It's all right, River. They're not going to hurt you here."

"They're not going to hurt me," River agreed.

Inara pried River's fingers from her arm and placed their hands palm to palm. "What are you worried about, then?"

River's eyes didn't meet hers, glazing over as her gaze drifted across the rug to the closed door. She took back her hand, balled it into a fist, and said, "Him."

7

Shepherd Book wasn't Mal's first choice, as far as allies went. He'd rather have Zoë by his side in a fight. In fact, he'd rather have Zoë with him in most situations, violent or not. There was a reason she was his first mate. Besides which, the Shepherd left Mal feeling judged more often than not. Still, as they placed the finishing touches on the goose enclosure, he couldn't help but think he'd picked the right man for the job.

They'd built a fence from a combination of wire they'd had lying around in the cargo bay and surprisingly sturdy bromegrass rope. The merchant who'd sold it to them promised it would hold as well as hempen but with half the weight. Mal hadn't expected that to be true, but it was what he could afford.

"You got a lot of experience with livestock, Shepherd?" Mal asked as he stepped back to admire their handiwork.

"Only if you count tending my flock."

"You callin' us animals?"

"Are we not all God's creatures?" Book gave Mal an appraising look.

"Don't belong to no one, preacher. Especially not God." He turned his back and rattled the fence to test its integrity. It held.

"Not half bad. Should keep them at bay."

Book appeared at Mal's side, hands clasped behind his back, gaze trained on the geese. "You've made your peace with the inevitable?"

It was at times like these that Mal weighed how much benefit there really was to having a preacher on board. None of his crew were particularly devout, but he knew some of them appreciated Book's spiritual wisdom. Inara, though she was Buddhist, got along with him well enough, and it was undeniable he'd done more than his share of looking after River. Even Jayne, perhaps the most irreverent of the lot, got along surprisingly well with the preacher. Mal didn't begrudge them whatever comforts they had out in the black. What he did take issue with was Book pushing his religiosity on him like Mal was a toddler and the Bible was a plate of Brussels sprouts.

"Preacher, if I ever want your sermon on the afterlife, you'll know."

The Shepherd looked sidelong at Mal, a quirk to his brow. "Very good to know, Captain. But I was speaking of the likelihood your captives will simply fly over our carefully erected enclosure."

"D'somebody say erect?" Jayne's voice, crackly and groggy, filtered in through the open door to the infirmary.

"The verb, I should hope," said Zoë as she led a beleaguered-looking Wash, Kaylee, and Simon back on board. They wore tired expressions and a fresh layer of dust. "As in to construct something?"

"Careful. If you define it, he may learn how to use it in a sentence." Wash glanced warily at the infirmary.

"Any luck?" Mal asked.

"Maybe." Zoë held out a folded bit of paper.

Mal glanced at the words. "What do you mean, maybe? Seems pretty straightforward."

"*Seems* being the operative word," muttered Wash.

"Refinery needs workers." Mal looked between the two, searching their gazes for subtext. "We can provide, but I'm guessing it ain't so simple as that?"

Married folks had a sort of shorthand. It was the closest thing to telepathy Mal had ever witnessed, and it was gorram annoying. It was why he'd told Zoë not to marry the pilot—that and the mustache.

"Had a bit of a run-in back in town," Zoë said, shrugging one shoulder.

"Literally, mind you." Wash gestured to a dirty patch on his trousers.

"Get to the point." Mal didn't like to let his impatience show if he could help it, but he was in no mood for this dance.

"Might be it's nothing." Zoë glanced from her husband to Mal. "Then again, might be it's somethin'."

"Can't be neither if you don't tell me."

"Folks in town were a mite dodgy," Zoë began, leaning forward to speak in a low voice. "Didn't like us askin' about work, for a start. Had some uncomplimentary words for the foreman. And one of them had this." She raised her arm, and only then did Mal notice she was carrying something. A sign, by the look of it, with a hand-printed message.

"'We're done with Blue Sun.'" Mal spoke the words aloud curiously. "You get a whiff of what this is about?"

"There wasn't a lot of time for sniffing around after we found it. Headed straight back here."

"Any chance they mean a different Blue Sun?" Shepherd Book asked resignedly. "Perhaps out here it has different meaning. Could be they're referring to the sun system, not the corporation."

"What's wrong with Blue Sun, exactly?" Simon asked. "Aren't they a food supplier?"

"I like their protein bars," said Jayne. He'd found his way to standing again, despite the sedative, and leaned limply against the door frame. "And their shirts."

"They're all sorts of things," Kaylee explained, voice soft like she was trying not to interfere with the rest of the conversation. They all stopped to listen anyway. "Make rations, clothing, supplies... stuff folks need everywhere from the Rim to the Core."

"Surprised you don't know that already, Doc," Wash said. "Would've thought a big corporation like them would've come up in your circles. Don't you fancy types always like to invest in things like that?"

Simon's cheeks went pink and he muttered something about diversifying funds and catering.

"The doc's upbringing aside, I don't like that our only option is working for a corporation that has almost as big a presence in the 'verse as the Alliance. Bigger, depending how far out you go." He eyed the sign carefully. Something about it struck him as being awfully sinister, like a warning. Still, he felt a warmth in his chest one degree removed from hope. "What were they doin' with a sign like this, anyhow?"

"I would think that's obvious, sir." Zoë stowed the sign upright against the control panel for the cargo bay. "Someone on this moon doesn't like the way they're being treated, and they've decided to do something about it."

"You mean like a strike?" asked Simon, eyebrows rising to alarming heights.

"Don't expect Brome has anything so organized as a union, but yeah, something like that." Zoë looked to Mal, a question in her gaze.

The thing about his history with Zoë was it meant they could read each other pretty damn well. And right now, her eyes spelled trouble.

"I ain't crossin' no picket line," Kaylee said. "My daddy's a union man."

"Yeah, but your daddy ain't here." Jayne pushed himself through the infirmary doors, his legs about as sturdy as the fence Mal and Book had built. "I say we do the work quick and get out of here."

"I'd really caution against you doing any labor for the time being," Simon said. "At least for the next few days."

"Shove off, Doc. I can work."

"Your cornea is scratched, so you'll need to keep the patch on."

"Just cause one of my eyes is broke—"

"You'd best leave operating machinery to those of us with full depth perception, son," said the Shepherd, placing a hand gently on the larger man's shoulder.

"Don't need no depth perception to push buttons," Jayne grumbled.

"Well, if you insist, I can stop administering pain medication, but I think you're going to want it."

Simon gave Jayne a subtle smirk, the kind that said he'd love nothing more than to see *Serenity*'s muscle suffer just a little.

"Is everything all right?" asked Inara, appearing on the walkway above, followed closely by River. "I heard arguing."

"River!" Simon's face lit up when he saw her, then a frown creased his lips. "What are you wearing?"

"She spilled tea on her other dress. Nothing to worry about, but I lent her something to wear in the meantime." Inara placed a hand on River's back, ushering her toward her brother. "This seemed easier than trying to find a replacement among her things."

Simon nodded, but there was an odd look to his face. Not that there wasn't always. Mal liked the boy well enough, but he did favor the sort of expression of a man who'd just smelled his own fart. Mal didn't take issue with the doctor's grimace most of the time, though he wished he'd turn on the smile more, at least for Kaylee's benefit. He didn't like seeing his mechanic upset, and when it wasn't his own fault, it was almost certainly Simon's.

"Are you all right, *mèi mèi*?" Simon asked.

River nodded, a smile playing at her lips.

"As much as I love family reunions, we've got more important business to discuss," Mal said, turning back to the matter at hand. "If we're going to take up work with Blue Sun, we'd best make sure we do this right. I don't want any complications."

"You rarely do, sir." Zoë cocked her head, glancing at Jayne. "Doesn't make them any less likely."

"Hey, don't look at me." Jayne held up his hands. He teetered a little, then caught himself on Shepherd Book's shoulder. "It weren't my fault, all that hero stuff on Higgins' Moon."

"One could argue that was a little bit your fault." Simon narrowed his eyes. "No, no, I'm wrong. It was entirely your fault."

"Oh, like you and the girl are any less trouble," Jayne sneered.

"Oh, I'm sorry. Is our status as fugitives inconvenient for you?" Simon took a step forward, brow furrowed.

"Not as inconvenient as it is for you, I'd reckon," Mal said. Squabbles among the crew were bound to break out now and again—nine people cooped up on a Firefly with nowhere to go wasn't exactly a recipe for getting along, after all—but now wasn't the time. They had bigger concerns. "Which is why I don't want either of you going anywhere near that refinery, *dǒng ma*?"

"I thought Brome was relatively safe." Simon's gaze flitted between Mal, Wash, and Zoë. "I didn't see any Alliance while we were out today."

"Alliance, no." Zoë shook her head. "But Blue Sun's got deep roots. Even if the folks on Brome aren't looking for a fugitive, that refinery might have surveillance, bring unwanted attention our way."

"Are you sure I can't be of any help?" Simon asked.

Kaylee reached out a hand, flexing her fingers, then balling them into a fist to hang limply at her side. "Might be for the best," she said at last. "You ain't exactly used to that kind of work."

"No offense, Doc, but they'd take one look at your hands and know you don't belong in a factory." Wash slapped Simon on the back twice. "You let the rest of us do the dirty work."

"Nobody's doing any work." Mal eyed them all carefully, driving the message home with his gaze. "Least, not till I've had words with the foreman. Want to see what he's about. By the sound of things, he's not well liked in town, and I ain't eager to hitch our wagon to someone likely to bring us down with him. What'd you say his name was?" Mal asked Zoë.

But Zoë wasn't looking at him anymore, along with the rest of his crew. Their attention had strayed over his shoulder to the cargo-bay entrance. He turned to follow their gazes to see an older man with flowing gray hair pulled back into a knot, a neat beard, and a scar along his cheek. Mal clocked a pistol at his hip but no other weapons. Despite his obvious age and the three deep wrinkles creasing his forehead, he had a youthful sheen to him and a hint of a smile that made Mal like him just a little.

"Hi there," Mal said, a jovial pep to his voice. He wasn't about to trust this stranger, not one inch, but he found geniality was almost as good as a gun in some cases. Behind him, Simon and River peeled off toward the guest quarters. Good. He didn't need any funny business, from the girl or from their new acquaintance. "I'm Captain Reynolds. Can we help you with something, Mr…" He trailed off, waiting for the man to introduce himself.

But the stranger didn't say a word. Didn't even look at Mal. His gaze was pinned somewhere past him. Mal glanced over his shoulder to see Shepherd Book a few paces away, staring right back.

"Lyle Horne." Book said his name like it was slippery, like it was oil. Like it might ignite on his tongue. "The foreman, I presume."

Leave it to a preacher to have more secrets than made sense. Still, Mal thought as he glanced from the newcomer to Book, maybe the Shepherd was good for more on this mission than tending the flock, after all.

8

Shepherd Book's first mistake was not running when he saw Lyle Horne. Time had stretched them both since the last time they'd stood face to face. They both had more wrinkles. They both had more scars—inside and out, he had to assume.

"How do you know the Shepherd?" Kaylee asked, a naive sparkle to the question as her attention centered on Lyle.

"The… Shepherd?" Lyle's tone was serpent-smooth, feeling out the shape of their little encounter. It was Book who'd taught him how to do that. "Don't think I've ever known a Shepherd. And they usually have a way of tellin' you, from what I hear."

"They do at that," Mal said. His tone was amused though his shoulders remained rigid.

"You haven't known me for some time, Lyle." Book stepped forward, slipping into a warm smile that didn't reach his heart. He needed to take back control, else Lyle could reveal more than Book was ready for the crew of *Serenity* to know. "Shepherd Derrial Book, they call me now."

"Shepherd Derrial Book." The name sounded familiar on Lyle's lips, even though he'd never used it before. "It's good to see you, old friend."

Lyle held out his hand. Book tried not to think of the last time he'd done that. Of what had come after.

"Likewise, *old friend*," Book echoed Lyle, clasping their hands together in a neat, perfunctory shake. No longer than necessary.

That was his second mistake.

The shock of seeing Lyle in the flesh, real and solid, was almost too much. He'd hoped for days, and prayed for more, but Lyle Horne was supposed to be *dead*. Book had watched him fall. For weeks after, he'd dreamed of the moment Lyle had slipped, or he'd let him go—he couldn't figure out which it was, not even after all these years—Book couldn't remember how many.

It was after he left home but before he changed his name. After he'd gone sour, before he'd gone worse.

He'd been called Henry Evans back then. He wasn't anything fancy, just a runaway with a chip on his shoulder and an ego to nurse. He'd been running a job on Valentine and been thrown to the wolves by his crew. Then Lyle had found him. Together, they'd recovered the bounty themselves. Beat his former crew to the punch and got paid double. A purse split between two men, Book learned, was a lot heavier than his share with a full team. He'd let the weight of coin wash away the guilt of what had come after, what he'd helped Lyle do to the folks who'd wronged him.

They were partners from then on—until they weren't. Lyle had saved Book, when it came down to it, and Book had repaid him with weak hands and a weaker will.

Lyle Horne knew the boy Book had been, not the man he'd become. Now, he'd know both.

"Derry," Lyle was saying to a rapt crowd of crew members. "S'what we used to call him. On account of the lactose intolerance, of course." He winked at Book.

It wasn't what Lyle had called him.

Hevans.

Neither flashy nor clever, just a neat shortening of his birth name. Ironic, maybe, that it was a homophone. Book prayed and preached and practiced his religion so he might go to heaven, all the while running from his past, where he used to be called exactly that.

"A lot has changed since then," Book said at last. He put his hands behind his back, flexing his palms.

"Wait, how is it you two know each other?" Wash asked, pointing to them each in turn with a pinched brow. "Childhood friends, former classmates, jilted ex-lovers…?"

"We were partners," Lyle answered with a sly, lopsided smile.

"In business," Book hurried to clarify. He didn't need Lyle spilling his secrets, not when he'd worked so hard to erase them. The crew of *Serenity* had been good to him this far, and he wasn't sure they'd still respect him if they knew what Henry Evans had done before it all. But that wasn't a part of him anymore. He'd worn many disguises: smuggler, soldier, spy, and now Shepherd. None of them mattered, though. God could see through them all. And Book was comfortable with that, as long as God was the only one.

"What sort of business was that, exactly?" Jayne asked.

"Not yours, son." Book didn't take his eyes off of Lyle's—the burnt hazel of a waning summer.

"I'm more interested in what business you have here with us," Mal said. "A little coincidental we were about to come find you when you showed up."

"Maybe it's a sign from God." Lyle smirked, nodding to Book.

It was the wrong thing to say to earn the captain's trust, but it was exactly the right thing to say to throw him off the scent of their past.

"Don't believe in signs, don't believe in God." Mal crossed his arms. "Now, you gonna tell me why you're on my boat?"

"Fair enough." Lyle put his hands up in surrender. "Well, as you so astutely deduced, I'm the foreman over at the refinery. Found myself in a bit of a pickle. Could use the help of some folks like you."

"And what kind of folks are we?"

"Savvy, strong, with the capacity to be airborne." Lyle's eyes traveled from Zoë to Jayne to Mal, and then finally landed on Book. "Folks I can trust."

"You don't have many of those, do you?" Mal asked. "Heard you're not so popular in town."

Lyle sighed, his shoulders dipping. "Hazards of the job, I suppose. Nobody likes you when you're the boss."

"Especially when you're the boss of a Blue Sun subsidiary." Zoë turned an icy gaze on Lyle. Good. Maybe she'd get some truth out of him. "Your workers don't like that much, do they?"

"No less than anyone else, I'd reckon. Folks never like it when someone else is in charge. There's always those that'd rather fight than work together."

"Used to be you were the one fighting, if memory serves," Book said before he could stop himself. He'd had decades to reflect on the sins he'd committed, sins Lyle had encouraged. Back then, he'd told himself he'd done what was necessary in order to survive. Now, he wasn't so sure the things he and Lyle had done had been in pursuit of anything as innocent as survival.

"Yes, well, things change." Lyle gave a wide smile. "Let's not linger on the past, though. I hear you need work and I've got it."

"In the refinery?" Mal asked.

"Not in it, no."

"You best not be askin' us to go scaring your workers into submission or anything." Mal said, narrowing his eyes. "We ain't interested in that sort of thing."

That was news to Book. Just before Lyle had arrived, scabbing had been very much on the table. But Mal worked in mysterious ways, he'd found. The captain of *Serenity* wasn't a loud man, and did no more talking than was necessary. But that meant a fair bit of maneuvering happened inside the man's head, where none of them could see it. Book was beginning to understand Malcolm Reynolds, in ways Mal would never truly know, but even that wasn't enough to keep up with him all the time.

"Then let me put your minds at ease." Lyle spread his hands wide as if showing them a battle map. "The refinery's got trouble. You're not wrong about that. I can handle folks unhappy with Blue Sun—hell, I can handle folks unhappy with me—but we're up against something worse."

"Worse than disgruntled workers?" Wash asked, a note of levity in his voice that Book considered inappropriate. "What could it be? Scylla and Charybdis? A dragon? The boogeyman?"

"You jest, but you're closer to the truth than you think." Lyle's lips twitched downward, a concentrated frown.

Book frowned, too. Once upon a time, he could read the muscles of Lyle's face like he could read his Bible now. He knew when he was being deceitful, and he knew when he was being honest. Maybe time had fogged Book's memory, or maybe Lyle had just gotten better at hiding things, but Book could have sworn that just then, Lyle was being neither truthful nor dishonest.

With a deep breath, Lyle continued, "Folks have been vanishing. One day they show up to the job, the next... they're gone."

"And you don't think maybe they're just sick of workin' for you?" Mal asked.

"Oh, I know they are. But that ain't why they're gone."

"And why is that, exactly?"

"Someone's takin' them." Lyle turned earnest eyes on Mal. "Brome ain't much, but to a lot of folks, it's home. Me included.

Not many choose this moon to settle down on. Not unless they have no other choice. About six months back, Brome got a new resident, Ms. Jenessa Leon. A lady. Not at all like the other folks here."

"How do you mean?" Mal asked.

"Well, for a start, she's got money. Enough to set up her own little compound on the other side of the moon. At first, she didn't bother us much. Just came in to town every so often, sometimes with visitors. Didn't really understand why—Brome's not much to look at, especially not to folks like her. But then things changed. Got weird."

"No offense, but Brome isn't exactly a bastion of normalcy." Wash gestured toward the open door and the town in the distance. "They tried to feed us grass burgers, for crying out loud."

Zoë put her hand on his shoulder and quieted him with a look. "Weird how?" she asked.

"Ms. Leon started asking folks questions, gettin' real nosy. And rude." Lyle wrinkled his nose. "Squalor—that's what she called living conditions out here. Right to our faces, too. She said Brome wasn't fit for civilized folks."

Mal scoffed. "Sounds to me like Brome wasn't fit for *her*. If she wanted civilization, there's a whole mess of central planets to choose from."

"Exactly! Why come here to our home and insult our way of life? That's why it's called *ours*, not *yours* or *hers*."

"What's this got to do with your missing workers?" Mal asked.

"That's what I'm getting to. See, Ms. Leon holes up in her compound and starts callin' herself Governess."

"Like... governor but for ladies?" Jayne asked.

"Or one of those live-in nannies?" suggested Wash.

"Either way, sounds like she's appropriating power that's not hers to take." Zoë turned to Lyle with a grim expression. "Let me guess, she's using her invented status to cause you trouble?"

Lyle nodded. "Started out just offering folks an alternative. Said they were welcome to join her if they were tired of how things are run on the outside. Says she's got a better life for 'em waiting inside her pretty walls. But now we got folks missing, and they ain't the sort to just up and leave their homes and families behind. Something's not right."

"So, you want us to go fetch 'em for you, is that it?" Mal asked, his expression unreadable. "Why can't you go yourself?"

Book wished he knew what was going on in the captain's head. Reynolds was not a stupid man, and Book had no doubt his mind was working double time to analyze all the information Lyle was providing. Still, he couldn't help but hold his breath as he watched their exchange.

"The Governess has a certain distaste for me. Can't imagine why." Lyle's smile was back, self-deprecating charm intact. "Not to mention a state-of-the-art security system. No one's getting in without express invitation from the Governess."

"So, we get an invite to this Governess's estate, find your missing people, and bring them to you?" Mal ticked each step off on his fingers.

"And you get the payout you need, and then some," Lyle said. His gaze traveled from the captain to land on Book. "Feels a bit like fate, you bein' here. I've got a good feeling about all this."

Book couldn't say he reciprocated.

"So, what do you say. Are we in business?" Lyle held out a hand to shake Mal's.

Mal eyed Lyle's outstretched hand. He didn't say yes, but he didn't say no either. Instead, he turned to look at Book.

"He's your friend, preacher. What do you say? Do you trust him?"

Book surveyed Lyle and saw all their history flash before his eyes. It meant something to him, it really did, but somewhere in

Book's mind he knew it would mean something to the captain, too—something he wasn't ready to discuss outside of his own prayers. Book hadn't made his first mistake today, nor the day before. He'd made plenty long before he ever met Lyle Horne, and countless more since. He just had to hope that trusting Lyle wasn't about to be another one. So he took one last look at Lyle, and did what he'd done all those years ago.

He said yes.

9

Jayne Cobb could usually tell when folks were lying. That was because people were lying a little bit most of the time.

Jayne lied plenty. To the crew, to his friends, to himself. So did everybody else. The doctor was lying when he told his sister everything would be all right, Kaylee was lying when she tried to act all refined for the doctor, and Wash was lying when he told Zoë he didn't want to have kids. Hell, Mal and Inara were lying every time they were in a room together and not ripping each other's clothes off. It was exhausting, but at least it was predictable.

There was only one truthful soul among them—or so Jayne had thought. The Shepherd was a holy man. Supposed to be righteous. But here he was, standing before the captain, the crew, and his old partner, lying like the rest of them.

Never put a man on a pedestal. He should've listened to his ma.

"Think we may be able to help you out, Mr. Horne," Mal said, reaching for the newcomer's hand and shaking it.

Jayne leaned heavily against the infirmary door, watching from afar. None of this sat right with him—the geese, the Shepherd, the unexpected guest. He couldn't put his finger on what exactly was so unsettling, but unsettling it was.

"Still," Mal continued, "I'd like to talk to some of the folks about town. Maybe start with the families of those taken?"

"Don't think you'll find them very interesting. Not much to know besides what I've already told you." Lyle Horne gave a half-hearted shrug. "You're better off using your time figuring out how to get through the Governess's security, if you ask me."

"Yes, well, I didn't, did I?" Mal's tone bit almost as hard as the geese. "No offense, Mr. Horne. I'm sure you've got your way of doin' things, which is why I know you'll respect that I've got mine."

"Who am I to argue with the experts? I hired you for a reason." The man's gaze swept over Book once more, searching for something but evidently failing to find it. "Just trying to get our people back promptly."

"I understand you're in a hurry." Mal indicated the open cargo-bay door and began to walk toward it. "Best we make haste, then."

"I, uh, all right then…" Lyle Horne allowed himself to be herded toward the exit.

Jayne had seen Mal handle nastier folk with as much finesse—Badger, for a start, not to mention Patience, Atherton Wing, and his own gorram wife. He didn't envy the captain that job. Jayne didn't much care one way or the other, as long as they got paid. He was more of a shoot-first-ask-questions-never sort of man. All this talk was making him dizzy. Or maybe that was just the pain medication.

Mal doled out orders like they were rations. "Zoë, you're with me. Kaylee, you talk to *Serenity*, see how much we can get out of her—the shuttles, too. Wash, I want you looking into this Governess and her compound."

"I may be able to help with that." Inara's voice floated down from the level above.

"She part of your world?" Mal asked, an edge to his voice.

"Not exactly, but women like her, sometimes they respond to a gentler touch."

Jayne looked at Mal with his one working eye, waiting to see if he'd say anything about that gentler touch. He didn't.

"Good. Appreciate it." Mal nodded curtly, then turned to go.

"What about me?" Jayne asked, wishing he sounded a mite less desperate. Sitting still was never his preference, and the captain had benched him all day. "Anything I can do?"

"You keep an eye on our guests here. Make sure none of 'em fly off."

Jayne flinched. He kept forgetting the geese were there. That was one benefit of wearing an eye patch—they were out of his line of sight most of the time. Then again, it could be a drawback if they all conspired to get the jump on him.

There was a general bustling as the crew got to work, following the captain's orders.

"I'm right behind you," Mal called after Zoë as she led Lyle Horne off *Serenity*. Then, he ducked back inside and made a beeline for Shepherd Book.

"Everything all right, Captain?" Kaylee asked.

"Ain't rightly sure," Mal turned his attention to the Shepherd. "Preacher, you got anything to you want to say?"

Jayne followed his gaze. Shepherd Book had seldom looked comfortable in all his months aboard *Serenity*. To be fair, they did an awful lot of crime under his godly nose and they didn't put much effort in toward hiding it. But now, in the wake of whatever all that was with Horne and the job, Jayne didn't think he'd ever seen him look like he did now, frozen.

"Nice to see old friends, isn't it?" Kaylee asked, chipper as always.

Jayne would've rolled his eyes, but the pain in his left peeper was enough to make a grown man weep. A different grown man. Not Jayne, of course.

"Not entirely certain *nice* is the word for it," Book finally said after a few moments' silence. "Strange, perhaps."

"Anything you want to share?" Mal pressed.

Book laughed hollowly. "You're asking the wrong question, Captain."

Mal crossed his arms. "Anything I should know you didn't care to say to his face?"

"Didn't think I'd ever see his face again, to tell the truth." Book's eyes were vacant as he stared at a blank spot in the distance. "I thought he was dead, but I should've known Lyle Horne wouldn't go down easy."

"You the one to put him down the first time?"

Book shook his head, paused, then shrugged. "Not on purpose."

Jayne pushed off the door, doing his best not to wobble. "Didn't think you had it in you, preacher."

"Jayne!" Kaylee shot him a dirty look. "He's obviously not proud of it."

"Oh, uh, right. Sorry." Jayne shuffled forward, arms outstretched as he went. He could see out of his right eye just fine, but it was a disorienting sort of vision. He couldn't quite tell what was close and what was far, and he didn't want to come up on anything out of the blue.

"You think he might hold a grudge?" Mal asked.

Book didn't respond, eyes misty with a bygone sheen.

"I ain't askin' to be nosy, preacher. If there's history might interfere with our dealings, I need to know."

"It won't." Book stood up straighter, a rigidity to his shoulders that wasn't there before. "Just... Be careful."

"Not exactly confidence inspiring words..."

Book sighed, clasped his hands behind his back, and turned his gaze to the captain, finally focused. "He's a loyal sort to those he's linked to. A good fighter, tenacious. He'll be a good ally—if that's what he wants to be."

"And if he don't?" Jayne asked.

"When I knew him, he was... unpredictable. But he could also be singularly focused. When he put his mind to something, he'd do it or die trying. Best not to stand in his way."

"My kind of man," Mal grunted.

Book's face broke into a smile. "You would've gotten along swimmingly, I think—or you would've killed each other."

"Well, guess we better find out which." Mal nodded toward the stairs. "You comin' with, Shepherd? Seems you know him best."

"*Knew.*"

"Sure. Whatever. Could use your insight."

"I'd rather not, if it's all the same to you."

"Suit yourself."

Mal headed out without a backward glance. Kaylee, too. She disappeared toward the engine room, muttering something about double-checking the fuel reserves, leaving Jayne and the Shepherd alone.

Jayne didn't speak for a while, just watched as muted honking filled the silence. Shepherd Book had, against all odds, become a friend. Jayne hadn't had many friends before, just partners he usually betrayed somewhere down the line, but Book... They were as unalike as two men could be, yet there was a kinship there Jayne would never have expected to find. He hadn't thought much about Book's life before *Serenity*, and it gave him a strange sort of unsettled feeling to know with certainty he'd had one at all. Shepherd Book had people—people like Lyle Horne. It just didn't line up.

"Why'd you lie?" Jayne asked eventually.

Shepherd Book didn't jump, exactly. It was instead the jarring quaver of a man lost in thought finally being found. "Pardon?"

"You know, about trustin' that Lyle guy."

"I don't know what you—"

"It's okay. We all do it." Jayne grimaced. "Just thought you knew, is all."

"Knew what?"

"Captain's got your back. He's got all our backs, even those of us he don't like all that much. Even when we don't have his." Jayne repressed a shudder. It wasn't all that long ago Mal had nearly thrown Jayne out of the airlock for what he'd done to the Tams. Simon and River weren't anywhere close to Mal's favorite passengers, but the captain had stood up for them right to the end. And then he'd given Jayne another shot. "Even when we don't deserve it."

Shepherd Book clapped Jayne on the arm. "We are all of us deserving of redemption."

"You think so?" Jayne couldn't help but ask. He wasn't too keen on religion most of the time, but the preacher had a way of seeing to the center of things. "I done a lot of things God wouldn't like, preacher, and I got no mind to stop." Between the thieving, the killing, and the things he liked doing out of wedlock, Jayne figured heaven wasn't really in the cards for him.

Book frowned, but then a chuckle burst from his lips. "You remind me of him—of Lyle. Back when I knew him, anyway."

Jayne didn't know what to make of that. Book had called Lyle Horne all sorts of words Jayne wasn't—like *loyal*—and more words Jayne didn't rightly understand—like *tenacious*—but he'd also called him a friend, and Jayne liked that well enough.

"Want to do a set?" Jayne pointed to the weights in the corner. They'd been moved to make room for the geese, but they were still usable.

"No, I don't think so."

"You sure? I might only have one workin' eyeball, but I can still spot you." Jayne crossed over to the weight rack, fumbling for the right combination for the Shepherd's starting bench. "Come on, just do a few. Stay sharp."

But the Shepherd shook his head, his expression drifting somewhere far off. "Already got plenty of weight on my shoulders today."

10

Two home visits later, Mal was no closer to understanding the situation.

"*Squalor* ain't exactly wrong, sir," Zoë said quietly as they came upon the third house. "I'm not saying I'd put it that way myself, just that maybe the Governess has a point."

With walls built from mud and a roof of dried grass, it was generous to call the structures the people of Brome lived in houses. They were more like large sheds or small barns. Mal had seen worse, but he'd also seen better.

"The way these people live ain't none of our concern."

Zoë gave him a withering look. "Could be if we end up stuck here."

That was true enough. Mal shaded his eyes with the flat of his palm. The heat beat down on them, heavy and bright. "Why is it so gorram hot?"

Zoë glanced up the sky. "Penglai's not far off. Must be a dual-sun kind of season."

"She's right," said Lyle Horne, who'd come to a halt outside a ramshackle structure. "Brome's always dry, but it ain't always hot. Right now is especially bad on account of us being on the short end of our orbit 'round Kalidasa and closing in on the Penglai triad."

Beylix, Newhouse, and Oberon. Mal had never done much in the way of studying the way planets, moons, and suns interacted in the 'verse. Still, he knew his planets.

"It's why we need you and your ship for this sort of mission." Horne grimaced at the bright sky. "No one could make the trek from here to the Governess's compound on foot and survive. This kind of heat ain't anything to sneeze at."

"The dust is, though," Zoë muttered through the cloth she'd tied around her face.

"The Archer residence. I'll see if anyone's home." Horne stepped forward to knock on the door, leaving Zoë and Mal a few paces behind.

"We better not be stuck here," Mal said under his breath. "It's hotter than *fèi fèi de pì yān* out here."

"You should've asked to borrow Kaylee's parasol," Zoë said.

"Wouldn't go with my outfit."

The door opened to reveal a short girl with freckles and a bushel of puffy copper hair. Her cheeks were round, but the circles under her eyes were hollow. She couldn't be older than River—maybe sixteen or seventeen.

"Mom!" she yelled as soon as she caught sight of them. "Boss man's here. Got company." Her eyes flicked to Mal, then Zoë. She let her gaze linger for a moment. "Oh... it's you."

"Friend of yours?" Mal asked.

"Not that I recall." Zoë cocked her head.

The girl ducked behind the door, muttering something about *town* and *strangers*.

"Hi, there. Sorry about that. I was in the back." A woman—Mrs. Archer, presumably—with the same curly hair red hair and shadowed eyes stepped into the doorway, shoulders rigid, gaze icy. "What can I do for you?"

Mal stepped forward. By now, he'd realized that Lyle Horne, well meaning as he might be, put people on edge. It was as he said: folks didn't like the man in charge.

"Hello, ma'am. My name is Malcolm Reynolds. I captain a Firefly ship."

"A Firefly?" came a muffled gasp from inside.

Mrs. Archer pressed a finger to her lips and swatted her hand behind her, shooing away the girl who'd answered the door. "Shh, Agate. Let me talk to 'em."

"Ugh, fine," the girl said before stomping off, her footsteps dull thunks against wooden planks.

"You were saying?" Mrs. Archer asked.

"Right. I mentioned that because Mr. Horne has employed me to help out with recovering the folks who were taken. I gather that's someone in your household?"

Mrs. Archer eyed Mal with trepidation, her gaze flicking to Lyle Horne once or twice before she said, "Yes, my wife. Just a few days back."

"Do you mind if we ask a few questions?" Mal gestured toward her house. He could feel the cooler air inside and longed to step out of the bright sun.

"Of course," Mrs. Archer said, but instead of opening the door wider for them, she stepped outside and shut the door with a click. "What d'you want to know?"

"Anything you can tell us," Zoë cut in. "When she left, if you noticed anything odd in the days before, any communication you've had since..."

"She didn't leave. She was taken. There's a difference," Mrs. Archer snapped. "And no, nothing strange. Dina went to work as usual. So did I, for that matter. We alternate shifts—she takes the day and I take the night. That way the girls are never on their own. Agate's old enough to watch the twins—they're only six—

but we don't like to put that on her if we can help it."

"And the day your wife was taken?" Mal pressed. To his right, Zoë took a few steps to the side, then peeled off. She had this way of vanishing in plain sight that would've unnerved him if he hadn't benefited from her stealthy maneuvers time and time again. Zoë knew what she was about. If something else pulled her focus, he trusted her to check it out without him. "Anything strange about that?"

"Other than the fact she disappeared, no. I came home near morning to trade off with her. Everything seemed normal, but then she didn't make it to her shift. At first, I thought it was—" Her eyes flashed to Horne for a split second.

"Family trouble?" Horne offered.

"No." Mrs. Archer's face pinched in disdain. "We have a happy home, despite... Just because we live modestly doesn't mean we love any less. Dina wouldn't have just left on her own. Besides which, where would she go? Not like there's another town just down the road."

"Wouldn't ever imply otherwise," Mal said. He wished Horne would back off. His presence was clearly putting the woman on edge, just as it had with the other people they'd visited, but every time Mal tried to speak to folks alone, Horne would cut in. It was like he wanted to stop Mal from digging too much. "Anything else you want to tell me? Anything I should know before we go lookin' for her?"

Mrs. Archer stared at Mal a few seconds too long before she said, "No. That just about covers it."

"Well, we thank you for your time, Mrs. Archer. Hopefully we'll have the other Mrs. Archer back to you in no time and this will all just be a little hiccup on the road back to normal."

Mrs. Archer gave them a smile that didn't reach her eyes before heading back inside.

"Well, there you have it," Horne brushed his hands together as though wiping away dirt. "Told you they wouldn't be much help."

Zoë reappeared at Mal's elbow as though she'd never left. "I think we got what we needed from them."

Mal decidedly did not feel that way. As Horne walked them back to *Serenity*, keeping up a steady stream of conversation with Zoë, Mal's mind wandered. Something just didn't add up. While he took Book's vote of confidence into consideration, he still wasn't certain Lyle Horne was a man they ought to be working with. No matter how well meaning the man was, he wasn't well liked, and that counted for something, as much as Mal wished it didn't.

Still, Mal was in no position to turn down the work, what with nine geese, empty fuel reserves, and a crew that needed to eat. They'd just have to do the job and hope it went smoothly. Not that he had any evidence to indicate it would.

"I'll come round in the morning with coordinates for the compound and we can discuss any further considerations then," Horne said as they approached *Serenity*. "I have a good feeling about this—about you." He gave them a grin and a wave before turning to walk into the tall, tall grass.

Mal frowned after him.

"Something the matter, sir?" Zoë asked.

"What ain't?"

"You know we have to help those people, don't you?"

"Yup," Mal grumbled. The truth of it was, even if *Serenity*'s fuel tanks were full, he couldn't walk away now. "It's just... Back there with those families, something didn't feel right."

Zoë nodded gravely as they climbed the ramp into the cargo bay. "Their families have been torn apart. I'd be surprised if it did."

11

"Here's the plan," said Captain Malcolm Reynolds.

River liked it when the captain spoke that way, with authority. It was like he had a gravitational pull they were all caught in. There was a rhythm to it, a pattern, like planets orbiting a sun. It made her want to cut loose and float along with them.

But River held her ground. The best she could do was watch. And feel. And dream.

"We can't all be everywhere at once, nor should we be. This job requires a multi-pronged approach. Everyone's gonna pitch in."

Everyone. He said it like it meant something.

She knew he didn't mean her.

River pressed against the wall, feeling the cool metal of *Serenity* through the fabric of her dress. The whole crew sat around the dining table. Together. A family.

River hadn't been invited.

She'd come anyway.

"What we've got here is a recovery mission. Basically, we've got cargo to steal, except that cargo is people. The more folks involved, the more potential for chaos, so I need you all sharp, *dōng ma*?"

People were too complex. People were too autonomous. That's what the captain meant.

If she were simple, would they bring her into the fold? River shuddered as a memory lanced through her. Sharp metal in the back of her mind. *Assimilate, assassinate, do as you are told. Be a weapon, not a girl. Two by two, hands of blue.*

River let the feeling course through her like her namesake. She leaned her head back and sank down to the floor. Breath came and went. She tried to hold on to the oxygen, tried to blink away the brightness.

It was like this sometimes when there were too many of them at once. Crowds did not agree with River. It was better if she knew them, but even the eight people one room over were overwhelming. There was certainty, anxiety, longing, anger, respect, and fervor all at once. It was everywhere. It was everyone.

She counted the things she could feel—the metal floor, the sweat on her brow, the smooth silk against her legs—but it was the sound of the captain's voice that brought her back to the present, grounding her.

"One group—we'll call them Team A—will meet the Governess. Inara's already reached out and gotten an invitation, so that's settled."

"She's expecting us for tea," Inara said, her voice clipped with unspoken angst. "Me and my… *husband*, that is. We'll be posing as potential donors to her philanthropic efforts on Brome."

"Husband, you say?" Wash asked. River could feel the joke in his throat before it took flight. "Which one of us lucky cads will it be, then?"

"Careful, or you won't be anybody's husband by the time we leave this godforsaken rock," Zoë smacked the side of his head playfully.

Jayne's gruff tone sailed over the sound of Wash's protests. "So, the captain and Inara will be playing decoy while—"

"Simon," Kaylee said in a small voice. "It should be Simon, don't you think?"

"What? Me?"

Simon's flustered face glowed like a beacon in River's mind. She didn't need to see him to know the pink tinge of his cheeks and the acceleration of his heart. It was a good heart. A stupid heart. Her brother wanted in strange patterns, reaching out and pushing back in equal measure. He wanted numbers and facts and lists of pro and con. He wanted without knowing what it was to *need*, and it all came out quiet and neglected like a planet far from the sun.

He had always been like this, she tried to reason, but lying to herself was harder now that her brain was no longer wired to protect her from painful truth. Simon sought only safety now when before he'd sought joy. She'd taken that from him.

"Makes sense, don't it?" Kaylee asked. "If you're supposed to be donors, you need to look the part. Like you've got money. No offense, Cap'n."

"None taken." The captain chuckled on the outside. River could feel his plaintive whine on the inside. "Probably for the best."

"Is it?" Simon asked, bewildered.

"You'll be a great fake husband," Zoë said, clapping him on the shoulder. "And you couldn't have a better fake wife."

It was the wrong thing to say. Simon was always tangled knots, but now Kaylee was too.

River sighed and leaned out to get a look at the crew. They were all huddled together around some kind of map or diagram in the center of the table. Mal stood in the middle, hands splayed wide, with Zoë and Wash on his right, Jayne on his left, and Kaylee, Simon, and Inara opposite. The Shepherd sat in the corner, unspeaking. His brain wasn't quiet, though. He was gone.

River tilted her head as his past washed over her in sepia tones—a different time, a different name, a different man.

Mal cleared his throat. "So, the newlyweds will take Inara's shuttle to the front gate and distract the Governess. Meanwhile, Team B—that's me and Zoë—we'll get in and find the folks who need rescuing."

"How exactly are you going to do that?" Simon asked. "If her compound is protected, you won't be able to get past her security system."

"See this here?" Wash's chair made a regrettable noise as he pushed it back to point at something River couldn't see. "There's a dome around the place. An electromagnetic field. No way in or out with that live."

"So, how do we disable it?" Jayne asked.

"We don't." Mal nodded to Inara. "The Governess is going to do it for us when you arrive. We'll have to time it right, but me and Zoë will approach from the rear—"

Jayne snorted. Everyone ignored him.

"—and when the field comes down, we'll slip through."

Simon leaned forward to look at the map. "And what about your retreat?"

"You and Inara will keep the Governess busy as long as you can. Keep her going—ask as many questions as you can think of. We're gonna need the time. Then, when you get the signal, you say goodbye. Me and Zoë will leave the same way we came in, cargo in tow."

"And what is the signal exactly?" Simon's brow furrowed in concentration.

"That's where the rest of you come in." Mal gestured to Wash. "Everyone else stays put on the ship. You get this place squared away for a few extra passengers, then when you hear from me, you fly overhead. You'll be able to see *Serenity* through the dome, or at the very least you'll hear her even if you're indoors. Then, you take the shuttle and you meet up with us here." Mal moved his finger to indicate another point on the map.

Jayne leaned back, all envy and pride, wrath and avarice waiting in the wings. "How are we gonna hear from you if you're in the compound with that electro-thingy up?"

"Little Kaylee? You got us covered?" Mal turned to the mechanic.

"I... I think so." Kaylee's fingers knit together, a tight weave of hesitance. "Getting the comms to work through the electromagnetic field is gonna be tricky."

"But..." Mal prompted. He believed in Kaylee stronger than any parent. River felt it radiating off of him in waves, his faith in her—that she would see them through, that she would see *Serenity* through. It was a shared world for only the two of them, the people who loved *Serenity* best. River skated by, trailing her fingers in the ripples of trust. She was there, too; they just couldn't see her.

"But if we reverse the polarity and Wash boosts the signal from the bridge, we should be able to bypass it entirely. Won't even notice we're there." Kaylee grinned. "Never done it before, but how hard can it be?"

"That's our girl." Mal rapped his knuckles once on the table. "Any questions?"

"Do I go with you and Zoë, then?" Jayne asked.

"You stay on *Serenity*," said Mal.

"*Cái bù shì*. You need me. What if there's shootin'?"

"There won't be." Mal set his jaw. "Besides, what kind of shot will you be with your eye all messed up? Jayne, you're as likely to shoot one of us as the enemy like that."

And there was wrath, all bruised and gutted. Jayne bristled with it, inside and out. "Now, that ain't fair."

"Yeah, well most things ain't." Mal turned to the others. "Everyone clear?"

"He's right." The Shepherd stood, finally breaking his silence. "You're a man down without Jayne."

"The captain and I have run plenty of missions just the two of us. I think we can handle it." Zoë exchanged a quick glance with Mal. Uncertainty bled between them, an open wound.

"Besides," Mal began, nodding in agreement, "I want you here in town. Somebody needs to keep an eye on our new friend, and who better than *his* old friend?"

"I'll go." Book took three paces to join them at the table. "You need the manpower. It would be a waste to have me stay behind when I'm a steady shot and you need backup."

River nearly drowned in the desperation the Shepherd carried. Fear prickled at his edges. He didn't want to be alone with a mirror, to look at his reflection and see the truth.

"You sure, Shepherd?" Zoë asked, giving him an apprehensive look. "Forecast says cloudy with a chance of violence."

"I wouldn't have offered if I didn't think I could handle it." Book bent his head and lowered his voice. "The captives might be bound or injured. You'll need an extra pair of hands. Besides, could be they'll be comforted by the presence of a Shepherd."

"They'll be the only ones," Mal grunted. The lie brushed up against River's forearms, making the hairs there stand on end. "All right. That's a plan. Let's hope it works."

"It won't," River said quietly. "They won't let it."

Everyone looked up at her, suddenly aware of her presence.

Concern, irritation, frustration, fear. River let the feelings wash over her for a moment, closing her eyes against the onslaught of attention.

"They will take her when your back is turned." She opened her eyes and focused on the captain, her arms rising beside her like wings. "And she will give them the sky."

12

It felt good to be moving. Mal wasn't good at sitting on his hands and waiting. Forward momentum was exactly what they needed. They had a job to do, and that was when his crew shone brightest. He took the stairs to the cargo bay two at a time.

"I should be able to get us near enough without detection," Wash said, following behind. "You'll have to take the shuttles from there."

"That's good. Don't want *Serenity* running out of fuel, anyhow. How long?" Mal asked.

"Few hours. Not a very big moon."

Wash put a hand on Mal's shoulder as they slowed. The geese, alerted to their presence, began to honk again. "You take care, all right?"

"You know Zoë can handle herself." After the recent business with Niska, Wash had backed off some when it came to his wife. Still, Mal could understand the worry in the pilot's eyes. Nothing was ever a sure thing in their line of business.

"I was talking about you." Wash's expression went somber. "Don't need any more close calls, all right?"

Before Mal had a chance to respond, Jayne's voice caught up to them. "Mal! Wait up, Mal!"

"I told you no, Jayne. I'm taking Zoë and the Shepherd and that's final. I ain't inclined to repeat myself." He turned to look at Jayne Cobb, a frown on both their faces.

It wasn't that long ago Mal had nearly fired the man. After his stunt on Ariel, Mal wasn't sure he could be trusted anymore. Trust, he knew, was all he had out in the black. Without it, they were just nine people in close proximity with nothing but *Serenity*'s outer shell separating them from the vacuum of space. With it, they were still nine people, still perilously close to an unpleasant death, but with a tether between them all. They were a crew, a family. Jayne had almost broken that.

"Nah, Mal, I just... I was thinkin'—"

"Yeah? You and what brain cell?" Wash asked, a chuckle in his throat.

"*Qù nǐ de*," spat Jayne. "I got ideas sometimes." He looked from Mal to Wash and back again. "Good ones."

"I'll believe that when I hear one." Mal crossed his arms and surveyed the man before him.

He took it upon himself to know exactly what drove each of his crew. It was his job as captain to understand their motivations and make sure they got what they needed to keep flying with him. Kaylee wanted to see places and tend to *Serenity*, Wash wanted to test his limits, and Zoë wanted to protect them all.

Jayne... Jayne was the easiest to understand and the hardest to satisfy. He wanted money. Lots of it. And right now, *Serenity*'s supply was drier than a Brome summer.

But now, Jayne was looking at him with an earnest expression Mal didn't see often. Jayne was good in a pinch, even those he brought down on them himself, but Mal was reluctant to put his trust in him so soon after his betrayal on Ariel.

"You don't gotta let me come with, but I can still help," Jayne said. "Shepherd doesn't wanna babysit Lyle Horne? Let me do it."

"Oh, I see what this is about." Wash chuckled. "You want to get away from the geese."

"What? No!" Jayne protested. "Just wanna be useful."

"You're scared of them." Wash grinned. "Do they give you *goosebumps*?"

"Wash..." Mal warned. Jayne was easily moved to violence and Wash couldn't take a punch nearly as well as Jayne. In a fight, it was easy to see who would win. Mal was hoping it wouldn't come to that. He turned to Jayne, aiming to steer the conversation in a less avian direction. "You think you're up for that sort of mission?"

Jayne nodded. "Yeah, Mal. I can do it."

"I don't want you tryin' to do too much. I just need you to watch him. Keep your head down and your eyes open..." Mal glanced up at the patch covering Jayne's left eye. "Eye open."

"Reconnaissance, Mal. I know how it's done."

Mal was surprised Jayne knew the word reconnaissance, let alone what it meant. Still, if Jayne wanted to make himself useful, Mal wasn't going to stand in his way. "Don't get too friendly with him. No need to complicate things. But see if you can't find out what's got the town all bent out of shape over him and Blue Sun. Might be it's none of our concern. Might be it is."

Jayne nodded eagerly. "I'll do it, you'll see."

Mal chewed the inside of his lip, eyes unfocusing as thoughts obscured his mind. "Lyle Horne. Something about him just smells—"

"*Fowl?*" Wash supplied with a significant glance at the gaggle of geese in the enclosure.

Jayne knocked Wash's shoulder hard with his own as he turned to go, and Wash toppled into the Mule with a loud bang.

"Ouch!" Wash yelped, holding his elbow. "My funny bone."

"That's enough, Wash." Mal's gaze followed Jayne as he went. He wasn't Mal's first choice for this sort of job, but he was at least more likely than Book to tell Mal if he learned anything about the connection between Lyle and the Shepherd. Book would've kept all that to himself. Maybe none of it mattered, but Mal was curious nonetheless.

"Do you think he got it? The joke?" Wash asked. "Because, you know, foul... fowl... because geese are—"

"Wash," Mal grunted, patience thin. "Go fly my damn spaceship."

13

Simon didn't make a habit of going to the Companion's shuttle. It wasn't that he didn't like Inara or her profession, it was that he respected them both. He never wanted to impose.

"Please, make yourself at home," Inara said, gesturing to the room with a sweeping motion.

Simon didn't have the heart to tell her the only place he felt truly at home was in an operating room. Bright lights, clean hands, and a problem before him he knew how to fix. A lot of people thought trauma surgery was chaos, but it wasn't. It was order. When Simon was in the OR, everything slowed down around him. He had to prioritize and move through a thousand bits of incoming data at once. Holding a life in his hands, knowing one wrong move would end it… It was easier to be responsible for a stranger. He couldn't really call anyone on *Serenity* that anymore.

Inara's shuttle was strangely lush. For a ship that was all exposed metal and sharp angles, she'd carved herself a corner of beauty in an otherwise starkly barren world. She had adorned her space in shades of maroon and red. He'd been told once that the color red made people angry, but here in the shuttle, it was coupled with soft draping fabric for an oddly calming effect.

Simon cast his gaze about the room for a suitable place to sit. Not the bed—that would be uncouth. Instead, he ventured toward the least obtrusive chair in sight, a black perfunctory-looking seat situated between two hanging curtains.

"Simon." Inara placed her hand on his shoulder gently.

Simon jumped at her touch. "Ah! Yes?"

Inara chuckled, a gentle tinkly sound like bells. "That's the pilot's seat. Why don't you sit here?" She gestured to a plush-looking red sofa. "Unless you want to fly the shuttle?"

Simon shook his head. "No, no. I better not." He scrambled over to sit on the very edge of the seat she'd indicated. "I have about as much experience with flying as I do with being married."

"Well, I'll take the wheel then, shall I?" Inara sat in the pilot's seat and made a quarter-turn, but paused to fix Simon with a curious expression. "At least we are on level playing field when it comes to the latter."

"We are?" Simon asked, surprised. "With your profession, I assumed you would have a great deal more knowledge in that realm than me."

"Knowledge of intimacy is not the same as knowledge of marriage." Inara twisted in her seat to face him fully. "Are we speaking of the former or the latter?"

Simon wished he'd never said anything at all. "I, uh, I didn't mean to imply… I simply…"

Inara, to her credit, seemed not to take offense. She was, perhaps, the only person aboard *Serenity* who did not look for insult in his words. Instead, she smiled curiously and tilted her head. "We don't have to speak of either, if you don't wish to, but I suspect we might both benefit from a frank conversation on the topic if we are to convince anyone we are husband and wife."

Simon nodded slowly. She had a point, of course. He just wished she didn't.

"Perhaps it would surprise you to know that Companions are permitted to marry," Inara said. "It's uncommon, but it is in no way forbidden."

"Is that not... potentially awkward?"

Inara laughed. "Many things worth pursuing are. The potential for tension is not reason enough to deny oneself one's desires, is it?"

Simon rather thought yes, it was, but he wasn't about to say so. "Is that something you want?" A long silence followed his question as Inara surveyed him. "I'm sorry. Is that too personal? Maybe I shouldn't have been so forward?"

Inara's gaze cut away and down, her eyes flickering with something housed between hope and regret. Simon had been a doctor long enough to know what pain looked like, and this... Inara was in agony.

"No," she said, finally.

He didn't know which of his questions she was answering at first, but then she continued.

"Marriage wouldn't mesh well with my business, I should think. For some, it is enough to love, but for many they need to possess. I do not believe that intimacy is a finite resource, but I know mine is a minority opinion." She paused and her gaze met his. "Do you know why I chose to fly with *Serenity*?"

Simon shook his head.

"Freedom," she said. "I wanted to see the world and meet interesting people, but I also wanted to be able to conduct my business my own way. A spouse would complicate that."

"The right spouse wouldn't."

Inara smiled sadly. "The heart doesn't always want what's right."

Simon's mind flashed to the little moments he'd seen over the past months on the ship—Inara and Mal exchanging a glance, sitting side by side, the way the air felt heavier when they were both in a room. It seemed so obvious—even to Simon, who was often the last to notice such things—that they shared some unspoken connection. But then he thought of all the times Mal had expressed his distaste for her profession. Sometimes he treated her like a queen, and others like an unwanted ingredient in an otherwise acceptable meal. He claimed to protect her honor as a woman, but not as a Companion, as if they were not one and the same.

"The heart is just a muscle," Simon said at last. "It can't want anything at all."

"You would say it like that." Inara shook her head, a fond smile playing at her lips. "What about you? Surely a strapping young doctor like you has had plenty of amorous attention. Did you ever consider getting married?"

"Oh, I, uh…" Now it was Simon's turn to look away. "Being a surgeon didn't leave me much room for social engagements, actually. It's not something I've thought about a great deal."

For as long as he could remember, Simon had felt as if he was delaying his life. His childhood had been spent with his nose in a book, studying to live up to his father's expectations. Then there had been medical school, where he'd lost himself in memorizing bones and nerves and cells and veins. And by the time adulthood had caught up to Simon, he'd thrown himself into finding River.

Now he'd found her, and still he was on the run.

"I've told a lot of lies about myself," Simon continued, a nervous laugh breaking from his chest. "But pretending to be married… I don't think I've ever felt like more of a fraud."

"Simon." Inara said his name so softly, like it was one of her velvets. "Inexperience is not a flaw."

"Inexperience?" Simon spluttered. "Oh, I… No. I didn't mean to imply—"

Inara held up a hand, her lips folding into a true smile. "You are under no obligation to disclose any history you do not wish to share with me. Fake married or not, I only want to know what you want to tell me."

Simon stilled. Part of him wanted to explain, to defend himself, to tell her he'd been with women before. He wouldn't mention how few, and he wouldn't mention how little it had mattered most of the time. There wasn't a lot of time for sex in a hospital; there was even less time for love. He didn't want Inara to think ill of him… but then, maybe she wouldn't. Of all the people who might understand, Inara wouldn't have been his first guess, but her words felt like a balm. *I only want to know what you want to tell me.*

"It's funny," he said after a long pause. "Of all the things I thought my life would be, I don't think I ever imagined that kind of future—a wedding, a wife, kids. I wonder if River… if I hadn't…" He trailed off, pain inching its way up his sternum as it always did when he allowed his mind to wander to a realm of *what if*.

"It's okay to talk about it." Inara pooled her hands in her lap, palms up. "Just because you can imagine that life, it doesn't mean you have to want it."

Simon's chest constricted. No one had ever granted him that sort of permission. When he talked about it with River, it felt like betrayal. When he talked about it with Kaylee, it felt like hope. Here with Inara, it didn't feel like anything. It just was.

"I miss a lot about what could have been. There were things I was going to do. I was going to save lives, learn new things. I was going to be someone." He gritted his teeth. "It sounds so egotistical when I say it like that, but I just… I had plans, and those all had to change."

"I understand," Inara said. "I left a lot of things behind myself as well."

Tension bled from Simon's neck and shoulders as she spoke. "I never thought about it—not before. Falling in love, getting married—they felt like boxes to check off later, things that could wait until I wasn't so busy. Strange how they finally caught up to me all the way out here."

"Not so strange," Inara said, a slight frown on her lips. "The way Mal flies this ship, we're always running. From the Alliance, from the past, from whatever enemies we make along the way. But I think the farther we are from everything, the more difficult it is to escape the little pieces of ourselves that tell us the truth. We can't ignore what we want when it's all we have to think about." Her words came in a long exhalation as she turned to face the central console, fingers ghosting over the controls.

Mal's voice crackled through the speaker. "Inara, you and the doc ready? Time to fly."

She pressed down on a button with her thumb and said, "Disembarking in five... four... three... two... one."

Simon scrambled to hold on as a rushing sound of changing pressure filled his ears. Inara gripped the steering console, pulling them up and away from the Firefly with finesse, and then they were level once more.

"So... I'm going to be your husband, then," Simon said eventually, the word awkward on his lips.

"Only for the next couple of hours." Inara glanced back at him, a question in her gaze. "I hope it won't be too uncomfortable for you."

"Likewise."

They flew in silence for a while, both staring at the golden horizon as the suns rose over a skyline of cracked earth and dry grass. Eventually, a structure came into view. Tall white walls of Grecian-style architecture stood stark in a valley of loose dirt and tumbleweeds. As they soared overhead, Simon got a glimpse of a shimmery haze surrounding the circular compound below—the electromagnetic dome. It was a hazy sort of barrier, distorting the estate as though through a heat cloud—blink and one might miss it entirely.

Inara pressed a few buttons and the shuttle slowed and began to descend.

"Are you ready?" she asked, standing and brushing out the wrinkles in her skirt.

"As I'll ever be."

Inara held out a hand, and he stared at it for a moment before taking it. Her touch was like a static shock. Maybe it was good that his first attempt at romance since leaving his old life behind was a farce. It would give him time to prepare himself if he ever got a chance at the real thing.

"I think I do want it," he said. "You asked before and I… I wasn't sure."

"It's okay to not be sure," Inara said. "But don't deny yourself happiness because you think you're not allowed to have it."

"It's just that I chose this. I chose to come after River. I chose to leave it all behind." Simon let out a long breath. He hadn't said any of this out loud before, and he found the weight of it overwhelming. "I chose this life."

"Sometimes the life you chose isn't the one you dreamed, but that doesn't make it less worthy." Inara squeezed his hand and led him toward the door. "Make sure you live it, anyway."

14

Jayne didn't like getting left behind. It didn't matter that he was the one who suggested it or that it was temporary. He always knew he'd watch *Serenity* fly off into the sky without him someday, he just thought it would be him doing the leaving. It almost always was.

"Well, Mr. Cobb, I sure hope your friends know what they're doing." Lyle Horne stood beside him, a frown creasing his brow as he squinted after the Firefly. "I don't much like entrustin' my affairs to strangers, but desperate times and all that."

"You ain't," Jayne said gruffly.

Horne cocked his head. "Sorry, don't follow."

"Shepherd's not a stranger, now, is he?" Jayne gave Horne a pointed look. It was the whole reason they'd taken the job in the first place. "You're old *friends*?" He twisted the last word with just a hint of a question.

Horne chuckled, but there was a steeliness to the sound. "Emphasis on *old*. Strange how time warps the memory."

"Can't imagine him young, if I'm being honest," said Jayne, glancing over at Horne. "Boggles the mind." He couldn't tell what the other man was trying to say. Of course, Horne might've been trying very specifically not to say anything at all. Maybe it was just the early hour—Horne wasn't at his most wakeful and cogent—or maybe the distrust between old friends was mutual. It wasn't exactly Jayne's job to stick his nose in the Shepherd's business, but it wasn't *not* his job either.

"We were barely grown when I knew him… don't think he's ever been *young*. The 'verse didn't let him have much of a childhood neither. He was always a worrier, thinkin' ten steps ahead on everything we did. Never did cut loose and just enjoy himself." Horne sighed and turned, beginning a slow trek toward town. "Gun to my head, never would've figured him for a preacher, though. That some kind of ruse?"

Jayne followed a few steps behind. "How d'ya mean?"

"Oh, maybe you put people at ease, make 'em think all's on the up-and-up since there's a Shepherd along with you. Then you get the drop on 'em."

"You done an awful lot of crime, Mr. Horne?"

"Now, why would you go askin' me something like that?"

"Just seems a fella like you would have to know a thing or two about foolin' folks to think up a con like that."

"I'm a businessman, Mr. Cobb."

Jayne scuffed his boots along the loose, dry Brome soil, kicking up a small cloud of it around his feet. Apologies didn't come to him naturally and he wasn't inclined to offer one up just for saying what he was thinking. Folks slung sorrys about like they were fists, easy to come by and just as dangerous, but Jayne was much more practiced with the latter.

Horne didn't seem offended, thankfully. Instead, he grinned at Jayne, a twinkle in his hazel-gray eyes. "You don't get far in my line of work thinkin' like a square. Success ain't a one-way ladder. You wanna climb it, you gotta be willin' to push folks out of your way, if you get my meaning."

Jayne surveyed the man before him. Book had said they were a little alike. He still wasn't sure whether he should take that as a compliment, but he was beginning to understand the two of them might have a thing or two in common after all.

"I think I do," Jayne said with a smile of his own. "Not like there's infinite money out there. You want more of it, you better be ready to take it from someone else."

"I bet you're a *gè zhēn de hún dàn*." Horne's gaze swept over Jayne, a calculation Jayne couldn't quite follow. Then he slugged Jayne on the arm and said, "Let me buy you a drink."

"A bit early for that," Jayne grumbled. The suns were barely cresting the horizon, lighting the town before them in eerie pre-dawn golden light. The structures of the town cast long shadows across the barren plane. Bromegrass reached for them like fingers. "I ain't even had breakfast yet."

Horne raised his eyebrows, fixing Jayne with an amused look. "In that case, let me buy you two."

15

Inara was not easily impressed. She'd seen no shortage of awe-inspiring sights in her life thus far. She'd been to extravagant temples and palaces, felt the most lavish fabrics on her skin, stood at the top of a plunging waterfall with a crystalline lake at its base, and dined with some of the most interesting people in the 'verse. But the scene that met her at the gates of the Governess's compound rendered her nearly speechless.

"It's uh... very green," Simon remarked. An understatement if ever there was one.

Visibility had been suboptimal in the early morning light as they'd landed the shuttle, but now that Inara and Simon stood before the translucent electromagnetic gates of the compound, the oasis before them was much clearer. Lush, green foliage the likes of which they'd not yet seen on Brome, was tidily spaced out on either side, and the trickling sound of water in the distance made Inara feel as though she were back on Sihnon rather than a barren border moon. The air around them suddenly felt cooler, as though the compound within was a temperature-controlled room rather than on a world with a punishingly hot climate.

"Welcome," said a delicate feminine voice as a crackle of electricity filled the air. The electromagnetic gate seemed to melt before them, like removing a pair of spectacles that were the wrong prescription, revealing a sharp view of the expansive grounds and the woman in the center of it all.

Mid-forties, with dark silken hair and glowing pale skin, the Governess had staved off the effects of age particularly well for someone residing on such a sun-blasted moon. She wore a dress of cerulean brocade and gold jewelry that sparkled in the sunlight. The Governess—Jenessa Leon—was a woman Inara did not know but felt she'd met a thousand times.

"Do come in. There's plenty of shade to go around." The Governess gestured around at the potted lemon trees placed around the edges of the compound. She stood in the middle of a stone pathway leading up to a large building made of white marble and large panels of glass, with an impressive number of stories and a balcony running all the way around. The architecture was an odd combination of neoclassical elements and more modern design. Light reflected from it at every angle so it was difficult to look directly at it. The Governess looked unbothered by the brightness, eyeing Inara with a careful gaze. "You must be Mrs. Gale."

Inara buried her discomfort at the honorific. It was a title she knew she'd never hold, and still it stirred something in her. No matter how she framed it in terms of business, there was always going to be a part of her that longed for connection, for love, for permanence. None were within her reach. Besides, she couldn't afford the sentimentality.

With an outstretched hand and the warmest smile she could muster, Inara stepped forward. "Governess. A pleasure. Please, call me Adaline."

"The pleasure's all mine, dear." The Governess took her hand in both of her own and squeezed. She had a soft touch, unburdened by labor, not unlike Inara's own. "And you've brought your husband, too."

Inara cleared her throat and extracted herself from the woman's grip to take Simon's arm. She prided herself on never taking clients she didn't want to be with so she rarely had to pretend at feelings she did not have. Still, she'd frequented the circles of elite members of society, and all of them had some charade or other in motion. She knew the ins and outs of playing a part. She just had to hope Simon would prove an adequate scene partner.

"Of course. Roland always likes to see potential investments before committing to them." Inara placed a hand on Simon's bicep. He bowed under her touch and she gave a slight squeeze.

"Well, let's get to business, then, shall we?" The Governess beckoned them forward down a stone path toward a central building—white, like the rest of the compound—with a high arched doorway.

Behind her back, Simon bent to look at her, a question in his gaze as he mouthed, "Roland?"

Inara shrugged. She'd needed to create believable aliases for them in case the Governess had a better connection to the Cortex than they did. Adaline and Roland were a couple she'd met many years ago from Londinium. If the Governess tried to research them, at the very least she would find a legitimate marriage license and a well-connected family. More importantly, she wouldn't find anything related to Simon or his sister, which was the more pressing matter at hand.

She took one last glance at the grounds, hoping for—or perhaps not—a glimpse of Mal and the others. Surely, they were inside already. But it was not her purview to ensure the rest of the crew performed their roles, so she turned her back on the stone pathway into the trees and followed the Governess into her fortress of glass.

The Governess led them inside, past a grand piano in the entryway and up a spiral staircase into a room with high ceilings and large windows. A waterfall inside a crystal casing lined one wall, light filtering in through the cascading water to catch in the gold joinery of kintsugi pottery displayed down the middle of a long banquet table that ran from one end of the room to the other. It was the sort of décor Inara encountered on the central planets, but this close to the Rim she hadn't expected to find such opulence.

"Do you host many dinner parties?" Simon asked.

"Alas, no." The Governess trailed a finger along the smooth finish of the table and sighed. "Bellerophon oak. Pity I don't get more use out of it."

"It's a beautiful piece," Inara said. They were delicate, these sorts of pleasantries. They couldn't dawdle too long, nor could they launch into talks of business without being impolite. The right balance was key to the art of conversation, though of course it mattered very little what they spoke of as long as they kept the Governess distracted. Inara positioned herself at the opposite end of the table, facing the entrance, so the Governess would have her back against window. It wouldn't do for her to catch sight of Mal and the others outside. "It must have been quite the ordeal to transport it here."

"Indeed! The first ship I contracted wanted to saw it in half so it would fit more easily in their cargo hold, but I wouldn't have it. Ended up paying an additional fare, but I think it was worth it." The Governess stepped behind the chair at the head of the table, bracing both hands on its back. Behind her, the large glass window overlooking the grounds behind the building was bright as the sun rose over the walls. Inara could just make out several small huts in the greenery—homes for the Governess's guests, perhaps, or for an as-yet invisible staff.

"There's no need to stand on ceremony, friends. Please, make yourselves comfortable, and ask me whatever you'd like to know."

Inara exchanged a brief glance with Simon. The time she'd allotted to discuss their fictitious marital arrangement back on the shuttle had been spent instead on their very real feelings on the subject instead. Perhaps not the best use of their time, given the circumstances. She knew Simon fairly well by now, but Simon as Roland Gale… that was another story.

"Well, I suppose an overview of what exactly it is you do here would be helpful," Simon began. "I'm afraid I'm not as well researched as Ina— as I'd like to be."

The Governess gave him a kind smile before turning to a side table to collect a tea tray that had been set out. She busied herself with pouring three cups of steaming liquid that smelled faintly of jasmine. It was not the level of ceremony Inara usually employed when serving tea, but she appreciated the show of hospitality all the same, accepting the proffered teacup—ceramic with painted pink and gold blossoms—with murmured thanks. Simon only blinked, failing to take his own cup of tea as the Governess held it out for him. Inara reached for it instead, placing it on Simon's open palm. It struck Inara as odd for a fleeting moment that the Governess did not have a butler or some other staff serving them instead of herself.

Once they all had their tea in hand, the Governess turned to Inara, addressing her answer to her, even though Simon had been the one to ask. "As I'm sure you've seen on your visit to Brome thus far, it offers very little to its residents. Life here is difficult. Your average Broman has shelter, clean water, or enough food for the family; rarely all three. Money is as scarce as resources, and the only thing that grows here is bromegrass."

Inara tried her best not to look too intently at the massive table before them. The credits it must have cost to build, let alone transport, might have saved countless families on Brome a great deal of hardship.

"Forgive me for saying it so bluntly, but it seems you're able to maintain a garden. Why can't they?" Simon asked.

Inara eyed him carefully. Either he was playing the role of a clueless moneybag expertly, or he was more naive than she thought.

"Come, let me show you."

The Governess beckoned them forward and, much like the dome outside, the large window overlooking the rest of the estate vanished, leaving room for them to walk directly out onto the veranda. Inara was once again struck by the odd sensation that, though they'd stepped outside, nothing about the climate around them had changed. Dread pooled low in her stomach as she swept her gaze over the scene below, hunting for any flashes of movement.

From their vantage point above, the estate looked even more impressive. The architecture itself was little more than perfunctory. Half a dozen single-story buildings made of a white-toned clay with shingled roofs were spaced evenly along either side of a trickling stream, shaded by tall trees with wide, flat leaves. It reminded Inara of a retreat or remote resort. She might have forgotten, if not for the faint hum of electricity from the dome above, that they were on such a barren planet. Near the edge of the enclosure, she spotted an electrical tower topped with a shimmering silver disk of some kind, curved along the edges so that it was reminiscent of a flower.

"Brome has a volatile orbit, affected by two suns. The inconsistent seasons make for poor harvests, so there's no point in farming without significant irrigational infrastructure." The Governess leaned against the railing, her flowing blue sleeves draping in an impressive imitation of the gentle stream below. Her gaze was, blessedly, fixed on Inara and Simon and not on the grounds below. "I've managed to do some of my own here to great effect, as you can see. The electromagnetic dome I have above us serves as something of a greenhouse environment, stabilizing the climate so growth can flourish."

"So, is that what we'd be funding?" Simon asked. "A garden?"

Inara winced. She would not have put it quite so starkly, but she shrugged off her instinct to intervene. Clumsy though he was at conversation, Simon was at least performing well as a distraction, holding the Governess's attention so she did not see the rustle of trees in the distance that could only be the rest of the crew making their way toward the center of the compound.

"Heavens, no!" The Governess let out a laugh. At least she found him funny instead of insulting. The last thing they needed was to be thrown out before Mal and the others were ready to leave. "Well, actually, yes, but not only a garden. You see, it isn't the Broman land I wish to cultivate, but its people."

With those words, the Governess gestured down at the houses, her gaze slipping from Simon's. Inara stepped forward, chin high, eyes focused. She leaned against the railing, mirroring the Governess so the filtered sunlight caught in the gold beading on her dress. The Governess's gaze slid back to her, away from the dangerous tapestry of infiltration below.

"You bring a great deal of wisdom and culture to a place like this, to be sure," Inara said. She would massage egos if she must. Better to flatter and keep the Governess's attention than the alternative. "But I fail to see how that can truly combat the effects of poverty on a region. Surely there is more we can do?"

They were the magic words. The Governess lit up. "Oh, indeed there is! That's why I built this compound. It is a rough-and-tumble world out there—the working conditions are abysmal and the climate even worse—but inside the dome, I have created paradise. It is my hope to find those who yearn for more and bring them here. Under my dome, they will have their basic needs met so they might pursue the deeper, truer need. I will feed their bodies, spirits, and intellects."

Inara found the words frozen in her throat. It was a strange endeavor, one whose merit she might have understood in a vacuum, but Brome was a community and the Governess's proposal sought to divide it. It was a marvel how those with money always believed they were the ones best suited to spend it. If the Governess gave a quarter of her funds to the people directly, Inara wagered they'd find ways to improve their lives on Brome in a far more efficient manner.

She opened her mouth, about to say as much, when Simon spoke up.

"A worthy venture, from the sound of it," he said. "But I'd still like to know more specifics. Is this some sort of restorative retreat? Rejuvenate them so they might return to their lives bettered? Or do those who come here stay permanently?"

They were good questions, ones Inara might have asked herself if she'd kept her emotions in check. She did not come here to pass judgment on the Governess, though someone ought to. The woman had an altogether backwards idea of how to help people. All this time, Inara had been concerned Simon would be the one to give them away. She should have been more concerned about herself.

"It's different for everyone," the Governess said. "They are, of course, free to come and go as they please. Some desire an escape from the harsh realities of Brome. Others need only temporary shelter due to unsavory circumstances in their lives. This way of life is meant to serve those who need it how they need it.

"Perhaps I can give you a tour," she went on, beginning to turn once more toward the lush landscape and the very obvious silhouettes of three people carving their way across the green in silence toward the huts.

"No!" Inara nearly shouted, fingers digging into Simon's shoulder. "We… should finish our tea first, at least."

Simon gave her a concerned look, then shifted his cup to his lips. "Indeed," he said. "We aren't on a central planet, I suppose. Waste not, and all that."

Inara let out a breath as the shapes of Mal, Zoë, and Book rounded the corner of one of the structures, vanishing from view.

"Well, drink up!" The Governess raised her cup in a toast.

Inara followed suit, but when the liquid passed her lips, it was bitter on her tongue.

16

"We sure they didn't come here on purpose?" Zoë asked, eyes skating the verdant surroundings.

"Don't see how it matters. We took a job, now we do it," Mal said. He fiddled with the comm Kaylee had given him. It didn't appear any different than the ones they usually used, but looks could be deceiving. "You readin' me?"

"Loud and clear!" came the response from Wash, chipper as always. "Everyone okay?"

Zoë plucked the device from Mal's hand and spoke into the receiver. "We all made it."

"Arms? Legs?"

Zoë let a small smile play across her face. "Yes, all limbs are accounted for."

"What about other parts? Not-limbs?"

"We're on a tight schedule here, Wash," Mal grumbled. "Save the flirting for when this is all over."

"Hey, maybe I was asking about non-sexy body parts like—"

"Yes, honey, do tell us. What parts of my body do you find unattractive?" Zoë asked.

There was a beat of silence on the other end before the comm crackled again, this time with Kaylee's voice. "Everything okay?"

"Coward," Zoë muttered.

"All good here," Mal said. "How's home?"

"It's been five minutes, Cap'n. Not much has changed since you left, except Wash throwin' this thing at me. Oh, and River's been staring at the geese a little more'n normal. Don't think it's nothin' to be worried about, though."

"Good. Let's hope it stays that way." Mal placed the comm in his pocket and motioned Zoë and Book forward. "Come on, we've got work that needs doin'."

The three of them crept forward through the Governess's compound. A smattering of small huts with rounded roofs lined the edges of a trickling stream, the water appearing almost artificially blue against a white stone riverbed. *Idyllic* was the word that came to Mal's mind, though he'd never found anything could be described that way for long. Everything had a catch, one way or another.

As they approached the center of the compound, no longer in the safety of the shadows, Mal's attention drifted toward the large structure at the center of everything, a building comprising mostly windows with a spire reaching up toward the top of the electromagnetic dome. There was some parable about glass houses, though he couldn't remember exactly what it was. All he knew was he wanted to throw the first stone. People like the Governess were why folks were hurting to begin with. Brome would be better off if, instead of building herself an oasis, she'd spent her wealth on roads or schools or irrigation for the planet. Same old, same old—those with the most money were the worst at knowing how to spend it.

With only the stream and a dozen or so yards of greenery between them and the central building, a movement caught Mal's eye and his vision snagged on Inara. She stood on a balcony on the east side of the main house, facing him as she leaned against the balcony. Simon stood just behind her, sipping a cup of tea in her shadow. They looked like a portrait, a husband and wife stitched together by class and coin. Something about it made Mal's stomach churn uncomfortably.

"Where are the people, do you suppose?" Book asked, pulling Mal from his thoughts.

"Asleep, I'd imagine." Zoë nodded toward the structures. "It's early still."

Mal tore his gaze from Inara and said, "Let's wake some people up, then."

They snuck around behind the huts, away from the main building. Mal's chest loosened with every step he took away from the strange alternate reality of Simon and Inara. Their romance wasn't real, and even if it were maybe that would be for the best. They were from the same world. It would make sense if they chose each other.

"Do we… knock?" Zoë asked, coming to a halt outside the first door.

"Would be the polite thing to do." Shepherd Book bent his head to speak quietly. "This is their home, after all."

"Can't be much of a home if it's also a prison," Mal said before grabbing hold of the doorknob and turning.

Inside were a number of cots with soft-looking linen blankets, some empty, some occupied. A table sat in one corner with half a dozen chairs crowded around it, and there was a water basin with neatly rolled cloths in a wicker basket beside it.

"It doesn't look like a prison," Zoë whispered.

"Looks like a spa," said the Shepherd.

A man wearing a sage-green tunic and trousers stepped in front of them. He had a halo of curly blond hair, pale skin, and deep-set watery eyes filled with fear. "Excuse me, are you lost?"

"In a manner of speaking," Mal said. "Lookin' for some folks—woulda turned up a few days ago. Dina, Eli, Tuan, and Julian." As he spoke the names Horne had given him, several heads swiveled to look at him. One in particular looked familiar, with freckles and voluminous auburn hair. "You wouldn't happen to know any of them, would you?"

"What do you want?" asked the first man, eyes narrowing. "You tell us that, first."

Mal knew this dance. He, Zoë, and Book were outsiders. It didn't matter that they were there to help; they were unknown. These folks probably didn't have much in the way of trust to spare. Mal would have to earn it.

"Not lookin' to start trouble," he began, raising his hands, palms empty and open. "Word back in town is they went missing. Folks thought they might've ended up here. We're just here to offer them a lift home."

The freckled woman came to stand beside the man. Her head only came up to his shoulder, but with her arms crossed and a frown etched across her lips, she seemed taller than them all.

"Who sent you?" she asked.

"I don't know if that—" the Shepherd began, but she silenced him with a glare.

"Who sent you?" she repeated, slower this time.

"Dina..." the first man murmured, a warning in his tone as he placed a hand on her shoulder.

"Get off me, Eli!" She shrugged him away and turned her gaze back on Mal, danger lacing her words. "I ain't playing around here. You tell me who's lining your pockets, or we sound the alarm."

"What alarm?" asked one of the others, short of stature with sharp cheekbones and a rosy-brown complexion. The fourth, younger than the rest with a round face and woven grass necklace, elbowed them and made a shushing motion. Julian and Tuan,

Mal decided, though he wasn't sure which was which.

Dina shot them both a look of utmost disdain. "The Governess don't take too kindly to intruders, I'd wager."

So, they didn't know their host all that well. That was something, at least. But Mal didn't relish the idea of taking captives captive. If they didn't want to go, there wasn't much he felt compelled to do about that. Still, it was clear these folks had something to fear. He just didn't think he and his crew were it.

"Your families said you'd been taken," Zoë said with a sidelong glance at Mal, asking him without asking what was the play here. Truth was, Mal wasn't rightly sure. Something told him invoking Lyle Horne's name wasn't going to get him anywhere good, but neither would lying.

"We met your wife and daughter. Seemed awfully worried about you." He nodded to Zoë, then turned his attention back to the woman—Dina. "But the fella paying our wage is Lyle Horne."

Dina glowered at him. "Get out."

"We just wanna talk," Mal said.

"Well, I don't." Dina looked him up and down, wrinkling her nose at what she saw.

"We're here to help," the Shepherd chimed in. "I promise, we mean you no harm."

"No offense, but not meanin' harm and not doin' harm are two very different things," said the man Dina had called Eli.

"Well, if you don't want to go home, suppose we can't force you," said Mal, exchanging a glance with Zoë. This was certainly an unexpected wrinkle in their plan. He'd anticipated resistance from the Governess and her cronies, not the folks they planned to rescue. "But I think there's a chance we can help, if you'd care to tell us what's really going on."

Eli bent to murmur in Dina's ear, still loudly enough to hear. "It would be good to head home…"

"Not while *he's* still in charge," Dina spat.

"Pardon my intrusion." Shepherd Book leaned in, his voice carrying over their whispers. "But if it's Horne you're concerned about, I think we may be able to help."

"Ain't nobody but us willing to stand up to that no-good *hún dàn*, and look where that got us." Dina gave him an incredulous look. "What makes you think you'd fare any different?"

Mal could think of a few things. They had guns, for a start. Lots of them. Not to mention his crew had a knack for managing tricky situations. They'd figure their way through this one, too.

But Book didn't mention any of that. Instead, he pulled back his shoulders, glanced up at the ceiling as though communicating with an unseen force, and said, "I believe I can help you deal with Lyle Horne because I've done it before."

17

Kaylee leaned against the metal railing above the cargo bay, swaying slightly to the metronome of intermittent honking. The geese had been at it for a while now, generating low rhythmic sounds that were more like conversation than screaming. It was nice once she'd gotten used to it. It made her feel less alone.

"Looks like it's just you and me," said Wash.

"And her." Kaylee didn't need to look down to know River was there. After the others had left, River had tiptoed into the cargo bay, quiet on her dancer's feet, and sat cross-legged in front of the enclosure. Didn't say a word, just stared down the flock with an intensity that made Kaylee want to hide in the engine room and not come out.

Wash joined her at the railing. "Who could forget our little anserine friend?"

"You did," said River from down below, unblinking. "Also, I am not stupid or gooselike. You should pick a better word."

Wash winced and exchanged a glance with Kaylee. "Good hearing."

"Yes, so please be quiet. I'm trying to listen."

Wash lowered his voice to almost a whisper. "You ever think

she hears more than we do? Or maybe just different?"

Kaylee suppressed a shudder, a memory flashing through her mind: River, unseeing, with a pistol in her hand. Three dead without looking.

No power in the 'verse can stop me.

Yes, Kaylee thought River was different. It wasn't just her hearing, either. It was everything. Kaylee didn't mind so much when folks were different. Hell, lots of people thought she was a bit strange, what with her affinity for engines. There was a big part of her that wanted to embrace every facet of River, no matter how odd. She was a girl untethered, a kindred spirit.

But there was danger there, too. If not from River herself, then from the world that wanted to put her in a cage.

"Maybe she feels a kinship with the geese," Kaylee said, shrugging one shoulder. "You know, they both..." She cast about for commonalities. "...have it out for Jayne."

"Who doesn't?" Wash cracked a grin.

To be fair, Jayne had it coming. Kaylee considered every member of the crew family in one way or another, but it didn't take a genius to see Jayne didn't feel the same. From the second the Tams had come aboard *Serenity*, he'd been less than welcoming. It was why Kaylee hadn't been surprised when River had slashed him a few months back, just before their job on Ariel. Well, she'd been a little surprised—that sort of violence wasn't exactly normal behavior—but she couldn't totally blame River for giving in to the impulse.

"I hope he's doing all right," she said. "Bein' on his own and all. Don't like that we left him behind."

"Jayne? I'm sure he's staying out of trouble..." Wash trailed off and cocked his head. "I'm marginally confident." Another beat of silence passed before he added, "I am not at all certain in any way, shape, or form. But... it's Jayne, right?"

Kaylee shrugged. "*Serenity* just feels so empty."

"They'll be back." Wash patted her arm gently. "Pretty soon, this ship will be full up and you'll be sick of hearing Mal and Zoë talk about their heroic deeds, and Jayne will find a way to take credit even though he wasn't there, and you can ask that doctor of yours how his part of it all went down."

"Yeah… I guess that'll be nice." Kaylee turned away, hiding the smile unfolding on her lips. Maybe Wash was right. She hadn't quite forgiven Simon his earlier slight, but it would be good for him to be useful on the mission. Maybe it would give him a little perspective. "It's just real quiet without 'em."

"Well, you say the word and I can start singing. I know some terrible shanties."

Kaylee's laughter echoed across the silent cargo bay, the sound rounding through the space and back again… and again… Her face fell.

Something wasn't right. It wasn't supposed to be this quiet.

Kaylee cast her gaze about for whatever was making her feel twitchy. Maybe *Serenity* needed tending, or maybe…

The honking had stopped. When she looked down, the enclosure was open, the geese were out, and River was nowhere in sight.

"They're coming."

Kaylee jumped. River stood inches from her, face still as stone. They locked eyes for a split second, River's gaze flickering with that bright intensity that so often accompanied her strange outbursts. Kaylee didn't have time to wonder if this was about to be one of those times when River didn't make any sense—or too much sense—and everything went sideways. Before she could so much as steady her heart rate, River had grabbed her hand and pulled.

"Run!"

Kaylee stumbled along behind her, barely staying on her feet. "River, what—"

"They're going to take her, they're going to hurt us and then take her." River led Kaylee away from the cargo bay and through the dining area, deeper into *Serenity*.

Kaylee's heart sank. She knew what this was about. Simon had told her, if not everything, then enough. The horrors River had experienced at the hands of the Alliance would make anyone a little paranoid. They did things to her brain that Kaylee didn't understand, would never understand. And River was smart enough to know they'd come back for her, one way or another.

"River," Kaylee said, grabbing hold of River's hand with both of hers and pulling to slow them down. "River, it's okay. They can't get you here." She glanced down the hallway toward the front end of the ship for Wash, who was only a few paces behind, to back her up.

"No one's going to hurt you," Wash said, panting a little as he jogged to catch up.

River nodded in agreement. "No one," she said firmly, then grabbed Wash's hand, too, and tugged them the rest of the way down the hall and through the door to the engine room.

"I promise you, we're gonna keep you safe," Kaylee said as she stumbled over the threshold. "The captain won't let anything happen to you."

"Not worried about me." River's gaze skated over the engine, then landed back on Kaylee. "I'm worried about *her*."

"Her?" Wash asked. "Is she… in the room with us now?"

River fixed him with a sardonic stare.

"She means the ship, Wash. *Serenity*," Kaylee murmured. River's behavior was sometimes odd, often unpredictable. It made her fun to play with, but something told Kaylee this wasn't one of her games.

"Can't get you in here," River said.

"What's going on? *Who* can't get us, River?" Kaylee asked.

"They want her wings." A small smile bloomed on River's lips as her fingers danced over the main engine actuator. "Jealous she can fly."

Kaylee glanced at Wash, who wore a befuddled expression.

"The geese? The geese are going to take *Serenity*?" Wash looked like his head was going to explode. "With what weapons? Their beaks?"

River took a single step back over the threshold and into the hallway, and said, "With guns." Then, she slammed the door shut, locking them both inside.

"Well..." Wash sighed, falling against the metal casing around the engine with a dull thunk. "Now it really is just you and me."

18

Book remembered Lyle Horne as a reckless, magnetic madcap. His plans were harebrained and genius in equal measure. He'd been a comfort in hard times. He'd saved Book's very life—never mind that he'd then risked it time and time again, like a man who didn't know how to quit the card table. He'd been a friend. But none of that mattered now.

Maybe he should have been more surprised to learn that Lyle was the source of all their present problems, given their history. Then again, maybe their history was the precise reason for his doubt. From the second Lyle Horne had set foot on *Serenity*, Book had felt uneasy. It was as if Lyle's very presence was a harbinger, an ill omen. The Shepherd had hoped to be wrong, but truth be told, he hadn't really believed he would be.

"So, what'd you do about him?" asked the freckled woman named Dina. She was a stout woman—not unlike the beverage—solid and strong in stature and demeanor. There was something in her eyes as well that made Book certain she wasn't one to cross. "You said you dealt with him before, so how did you do it? How'd you get rid of him?"

"Well, I dropped him off the side of a cliff." That was only a sliver of the story, of course, but he couldn't very well tell these people the truth—that it was an accident, a failure, the greatest loss he'd ever felt.

"Brutal," said the one called Julian. They cut an androgynous figure and wore their sleek black hair in two braids that framed their face.

They'd all settled round the table to talk. Dina, Tuan, Julian, and Eli all stared at Book with expectant expressions. He was used to that reaction on account of being a Shepherd in a world that needed a little faith from time to time. But this was the first time he'd been given deference for his less savory past.

"I let gravity do most of the work," he said by way of explanation. He needed to strike the right balance of truth. He wasn't willing to lie outright—not anymore, at least—nor was he willing to put his history on display for anyone but God. Trouble was, these people weren't going to trust him or the crew of *Serenity* unless he did a little of both.

"Didn't stick, though, did it?" Dina crossed her arms and settled back into her chair. "Like a cockroach, that one."

"'Scuse me for interruptin', but it would help an awful lot if you could tell us what exactly your grievance is with Horne. Can't help much if we don't have a clear picture of what we're helping with." The captain leaned forward on his elbows, looking conspiratorially from one of their new acquaintances to the other.

Dina sniffed. "Waste of our time," she said with a sneer. "Knew you weren't for real. Won't turn on your employer—money's too good."

"I'm not saying we won't turn on Horne, I'm saying we need more information if we're going to do this right," Mal said, measured and low.

"Don't see how you knowing our business makes you any better of a shot with that pistol of yours," Dina grumbled.

Book sincerely hoped it didn't come to that. In a good old-fashioned shoot out, he wasn't confident Mal would win, not to mention he wasn't sure who he'd be rooting for.

Zoë fixed Dina with a warrior's stare. "You want our help, you tell us what we need to know."

"Never said we wanted your help."

"Dina, shut up," Tuan snapped. He was the youngest of the group, perhaps Kaylee's age, with hair clipped close to his skull. A few pieces of woven bromegrass adorned his neck and wrists like jewelry. "Not like we were getting anywhere on our own. Besides, what do we have to tell 'em that Horne doesn't already know?"

The others nodded. Dina grunted noncommittally.

Seeming to take that as permission, Eli pushed on. "It all started a few weeks back with the protest."

Dina grunted again.

"Okay, it started before then. When Horne extended our hours—"

Dina sighed.

"You wanna say something, Dina?" Eli snapped. "If you're gonna keep interruptin' me, you might as well be the one to tell it."

Dina leaned forward, eyes narrowed in concentration. "Horne is a no-good rotten *qīng wā cāo de liú máng*."

"Tell me something I don't already know," Book muttered.

Zoë and Mal both shot him identical looks of curious appraisal.

"Well, I wouldn't put it in quite those words, but..." Book averted his eyes. He wouldn't have put it in any words at all if he could've helped it. Had it been entirely up to him, he would have left Horne behind in the past just as he'd left him behind on Valentine. Digging up their history would do neither of them any good.

"Any chance you were gonna tell the rest of us?" Mal asked. "I seem to recall askin' your opinion and gettin' nothin' but a *zhēng qì de gǒu shǐ duī*."

"Mal," Zoë said softly, a warning in her voice. She turned back to Dina and added, "Maybe you could be more specific."

Book silently thanked her. It wasn't his intention to mislead the captain, but it also wasn't his intention to share all his secrets.

Dina wrinkled her nose, folding freckles upon freckles. "Horne's our Blue Sun rep. Has been goin' on a year now. Showed up one day with a crate of logo T-shirts and signing bonuses. More money than a lot of us had seen in one place before. Course, we didn't realize what we were signing on to."

"Blue Sun ain't exactly my favorite mega corporation," Zoë began, "but I'll admit I thought they'd have a fairly standard labor contract."

"Oh, they do," Eli said with a sigh. "It's what we had before Lyle Horne."

"And after?" Mal prompted.

"Long hours, no overtime, and dwindling wages." Julian shook their head. "The sum he gave us all in the beginning doesn't even cover half of what he's taken from us."

"Why not complain to Blue Sun, then?" Mal asked.

Book put his fingers to his temples. "If Horne is their liaison, I hardly think that's a viable option. It's a classic setup. He's placed himself between them and their only avenue for recourse."

"Not our only avenue, thank you very much." Dina shot him a mighty glare. "Maybe we couldn't go direct to the big boss, but we weren't going to sit around and watch him take advantage. We organized."

"That's one way to put it," muttered Eli.

"You got somethin' to say?" Dina turned her attention to the wiry man at her side.

Eli just shrugged and said, "I seem to remember you suggesting we hog tie him to the radiator and crank up the dial."

Dina shrugged. "I don't see how that's not organizing."

"We ended up planning a rally," Eli told Mal. "Folks were supposed to walk out on the job and congregate in the square. We were going to show him how united Brome is. Even the Governess here was on our side. We're a family here. We stick together."

"Only that ain't what happened," Dina said.

"Horne got wind of it all somehow. Found out we four were the ones planning the walkout." Eli shook his head, somber. "Fired all four of us on the spot."

"Shoulda fired him, if you know what I mean," Dina grumbled.

"Shoulda done a lot of things." Eli placed his hands, calloused and worn, on top of the table. He stared with empty eyes, looking at something that wasn't there. "He threatened to do the same to our families. And worse."

"And this ain't the first time he's lashed out. Plenty of folk been on the receiving end of his wrath. Not many of them came back to work after." Tuan clutched the woven grass necklace he wore in a tight grip, his jaw tense.

"Horne's just one man. How's he fixin' to have the advantage?" Mal asked.

"Oh, he ain't just one man. Got himself a bunch of enforcers—big men with big guns," said Eli. "There ain't no crossin' Lyle Horne and livin' to tell the tale."

Book's heart sank. The Horne he knew… well, he wasn't exactly a decent man, but at least he was more graceful than this. A pain emerged somewhere beneath his ribs, dull and aching like an old wound.

"The Governess got us out. Maybe she knew we wouldn't stop." Julian's eyes flicked to Dina, a mixture of admiration and disdain in their gaze. "Or maybe she just knew Horne wouldn't. Either way, she saved our lives."

"Can't help but notice she didn't save your jobs, or your families, or your town," Mal began.

"All she did was take you from them," Book finished.

Tuan and Eli nodded. Julian wrinkled their nose. Dina sighed heavily.

"We gotta go back," Dina said after a long moment. "He's right. Ain't nothing gonna get fixed without us." She looked to Mal, rightfully judging him to be their leader. "Well? What's the plan?"

Book could tell the woman was a firecracker, to say the least—impulsive and more than a little volatile—but in Book's experience, most movements needed that spark to get started.

Mal smiled, reaching into his pocket and withdrawing the communicator Kaylee had given him. "Got a ship stationed just a little way away. Once we're to the wall, I'll call 'em. They'll fly overhead, alerting our other team it's time to go. Then we'll slip through over the wall undetected and rendezvous with the others."

Dina looked, if possible, marginally impressed. "A ship, you say? I'd like to see that."

There was a roar of an engine, crackling and bright. Book was alarmed to find he associated the sound with the feeling of home. Almost as alarmed as he was to see a Firefly passing overhead as he rushed to the door and poked his head outside.

"You can see her right now if you hurry," he said, gesturing them all toward the door.

"*Wǒ men wán le*," Zoë muttered, turning to Mal. "You didn't call them, did you?"

Mal held the communicator limp in his hand, staring at the sky where the contrails of *Serenity* lingered above in her wake. "I surely did not! Somethin' got that husband of yours flying early." He pushed through the door and ducked outside. "We best make haste. There's no tellin' what's got him spooked."

Book didn't say so as he and Zoë followed, quick and quiet, but he thought he had a pretty good idea what—or rather who—was to blame for their pilot's premature takeoff. Lyle Horne wasn't the man Book had thought he was, and that scared him almost as much as the alternative.

19

Inara breathed easier once Mal and the others were gone. They'd vanished inside one of the huts and not come out again. Still, she was far from comfortable.

The Governess was no more imposing a figure than any she'd faced before. Inara had unraveled far more impressive people. Far more villainous, as well. It was not the Governess's status, nor her poor excuse for philanthropy, that put Inara off. It was the way she seemed to believe her own lies, that she was truly helping people when all she was doing was turning money around and around like wine in a glass she never intended to drink.

"If I understand you correctly, Governess," Simon said, "our funds would go directly toward bettering the lives of those selected to join your compound."

He was good at this—sounding like he belonged. Maybe it was because once upon a time, he had. Simon had a way of repeating exactly what the Governess had already said in slightly altered words, showing he was listening without actually progressing the conversation further. A waste of time, really, but that's what they were there to do.

"And you would use our donation to create a viable alternative to the impoverished lives they lead now?" he asked, tilting his head *just so* to imply interest.

It would be so easy to let Simon steer the conversation. He would lead them through innocuous pastures, never straying from the proper path.

Inara was once like him—good with authority. When had that changed? The answer rose in her like a ship taking flight.

"Tell me, Governess," she began, despite her best efforts to subdue her own feelings. "What makes you think investing in this compound is a better use of money than investing in the infrastructure that already exists here? Wouldn't it be better to help them improve what they've built and bolster the communities that already exist?"

Simon shot her a wary look. "In— My darling, I think the woman who actually lives here knows better than we do what the people need."

Inara gritted her teeth. He was right—not about the Governess knowing better, but about letting the matter go. There was no need to antagonize her. Had Mal been there, she would undoubtedly be holding him back from doing the same. In his absence, apparently, she'd undertaken the task herself.

"I'd like to hear the Governess's answer, if it's all the same to you."

Simon reached for her, his fingers closing around her arm. She wrenched herself free.

"It's our money, after all, dear." She'd forgotten the fake names they'd established, the fake people. Now she was just Inara, and she was angry.

"I did, of course, consider that," the Governess said in a measured tone. Her countenance remained stony, her blue eyes an unreadable echo of the lush landscape below them. "The problem is, Brome doesn't have much to begin with. Besides, the people here don't have any real leadership. I could give them what I have, but I'm not convinced they'd know how to spend it wisely."

Inara opened her mouth, ready to tell his woman she couldn't have a cent of her money, real or fake, because she wasn't convinced the *Governess* knew how to spend it wisely. Before she could utter a single word, however, the roar of an engine sounded overhead. A cry of anguish in a world too cracked and dry for tears.

They all looked up—even Inara, who knew that sound better than most. The sun had risen further in the sky by now—Kalidasa, by the looks of it, with Penglai not far behind. A flash of silver passed above them. Even through the Governess's dome, *Serenity* was unmistakable. With her engines ablaze, the ship was a set of twin suns herself, bright and warm and calling them home.

"What was that?" the Governess asked, craning her neck to get a better look.

Inara exchanged a glance with Simon. They needed to get out of there, and quick.

Simon cleared his throat. "Well, my wife and I ought to discuss this, I think. Perhaps we'll see the sights—really get a good picture of what our money can help people escape." Simon gave the Governess a curt nod before offering his arm to Inara. "Shall we?"

"Indeed," Inara managed. She looped her arm through his and tried not to appear too eager to leave the strange estate and its proprietor.

The Governess was not so quick to be rid of them, however. She simply smiled as she kept pace, following them past the enormous center table toward the stairs. "I'll see you off, then, shall I?"

"There's no need—" Inara began, but the Governess waved her off.

"Nonsense! Hospitality need not be lost just because we're all the way out here."

Inara's fingers tightened around Simon's arm as they followed the Governess downstairs at a glacial pace, then finally through the front doors and back outside.

"It's been a pleasure, Governess," Inara said with a bow of her head. "We'll be in touch shortly. If you could just..." She gestured to the electromagnetic dome.

The Governess gave her a long, considering look, then moved to a control panel at the gate. Before she could turn off the dome, however, a chirp sounded from one of her dangling bracelets, and her gaze snapped to alertness, her eyes darting every which way as she listened to her comm.

"Governess?" Simon asked. "Is everything all right?"

"I'm afraid not," the Governess said.

"Well, you obviously have important business to attend to." Inara stepped toward the gate, but the Governess held out an arm, blocking her.

"You're not going anywhere." Her eyes—a deep, inky blue—rose to meet Inara's. "There's been a security breach. Someone's in the compound who shouldn't be, and we can't lower the dome until the trespassers have been secured."

"Surely that won't be necessary," Simon said.

Inara's heart sank. The Governess might not have gotten wind of their deception just yet, but if she found the others...

Before Inara could so much as complete the thought, movement caught her eye, a flash of burnished red amidst the greenery.

Malcolm Reynolds stepped out from the topiary and onto the path, shoulders set, a grim expression on his face. He was bracketed by Zoë and Book.

"Governess," he called out.

"Identify yourself!" the Governess shot back.

"Name's Malcolm Reynolds," Mal replied, hooking his thumbs through the loops of his suspenders. "Seems you and I have got business to discuss."

"Oh, is that so?" The Governess's voice was dry with impatience. "I don't usually do business with people I don't know."

"Well, that ain't what I've heard."

"Tell me, what *have* you heard?"

Inara stiffened as the Governess reached into the folds of her dress for what Inara could only imagine was a weapon of some kind. From Inara's position, up against the gate a few feet behind the Governess, she tried to communicate the danger to Mal with her eyes, but it was no use. Mal had never been as good at reading her as she was at reading him.

"I heard you're here to help," Mal replied. Behind him, four figures came into view—strangers to Inara, though she assumed they were the people Lyle Horne had sent them to rescue.

"You heard right," the Governess said, an edge to her voice. "But that doesn't explain why you broke into my compound."

"Only way to get the truth, wasn't it?" Mal took a step forward, then another, and another.

Danger flashed in the Governess's eyes. Inara didn't think before she lunged. The Governess whipped her hand out from the folds of her cerulean skirts, a tiny ivory pistol in her hand. Inara's fingers closed around the handle and she tugged, pulling the Governess with her.

It was a mistake. Inara, lithe though she was on a dance floor, was no warrior. The Governess brought her elbow up and jammed it into her ribs, then her throat. The air left her body as she stumbled back, pain lancing through her body.

Strong arms caught her. Simon took her weight, then steadied her. He wasn't really her husband, but in that moment Inara thought he'd make a good one someday, if he decided to walk that path.

"If we're going to talk about the truth, it seems I'm owed an explanation as well," the Governess said, eyeing Inara as she raised her gun to point it at Mal once more.

But Mal wasn't stupid. Well, he wasn't *not* stupid either, but that was beside the point. In the chaos, he'd drawn his own weapon, as had Zoë.

"You're outgunned, Governess," Shepherd Book said as he stepped out from behind Mal, notably not brandishing a weapon himself. "I'd hear the man out."

The Governess glared, but lowered her weapon slowly. "What do you want?"

"I want you to let the shield down," Mal said. "I want you to let us walk away. I want to get through this with no bloodshed. And then, I want to eat a hot meal, get paid, and leave this gorram moon behind."

"And why exactly should I help you?"

"Well, Governess, because there's more of us than there are of you, for a start. And that bit about bloodshed's more of a bonus than a true objective." Mal shrugged and clicked the safety off as if to prove his point. "But more than that, these folks said you tried to help them. You tried, and even though it didn't work, and that ain't nothin'. Now, I'm offerin' you an opportunity to do more than try. What do you say?"

"More than try? You think you can go up against Lyle Horne?" the Governess asked. Her tone was derisive, but Inara saw beyond it. The woman was doubtful, but she was also a little impressed.

"Oh, I know so." Mal smiled—that smug, superior grin he wore when he knew he'd won. It made Inara want to smack him upside the head. "What do you say? You want to do some good around here or what?"

Inara's gaze snapped to the Governess. This was not a woman who'd ever done any real good in her life. No matter how good her intentions, the Governess was more of a nuisance than a help to the people of Brome. If she hadn't wanted to dirty her hands with any actual work before, why would she now?

But the Governess flipped the gun over, handle out in surrender, and said, "I do."

20

"Did she just lock us in the engine room?" Wash asked, blinking at the place where River had been moments before.

"Seems so," replied Kaylee.

"Is this some kind of game you two play, then?"

"Not that I know of."

"Okay, okay, *okay*..."

"I... don't think it is okay," Kaylee muttered. "She's out there on her own."

"No, she's got the geese, remember?" Wash threw his hands in the air and gave Kaylee an exasperated look. "You got the comm on you?"

Kaylee flexed her empty hands and patted her jumpsuit down, but it was no use. She shook her head. "Must've dropped it while we were running."

"Well, this is grand." Wash leaned his head against the cool metal of the engine-room door, staring out through the small round window for signs of movement. If River was doing something, she wasn't doing it anywhere near them. "This is why Mal leaves me behind, you know. Because my part of the plan always goes wrong."

"I thought it was because you can fly."

"Well, I can't fly now, can I?" That, more than anything, was what had Wash wound tight as a compression coil. He'd been nervous before with *Serenity*'s fuel reserves low, but this was another level entirely. He made a grabbing motion with his hand and motioned to Kaylee. "Hand me the pry bar. Hoban Washburne doesn't get grounded."

Kaylee raised her eyebrows.

"Okay… well, only one time when I was thirteen. My parents looked under my bed and found—"

"I don't need to know." Kaylee tossed him the pry bar and grabbed a few wrenches to boot. "You think she'll be okay?"

"It's just a door, Kaylee. Couple dents won't hurt her." He leveraged the pry bar into the gap, biting his lip in concentration. He wasn't exactly a strongman—Jayne had offered to spot him on occasion at the bench press, but Wash was more inclined to lift spirits than weights. In this moment, however, he wished he'd done a few reps. His muscles weren't built for brute force. "Phew, okay. Trying again…" He wiped the sweat from this brow and returned to work.

"I was talking about River," Kaylee said.

"What about River?" Wash could barely hear her over the rush of his blood in his ears.

"If she's right—if there's a crew coming to steal *Serenity*—she's out there by herself. What if they hurt her?"

"I think you mean what if *she* hurts *them*." The first time Wash had seen River, he'd thought she was just a fragile little girl. He was quickly disabused of that notion. River was resilient and clever and empathetic but, yes, still fragile. She was too many things to count, and Wash had never been good with numbers.

Kaylee leaned against the wall and sank down to a crouch.

Wash put down the pry bar. "You're really worried about her."

Kaylee nodded, eyes watery. “I know it’s just River. I know sometimes she says things that don’t mean nothin’, but… she said they’d have guns.”

Wash reached out to squeeze her shoulder. Kaylee was very much the sister he didn’t have—less acerbic than the one he did—and he couldn’t help but feel a twinge of discomfort at her obvious distress.

“They’ve got guns, and they’re gonna take *Serenity*, and we’re stuck in here like a couple of useless pigs in a pen.”

“We may be stuck here, and we may be pigs, but we’re not useless.” Wash stood up straight and reached down to help her up. “Come on.”

Kaylee took his hand and pulled herself up. “What are we gonna do? Can’t exactly fly from the engine room.”

“No, we certainly can’t. But we can stop *them* from flying.” He gestured at the engine. Wash was no scruff when it came to understanding the inner workings of *Serenity*, but Kaylee was on a whole other level. He saw the moment it all clicked, her eyes brightening as her brain jumped into gear. It was a sight to see, Kaylee with a wrench in her hand and a spark in her mind.

“If I cut the hydraulics and rewire the drive feed, that should keep us on the ground.” Kaylee slid the cover back, exposing *Serenity*’s core. “Easy peasy, just need a few minutes…”

The engine roared to life.

“You don’t have a few minutes.” Wash rushed to her side as the engine began to spin and light permeated the dark metal room. “You don’t have any minutes.”

Kaylee chewed her lip, turning the wrench over in her hand. “I can still do it, force them to land. Just gonna be a little tricky.”

“How can I help?” Wash knew better than to take charge. The engine room was Kaylee’s world and he was just living in it.

“Hold this, and stay out of the way.”

She slapped a wrench into his hands and got to work. There were a lot of fast movements, followed by still waiting periods as the engine cycled back around. Wash glanced at the door a few times, but there was no sign of River or the geese or whoever stole the ship. It was just him and Kaylee.

"There. That oughta do it." Kaylee brushed her hands together as the sound of the engine whined and waned.

"You did it!" Wash grabbed her shoulders and squeezed. But it was a short-lived victory as gravity kicked in and *Serenity* began its descent. "Strap in!"

Kaylee pushed him toward a small seat in the corner—the only seat.

"No way, you take it," he said. He'd never forgive himself if Kaylee got hurt on his watch.

"I've got it covered." She shoved him again just as the Firefly tipped to the side, sending them both to the floor. "Or maybe I don't."

Serenity impacted before either of them had a chance to stand. A sloppy landing, but not a full-on crash. It could've been worse—for the ship and for them.

"You've got a little…" Kaylee gestured to her nose.

He wiped at his own, his hand coming away with a rusty residue. "*Āiya!* Is that blood?"

"Engine grease."

Wash let out a long sigh and rolled onto his back. "We did it."

Kaylee's face split into a smile. "We did. But, uh… what happens next?"

Dragging himself upright, Wash looked at the door, barely dented from his ill-advised attempt to force it open. "We wait, I guess. If they want to take off again, they'll have to come back here eventually."

"And then what? Wash, we don't got any guns."

"We have..." Wash cast his gaze about, landing on the discarded wrench and pry bar. He handed one to Kaylee and raised the other himself, preparing to strike.

Kaylee followed suit, a dubious expression on her face.

They framed the door, Kaylee on the right and Wash on the left, and waited. It took only a few minutes before they heard footsteps. Wash pressed his finger to his lips and mouthed, "Not a sound."

Metal ground on metal, and the door slid open.

"Ahh!" Wash yelled, rushing forward to take down their would-be-assailant. He didn't make it very far. A hand hit him in the chest and the air left his body as he staggered back, blinking. He had the vague impression of a figure stepping over the threshold, barefoot and familiar.

"River?" Kaylee's voice sounded strained and far away. "Is that you?"

Wash blinked his vision back into focus. River stood in the doorway, fists balled, a dead stare in her eyes. For a split second, Wash was willing to entertain the notion that it was not, in fact, River, or at least that it was some new version of her they didn't yet know. But then, River lifted her chin and gave Kaylee a scathing look.

"Of course it's me." She took another step inside and looked to Wash. "Put that down. You're going to hurt someone," she added, eyes flickering to the wrench in his hand.

"That was the idea," he muttered, but set it down all the same. "If you hadn't locked us in here, we could've—"

"Gotten in the way," River said. "I needed you here so I could talk to them."

"Talk? You wanted to *talk* to them?" Wash threw his hands in the air. "I could've helped with that. I'm great at talking!"

River rolled her eyes. "You talk a lot. There's a difference."

"Ouch." Wash pressed a hand to his chest. He didn't even have to fake the pain; the place where she hit him was still sore.

River beckoned them both forward. "Are you ready?"

"Ready?" Kaylee repeated.

"For what?" asked Wash.

River paused in the doorway to look over her shoulder, a devious glint in her eye that Wash didn't like one bit. "To meet the new captain, of course."

As they followed, Wash leaned in to Kaylee and whispered, "I swear to God, if the new captain's a goose, I'm going to lose it."

21

"I don't like her," said Zoë, eyes trained on the Governess as they made their retreat.

The Governess, Simon, and Inara loaded into their shuttle along with Shepherd Book while Zoë and Mal ushered Dina, Eli, Tuan, and Julian to the other, parked a ways off behind a curtain of bromegrass. It would be a tight squeeze—shuttles weren't built for more than four passengers—but they'd make do.

Mal eyed his first mate warily. "You don't like anybody when you first meet them."

"Now, that ain't true—"

"Remember when I hired Wash? You said he bothered you." He chuckled, pointing an accusatory finger at her. "And see how that turned out?"

Zoë glared. This wasn't the first time Mal had needled her over her reaction to Wash, nor would it be the last, he reckoned. It was just that Zoë so seldom did anything worth laughing about—not because she wasn't funny, but because Mal valued keeping his head attached to his body.

"Not just Wash, though, was it? You thought bringing Inara

on board was too risky, and at first you thought Jayne was too impulsive—"

"I *still* think Jayne is too impulsive."

"Admit it—it takes you a minute to warm up to everybody, doesn't it?"

"I liked the Shepherd on the first day."

"And notice how I'm not holding that against you." Mal flashed her a smirk. "Come on, Zoë. What's not to like? She's powerful, beautiful, rich…"

"Seems to me anyone on Brome who's all three of those is probably takin' advantage of someone or other."

She had a point. The folks they'd come to rescue seemed to like her well enough, and she'd agreed to help them with Horne, but there was a piece of the puzzle still missing.

"It was the mustache," Zoë said after a few beats of silence.

Mal blinked. "Pardon?"

"Something about it didn't sit right. I can't explain why." She shrugged. "Soon as he shaved, I changed my mind about him."

Most people thought Wash and Zoë were a perfect balance of opposites—Zoë the serious and capable warrior and Wash the lovable clown—but they were more alike than folks expected. They were both good judges of character, for a start. The one time Zoë had been truly wrong, there'd been honest-to-goodness love in the mix, so Mal would cut her some slack. But only some.

"Good to know your opinion can be swayed so easily," he said with a roll of his eyes. "I'll be sure not to grow out my beard, then."

"I'd take that as a kindness, sir."

They loaded up the shuttle with little fanfare. Eli made a squeak like a startled chipmunk and Dina hollered in delight when they took off, leaving the ground behind.

"I take it none of you have ever flown before?" asked Zoë.

Julian gave her a queasy nod.

It was strange to think of folks being moon-locked. Damn near everyone was born to one planet or another and called a globe home. Mal had been one of them once. The prairies of Shadow had been a lively place in his youth, but they lived only in memory now, taken, like so many things, by the war. He learned quickly that home could be a lot of things—a ship, a crew, a plan to keep flying. This detour on Brome was testing all three.

He navigated east, following the path of *Serenity*. He couldn't lose her. Not today.

"Mal," Zoë said.

"What is it?"

"You seeing this?"

He was not, in fact, seeing anything, steering by force of habit more than anything else. He blinked and the view came into focus.

Burnt and flattened bromegrass spread out before them, a pathway leading to *Serenity*, light bouncing off her metal frame.

"*Āiya,*" Mal breathed as his fingers danced across the controls. His heart beat faster, his chest constricting at the sight. "Looks like they had a rough landing."

"Maybe Horne hasn't done much flying either," Zoë muttered.

"If he's gone and banged up my ship, he's got another think comin' to him."

Mal set the shuttle down a good dozen yards from *Serenity*. The other shuttle landed not far behind.

"He'll have his enforcers with him," Eli said.

Mal nodded. "You got weapons? Don't wanna find ourselves outnumbered."

Dina raised her fists with a smirk. "I've been armed and dangerous since birth."

"Right..." Zoë glanced at the others. "No guns, though, I gather?"

They shook their heads.

"Which of you's the best shot?" Mal asked, wishing he'd thought to bring more weaponry. As it was, they had only three guns: his and Zoë's pistols, and her rifle.

Dina stepped forward, but Eli put his arm out to block her path. "Tuan's got the eyes of an eagle and he ain't too trigger happy."

"Hey!" Dina gave him a wounded look.

"Good." Mal turned to Tuan, the younger-looking fella. Mal thought he might be the eldest child of one of the families they'd spoken to, only a few years past twenty. "Think a pistol would suit."

Zoë was at his side before he could even look for her, holding out her pistol to Tuan, who took it after only a moment's hesitation.

"The rest of you stay hidden until we can assess the situation," Mal pulled out his Liberty Hammer, finding comfort in the familiar heft of his own weapon. "Zoë?"

"With you." She retrieved her Mare's Leg rifle from the corner.

The others egged Tuan on—Eli gave his shoulder a paternal squeeze, Dina whooped, and Julian rose onto their tiptoes to kiss his cheek—then the three of them exited the shuttle.

Inara's shuttle had landed only a few yards away, and she and her passengers were piling out onto the flattened bromegrass.

"You don't think it's strange, sir?" Zoë asked in a low voice.

"I think a lot of things are strange. You're gonna have to be more specific."

"Sounds like Horne's got a crew of enforcers backing him up." Zoë glanced from Mal to the Governess, who was delicately stepping out of Inara's shuttle, assisted by Simon. "Why doesn't she?"

Mal's eyes followed the Governess as she brushed out her skirt, stepping carefully so as not to collect too many bromegrass seeds in the brocade weave. Mal was never one to judge a book by its cover, but she didn't look the sort to dirty her hands with something so undignified as bloodshed. She had a gun, but whether or not she could wield it with any finesse was yet to be seen. Zoë was right: she ought to have some sort of fighting force.

"Suppose she thinks she's safe cause of the dome," Mal said, but he didn't really believe it. Something didn't add up. He didn't have time to run theories just now, though, so he filed it away for later examination. "Come on."

The others met them halfway between the shuttles.

"Are we expecting trouble?" Simon asked, eyeing their guns.

"Better to expect it than the alternative." Shepherd Book pushed past him, rolling up his sleeves as he went.

"You prepared for what this could mean?" Mal asked, catching the Shepherd's eye. He didn't know the finer details of Book's relationship with Horne, but if it was anything like Mal's with his old war buddies, he could imagine the inner turmoil going on in Book's mind. "If you wanna sit this one out, ain't nobody gonna blame you."

"Perhaps it's naive to hope for a peaceful resolution to all this." Book tucked his chin and balled his hands into fists. "But I'd rather be there, one way or the other."

Mal nodded, then turned toward *Serenity*. Though he didn't expect it to work, Mal tried the comm in his pocket a few times, calling for Kaylee, Wash, and even River—all to no avail. With a sigh, he returned it to his pocket. It was time to take his home back.

They situated themselves as advantageously as possible. The terrain didn't lend itself well to an ambush. There weren't any big rocks or trees to position behind, so instead he directed them to use the shuttles as cover. Zoë could hit a target dead on at near a hundred yards with her rifle, so he had her take a hike behind a curtain of undisturbed bromegrass. Tuan with his pistol and the Governess with hers were set up near the shuttles. Finally, Mal and the Shepherd would do what had to be done and knock.

"Howdy!" Mal shouted through the cargo-bay door. "Seems you've taken my spaceship for a little joy ride, Horne. Don't take too kindly to that sort of thing. Course, if you'd asked permission, we might be in a different situation here."

He exchanged a glance with Book, who shrugged.

"Now, I'm suggestin' you come on out of there and we talk this over like civilized folk." Mal rapped his knuckles on the door once more. "You hearin' me, Horne?"

"Lyle," Book said, his voice raised to nearly a shout. "It's time to come out."

There was a gushing sound as the pressure on the door released, followed by a chatter of goose honks, but when the door came down at last, it wasn't Lyle Horne who stood on the other side. It was a girl. A teenager. A group of them.

There were four of them, each with a weapon Mal recognized all too well: on the left was a wiry-looking white boy with shaggy blond curls holding a pistol; to the right was a light-brown-skinned boy with a buzz cut and goggles, carrying—or attempting to carry—Jayne's machine gun, Lux; and near the door control panel was the youngest among them, with dark hair and a round face, holding what was unmistakably the rainstick Jayne had picked up back on Triumph. At the center, though, was a girl with fluffy red hair, freckles, and a gaze more piercing than a flesh wound. She held the Callahan full-bore auto-lock, Vera.

Mal knew when he was outgunned. This wasn't one of those times. Four on four—maybe four and a half if he counted the Governess—were generally favorable odds. He knew his aim, not to mention Zoë's, would be more accurate. It wasn't the guns that had him worried; it was the targets.

Mal put his hands up, taking his finger off the trigger of his Liberty Hammer, and said, "Think there's been some kind of misunderstanding. Seems you've taken my ship. I'd love to have it back if you care to parlay."

"*Your* ship?" said the girl at the center. "I think you mean *my* ship. I'd kindly ask you to get off it."

"Let's not be hasty." Mal eyed her carefully—she was the girl from town he'd met at the Archer household. He'd thought at the time she'd sounded interested in *Serenity*, but he'd just assumed she liked ships, and who could blame her? Seemed she had a bit more of a nefarious interest in his, though. "Looks like you've run down. Maybe we can help you get back in the air."

She fixed him with a pitying stare. "But why would I need you when I've already got your mechanic?"

"Kaylee?" Mal shouted, leaning to get a better look. She wasn't anywhere to be seen. Mal's heart beat faster. "Where's my crew?"

"Can you really call them your crew? You don't have a ship anymore." A sly smile crept across her round face.

"I'm still the captain of *Serenity*." It was the wrong thing to say. Mal could tell even before she leveled Vera directly at him, finger on the trigger like she knew how to use it.

"*Serenity*'s got a new captain now—Captain Agate. Got a nice ring to it, eh?"

"Agate?" The name sounded from far away, equal parts surprise and scolding. "Agate, honey? Is that you?"

"*Mom?*" Agate's body tensed and her attention swung from Mal to just beyond the shuttles. So did her gun.

There was a split second where Mal considered taking advantage of the distraction. If he could clear the ramp fast enough, he could overpower her, tackle her to the floor, and take the gun away. Maybe he could do all that without the others turning their weapons on him first. And if they were all very lucky, no one would get hurt. But Mal wasn't in the business of counting on luck. It hadn't served him well of late and he wasn't about to put the lives of his crew and then some in the hands of chance. Nobody's gun was going to go off on his account, especially not Vera.

It went off anyway.

Mal slammed his body into the Shepherd's and took him down without hesitation. They hit the ground together, the impact nowhere near as jarring as a bullet wound. Mal could hear the zing of bullets ricocheting around the cargo bay, only to be drowned out by loud honking. He waited a beat before getting to his feet, cursing himself for not acting faster, but when the cargo bay came back into view, all he saw were four surprised-looking faces and a cascade of feathers in the air.

"Agate!" Dina shouted as she ran toward them.

Mal put up a hand, but it was plain as day on the woman's face: nothing short of being shot at herself would stop the mother from getting to her daughter.

The others weren't far behind, eyes wide with panic at the sound of gunfire.

"Everybody all right up there?" Mal called.

Agate lay on the ground, knocked over by the recoil from Vera, staring wide-eyed and shell-shocked at the feathers raining from the ceiling. Dina pushed past Mal, pulling her daughter into her arms in a rough embrace with a sound halfway between a sob and a laugh. Vera lay on the floor at her feet, no longer a threat.

"Mom, get off," Agate whined.

Mal took a tentative step up the ramp.

"Don't… Don't come any closer!" said one of the others half-heartedly, holding their own gun like it was an unpredictable explosive. The safety was still on, to Mal's relief.

"These ain't toys," Mal said, kneeling beside them and wrapping his hands around the machine gun. "You give that to me, else someone might get hurt."

"Someone's already hurt," murmured the Shepherd, who'd followed in Mal's wake.

Mal quickly glanced at each of the would-be-hijackers, searching for injury, his blood pressure spiking dangerously at the thought. But the Shepherd's gaze was fixed on the top of the stairs.

There, a flurry of white passed back and forth, honks of anguish filling the room. One of the geese had been hit. They'd been suspiciously quiet—and absent, now that Mal thought about it. The bromegrass Mal and Book had used to secure the enclosure was strewn about the floor.

"Damn things chewed through it," Mal muttered.

"Anyone hit?" Zoë asked, slowing to a jog. The others followed, curious but cautious looks on their faces.

"I can… ready the infirmary," Simon panted as as he came to a stop next to Zoë.

"No need for that." Mal shook his head. "Just a goose."

"No!" Agate let out a high wail. "You have to fix her!" She pushed off Dina and got to her feet, clutching her arm. The recoil on Vera was enough to dislocate a grown man's shoulder if he wasn't ready for it. Mal was surprised she was still conscious.

The other former captives—Eli, Tuan, and Julian—joined the throng now, each making a beeline for one of the teenagers. The likenesses between family members became immediately apparent. Eli swept the lanky teen who'd held Jayne's pistol into a hug, disarming him at the same time, while Tuan gripped the hand of the smallest of *Serenity*'s hijackers and shook his head, speaking in a low voice with a grave expression on his face.

"You can fix her, right?" Agate turned teary eyes up at Mal as she pointed at where the goose lay on the floor.

He shrugged and glanced at Simon. "What do you say, doc?"

"I'm not a veterinarian," Simon said. "But you should let me look at your shoulder."

"I'm fine," Agate grumbled, then stepped away from him, eyes narrowing.

Mal sighed. "Will you let us come aboard, put the weapons down, and talk to us?"

Agate gave him a hard look, as though sizing him up. Even with her injured arm, Mal didn't relish the thought of fighting her.

"Only if you save the goose," she said finally.

Simon groaned. "I'm really not equipped for avian—"

"She said save the goose," Mal barked, indicating Agate beside him. "That's an order from your captain."

22

If there was one lesson Wash had well and truly learned during his career as a pilot, it was to expect the unexpected. Still, there was no universe in which he was mentally prepared for the scene that met him in the cargo bay. Guns and geese—fun to say, less fun to mix. There was a lot of honking, to say the least. He narrowly avoided the flock's stampede as they scattered, making room for Zoë and Book, who between them carried the wounded goose, struggling and straining, toward the infirmary.

"There you are," Mal said on finding Wash, Kaylee, and River clustered together on the stairs.

"Welcome back... Captain?" Kaylee looked from Mal to the new girl—the one who'd called herself captain.

She was a strange creature, only about five feet tall and with round cheeks like a cherub, but with a razor-sharp gaze. Wash wasn't entirely sure which of the captains he'd rather cross—neither, probably. He wasn't a confrontational sort, and the prospect of being on the receiving end of either of their tempers left him feeling almost as chilled as having someone else fly *Serenity* with him on board.

"Is it just me or did Mal get shorter?" Wash asked in a conspiratorial tone.

Kaylee nodded, eyes tracking the girl as she was led into the dining area. “I like his hair long. It makes him look powerful.”

“That’s enough out of you,” Mal grunted. “Where were you, anyhow? Seems a mite fishy that four teenagers got the jump on my ace pilot and top-notch mechanic.”

“Locked in the engine room.” Wash shook his head. “You have to know, Mal, I wouldn’t give up *Serenity* so easily. I would have defended her with my very life. Well, maybe with Kaylee’s life.”

“Hey!” Kaylee gave him a shove.

“Well, maybe River’s…” Wash glanced around for her, but she was nowhere to be found. Seconds ago, she’d been right with them, leading the way toward the cargo bay. Now, she was gone, just like a ghost.

“Who’s to say it wouldn’t be us defending her with *your* life, huh?” Kaylee shot back, hands on her hips.

“Good thing it didn’t come to that.” Zoë joined them at the door and folded her arms around Wash’s middle. “You might be my husband, but don’t think for a second I’d forgive you if anything happened to our girl here.”

“Please,” Wash grumbled. “*Serenity*’s withstood worse.”

Zoë and Kaylee exchanged a weary glance as Wash looked on. It was a common occurrence, one he’d made his peace with. Sometimes, significant looks weren’t for him to understand, and that was all right.

In the kitchen, Inara grabbed the kettle to make tea for them all while Shepherd Book poured some stale crackers into a bowl to share. When they were done serving these meager refreshments, Mal cleared his throat.

“Now, I think we’re all overdue for a conversation,” he said, turning to face their guests. “Hear each other out and whatnot, find out what page we’re all on, then see if we can find our way to gettin’ on the same one. How’s that sound?”

There was some hesitant nodding among the newcomers—family members, now that Wash got a good look at them. Some looked to be parent and child, where others were clearly siblings. He'd seen them before in the cargo bay, some embracing, some locked in stern conversation, no doubt facing a scolding for their madcap behavior. Now, they were all huddled close together, a reunion charged with the tension of recent events. Wash didn't clock any weapons in sight, but that didn't mean they were out of the woods just yet.

"Not until you save the goose," said the one at the center—"Captain" Agate. Her red-tinged face settled into a stern pout, giving her the look of an angry tomato. "No point in discussing anything if you can't even do that." She crossed her arms and fixed Mal with an incinerating stare.

"I hear you, loud and clear," Mal said, a placating tone to his voice. "But there's only so much we can do for her. Could be she don't make it, and I want you to prepare yourselves for that."

One of the other hijackers let out a soft whine of despair.

"I ain't sayin' that's a certainty," Mal hurried to add. "Just that we may not want to wait before beginning discussions. There's lots for us to talk about, and I don't think—"

"I said, not until you prove you're worthy." Agate crossed her arms.

The whole thing struck Wash as incredibly funny. Malcolm Reynolds was not an easy man to put in his place, but somehow this teenage girl had forced him into a corner. Wash was not above enjoying that—at least for now.

"Right..." Mal balled his hands into fists. "I'll check on the patient, then." He sidled up to where Zoë and Wash stood off to the side. Though he'd stowed his gun—and forced them all to follow suit—his hand still rested on his holster out of habit. "Keep an eye on 'em while I'm gone. Don't want this place turning into a daycare."

Zoë gave him a nod, but her lips split into a smile as she turned back toward Wash. "Wouldn't be so bad, would it?"

"Spoken like someone who's never been a babysitter." Wash wrapped an arm around her waist and pulled her in close. It was a hazard of the job, being away from her. Every mission pulled them apart. Still, he liked the bit where they came back together.

"Excuse me?" Zoë leaned away with an indignant expression. "I babysit plenty on this boat, and you all are grown adults."

"Should I be offended? I feel like I should be offended."

Zoë took his face between her hands and pressed a kiss to his cheek. "Not if you know what's good for you."

Wash did, and arguing with his wife certainly didn't make the list. Instead, he turned his attention to their guests. They weren't babies by any stretch of the imagination. Teenagers, certainly. Their leader, Agate, looked to be firmly in the middle somewhere. All of them were too young for this sort of trouble.

"Can you imagine *Serenity* with a baby on board?"

"Yes," said Zoë instantly, and her gaze bored into him. Her eyes, brown and flecked with gold, were prettier than any gorram planet. He wouldn't mind being landlocked there. Not at all. "I can, in fact, imagine it. Have done plenty of times."

"What? Why?" Wash looked around at the sharp corners and exposed wires all around them. A ship was a series of disasters waiting to happen. "This place is a death trap."

"Well, it's our home, and I imagine any child of ours would learn to live here just as we have."

Wash blinked, his vision sparking with bright lights as his head filled with a ringing in his ears—or maybe it was just muted honking. "Child... of ours? You and me?" He pointed to her and then himself.

"Can't think of anyone else on this boat I'd want to start a family with." She caught his hand in hers and pressed it to her sternum. "We've got a lot of love to give, don't you think?"

They'd broached the topic before, of course, but it had always felt hypothetical, like it was for a different version of them. He'd sort of assumed when he'd married her that having a family wasn't in the cards for them. Babies were for folks with houses and bank accounts and a stable environment that wasn't under constant threat of being blown up by the Alliance. He'd put that dream to bed long ago.

"I, uh, haven't put much thought to it," Wash said, a nervous laugh stuck in the back of his throat.

"Well, do." Zoë gave his rear a swift pat and added, "I'm serious, Wash."

Truth be told, being a father was one on a very short list of things Wash knew with certainty he wanted to be good at. The problem was, he wasn't sure that truth held out here in the black. Yes, he had the playful disposition and the dinosaur toys to prove it, but he didn't have the power to make the 'verse a softer place for their little one. It was harsh world after harsh world for them, and the thought of asking an innocent soul to carry that on their little shoulders without choosing it… well, it didn't sit right with him.

"I don't know." Wash's brow furrowed, the muscles tensing as his face pulled into a pinched expression he seldom wore. His gaze swept over their collected guests, lingering on the younger ones. They were grown—or at least more grown than the fictional baby Zoë was talking about—but still, his heart clenched a little at the thought of any of them falling into the sort of dangerous lives he and the crew led aboard *Serenity*. "The first time we have youths aboard and already there's a bullet wound on this ship."

"It's a goose, Wash."

"Yeah, but it could've been a person. It could've been me. It could've been you." Wash's fingers found the nape of Zoë's neck, making small circles on her skin. "And today's not even close to the most dangerous we've had recently. Can you imagine dealing with a baby and Niska? A baby and the Alliance? What happens if one of us dies?"

Zoë nodded, her expression grave. "I know, I know. I'm not saying it won't be difficult, but most things worth having are."

Wash's brain churned on and on, listing all the things that could go wrong. "We can't baby-proof a spaceship. Hell, we can't even baby-proof Jayne. And you know the captain will have something to say about it."

"Yeah, well, the captain isn't married to either one of us, so I'm not sure his opinion matters." Zoë laced their fingers together and inclined her head so their foreheads touched. "Think on it, okay?"

Wash chewed his lip, casting his gaze around the ship. Their new captain sat resolute at the dining table wearing a sour expression. For a moment, Wash imagined another face there—one equal parts him and Zoë. He imagined his own daughter with them all, eating dinner—mostly protein, seasoned with the Shepherd's herbs. Mal and Zoë would tell her war stories, appropriately scrubbed of the gorier details if Wash had any say over it. Kaylee would help her learn to take things apart and put them back together again, Inara would show her how to care for her curls, and Simon would tell her about all the bones and muscles in her body. Jayne would probably teach her how to swear. Wash would do his best to forgive him for it.

And maybe she would love to fly, just like him. She'd sit in his lap and he'd let her steer. They would play make-believe and hide-and-seek and while away the hours while they waited for her mom to come home from doing profitable crime.

It was all too much, too wonderful. He wanted it, the same as Zoë. That didn't mean it was a good idea, but then again Wash had never let that stop him before. Maybe it was possible. Maybe they could be happy. Maybe he'd think about it later. There was plenty of time for all of it someday.

23

In his time as a trauma surgeon, Simon had reattached limbs, repaired shattered bones, and even once removed a live snake from a man's colon, but he'd never operated on a goose before.

With the help of Shepherd Book and Zoë, he was able to subdue the bird and stop her from thrashing long enough to sedate her. He hadn't even been sure it would work, or if it was the proper protocol, but it was what he knew, so it would have to do. Now, it was only a matter of patience, dexterity, and a little luck as he navigated repairing the wing the bullet had torn through and removing the bullet from the bird's flank.

"How's the patient, Doc?" Mal asked. "Would love to have a positive update to share with the others soon."

Simon didn't look up. "I'm doing my best not to cause further damage. Her anatomy isn't familiar to me, so that takes additional time."

"Time. Of course. Not intendin' to rush you." There was the sound of fingers drumming on the doorframe, then Mal took a few steps inside. "It's just that they're refusin' to discuss anything with us till they know one way or the other."

Simon tried to focus on the bullet wound, the nerves and

vessels at play. It would do none of them any good if he nicked an artery while trying to prevent further blood loss.

"Need a hand?" Mal asked.

Simon hesitated. "Yes, but… I'm not sure yours—"

"Did my fair share of field medicine during the war, Doc. I can handle most anything you throw at me."

"I don't doubt your mettle, it's just that—"

"Come on. What d'ya need?"

"Well…" Simon trailed off. The indignity of it all was rather acute. "My, uh… My brow is a bit… sweaty."

Mal turned stiffly, waving his finger wildly as he scanned the room. "I'll, uh, get a cloth?" He fished around on the other side of the infirmary before returning to Simon's side.

"I'll just reach around here and—" Mal gingerly patted the cloth across Simon's brow and sighed. "So… this is what it's come to."

"I apologize if this is humiliating for you. There's a life in the balance—albeit an avian life—but your poor masculinity is the real victim here."

"Takes more than a little brow moppage to test my masculinity." Mal set the cloth down, but didn't make for the door. Instead, he stood there at Simon's elbow for a beat before adding, "I ain't too proud to admit it, letting someone else give orders on my ship might do the trick, though."

"Ah, are the captains not getting along?" Simon adjusted his grip on the retractor.

"This ship's only got one captain, and that's me."

"I don't know about you, but my mother taught me to share."

"Now ain't the time," Mal growled.

Simon didn't need to be told twice. The captain was difficult to read at times, but Simon usually had a fairly accurate pulse on his moods—when a joke might be appreciated and when to shut the hell up. At first he'd found it taxing, the mental whiplash of the ups and downs of this life they all led, but now he was used to it—or as used to it as it was possible to be when nothing was truly predictable and everything could change at a moment's notice. Case in point: the teenager calling herself captain.

Mal leaned back against the wall and let out a heavy sigh. "Truth be told, I'm not half so bothered by her as I am by that *woman.*"

From the way he said it, there was no question as to whom the captain was referring. The Governess wasn't exactly *Serenity*'s usual sort of guest, and Simon could only imagine how discomfiting her presence might be to Mal.

"She does have a rather repugnant air about her."

Mal wrinkled his nose. "So do you when you casually use words like *repugnant.*"

"Sorry if my vocabulary offends you."

A few minutes of silence passed in which Simon was able to finish clearing a pathway through which to remove the bullet. He grasped it between his forceps, pulled it out, and let it drop onto the metal tray with a soft plink.

"What's your read on her?" Mal asked.

"Me?" Simon pointed to himself with the bloody forceps. It was an odd occasion indeed when the captain asked Simon anything at all. Most of their exploits were far outside Simon's realm of expertise, aside from the increasingly frequent medical emergencies he attended to on *Serenity*. Indeed, unless the Governess had a bullet hole Mal hadn't expressly put there himself, Simon hadn't expected to weigh in on the matter. "You want my opinion?"

"Wouldn't have asked for it if I didn't."

Simon raised his eyebrows but didn't press further. "Well, she's dignified, I suppose. Carries herself with a modicum of decorum and has an eloquence I'd expect of a woman of her status."

"Should've known you'd like her. All you rich folks care about is decorum."

"I didn't say I liked her." Now that the bullet was out, Simon turned his attention toward cleaning the wound. It helped to have something to do. Conversations with Mal seldom went how he expected, but it was a comfort to have his hands busy while they talked. "Just because her manners are familiar doesn't mean I find them pleasant."

"That so?"

"It is." Simon set his jaw, trying not to hold any tension in his hands as he worked. It wouldn't do for him to cramp up now, not when he was about to begin suturing. He needed his fingers limber and his movements fluid. "Besides, there was something about her whole presentation that rang false, like she was performing rather than being. She dressed and spoke and acted exactly like she was supposed to, for who she is, but it all struck me as practiced, if that makes sense."

"You mean she's putting on an act?"

"Maybe. It's hard to tell. If it were all an act, one would think she'd do a better job of hiding it."

"How do you mean?"

"Her estate was impressive, don't get me wrong, but someone of her status, with her resources, ought to have a staff of some kind. A butler, at the very least."

"You've got your prissy pants in a wad over being served by your host instead of a servant?" Mal asked.

"Let's leave my pants out of it, shall we?" Simon threaded the stitches evenly, closing the wound with practiced ease. "All I'm saying is it's odd that someone like her is all the way out here alone. I wouldn't trust her if I were you."

"Oh, I won't. I don't make a habit of trustin' people for a good long while—longer than I plan to be on this moon, anyhow."

Simon finished off the stitches and cut the sutures. He'd have to find a way to keep the goose from picking at them. Maybe he could fashion some sort of cone...

"Well, the good news is you can tell our young captain that the patient cleared surgery with flying colors."

Mal groaned. "Wash put you up to that?" Mal asked with a groan.

"What? No, I..." Simon deflated. "Ah. Flying. Yes, I see. No, that was just a fortuitous coincidence, I suppose."

"Excuse me if I choose not to believe you." Mal rapped his knuckles on the wall once as he made for the exit, but lingered in the doorway. "It was after the duel on Persephone, in case you were wonderin'. When I got stabbed by that pompous, spoiled, *bèn tiān shēng de yī duī ròu*. You patched me up good. Barely even a scar."

"What?" Simon blinked at him in confusion.

A grin flashed across Mal's face for just a moment. "That was the moment when I decided to finally start trustin' you," he said.

And then, just like his smile, he was gone.

24

Malcolm Reynolds was good in a crisis. That didn't mean he enjoyed them. Just once, he wished a job would go according to plan.

With a heavy sigh, he surveyed the cargo bay. Feathers and goose droppings coated the floor in a carnage of white. It was better than cow dung, if only because the smell wasn't so rank, but in the grand scheme of things, birds were far from his favorite cargo.

They were also nowhere to be seen, which wasn't particularly encouraging. He liked cargo that he could see, cargo he could trust. Geese on the loose was a whole mess of chaos he wasn't prepared for.

"What happened to our feathered friends?" he asked the first person he encountered on his way up to the dining area without looking to see who it was.

"They got hungry," River replied with an unsettling head tilt. "Chewed through the grass."

"And have you seen them lately?"

"Heard loud noises. Got scared."

"Right…" Mal gave the ship a last once over before continuing on. "If you see 'em, uh…" He'd been about to say she ought to round them up again, but River wasn't the most reliable among them. That wasn't to say he didn't think she was capable—River had proven herself time and time again to be a valuable member of the team in ways he'd never expected. It was just that he wasn't so sure River and the geese were a good mix. They'd either end up killing each other or becoming a dynamic combination no one anticipated. Either way, it would spell trouble for the rest of them. "Tell somebody, okay? Don't want them mucking up the engine."

With that, he bounded up the rest of the stairs to the dining area, not waiting for River's reply.

"Bullet's out. Goose is sleeping, but she's going to live."

There was a palpable release of tension in the room.

"Well, that's cause for celebration, indeed," said the Shepherd, handing Mal a mug of tea.

Mal frowned into his glass. "No offense, Shepherd, but I usually celebrate with something stronger."

Book gave him a withering look. "There are impressionable minds present."

"I've got a bottle of whiskey stowed away on the bridge somewhere," Wash said.

"Less talking, more fetching." Mal gestured him toward the door.

"I'll help," Zoë said. "Might be... heavy."

Mal rolled his eyes, but let them go. There were too many bodies in the dining area anyway.

"So." Mal stepped up to the table, setting both hands out wide as he stared down Agate, the would-be captain. He remembered what it was like to be young and headstrong. He and his friends back on Shadow had done plenty of foolhardy things when they were her age. They'd gotten away with a fair bit of mischief, too. Part of him respected her for it. The rest of him was gorram fed up. "You want to tell me what you're plannin' to do with my ship here?"

"I think you'll find it's *my* ship, actually," she said with a haughty glare. "And I thought that was obvious."

"Well, it ain't." Mal sighed. "I'm operatin' on only half the story here, or so it would seem. Explain it to me like I don't know a thing."

Agate scoffed. "That'll be easy since you obviously don't."

Mal opted to ignore that particular jab at his intellect, instead motioning for her to continue.

"It's pretty simple, actually," Agate said. "Heard about your ship, decided to take it, took it." She ticked each step off on her fingers.

"Right, but why?" asked Eli. "That's an awful lot of danger to be putting yourselves in on our behalf."

Dina, whose face was arranged in a precise copy of her daughter's unamused expression, huffed. "It's a spaceship, Eli. Is that not enough for you?"

"It's not *just* a ship," Agate shot back. "It's a *Firefly*."

The girl had good taste—Mal had to give her that.

Eli shook his head. "Well, at least we know where she gets it from."

"Had to do it, didn't we?" one of the other hijackers chimed in—the older boy with dark hair and warm brown skin who looked like a younger copy of Julian. "*Someone* had to come save you."

"Lenny's right," said the one next to Eli, his blond curls an echo of his father's. "You'd been gone for days and we couldn't trust Horne to do it."

"Russell… you really shouldn't have." Eli shook his head, but there was a glow in his eyes that looked an awful lot like pride.

"We had to!" Russell replied, throwing his hands in the air.

The third and youngest member of Agate's young crew—a likely relation of Tuan's, by the look of them—nodded emphatically, but didn't say anything.

"Well, one way or another, we got your relatives back," Mal said. "So you won't be needin' *Serenity* anymore. We'll drop you off in town, you can have your little reunions, and then we'll be off."

The adults all exchanged wary glances, an unspoken reservation passed between them.

"That's not how it's going to go, actually," said Agate. "See, if we go back to town, Horne will just round *them* up and make an example of 'em. He's done it before—anyone who stands up to him is punished."

Julian nodded gravely. "A few months back, a couple folks started taking breaks during their shift—said it was too hot inside to work and they needed to go outside to cool off. Horne told 'em to deal with it or he'd show them real heat. When they asked him to bring in some fans or prop open doors, he burned the skin right off their hands. Now they can't even work the machines. Lost the fight, lost their jobs."

"That's true, I think," Kaylee said. "Simon and I met someone with burns on their hands at the market. Wouldn't tell us what happened, but..."

Mal grimaced. Labor conditions weren't good damn near anywhere. Even on the central planets, folk like them didn't get much better. He was reminded of the mudders back on Higgins' Moon, given the worst deal he'd seen in a long time, and somehow still fighting to make something resembling community and home out of it all. Of course, a lot of them were drunk most of the time, which either hindered or helped depending on how you looked at it.

"So, you reckon if you try to go back to the way things were, you won't just be dealing with bad wages and long hours. You'll be up against Horne's nastier side."

"You say that like he's got a good side," Dina grumbled.

Mal's gaze drifted over to Shepherd Book, but the preacher was engrossed in cleaning the dishes. Of course, it wasn't unlike him to work hard—not a one of them liked chores, but the Shepherd always picked up the slack where he could without complaint.

Some kind of godly notion or other, Mal supposed—carry each other's burdens, or serve one another humbly, or do unto others. Those verses used to bring him comfort, give him purpose. Now they just served as a reminder of times he'd rather forget.

A man like Book, who did what was not asked of him, who helped others for no ulterior motive, must have had a reason to trust Horne once upon a time. Either Lyle Horne was once a good man or Shepherd Book was a bad one. Either way, Mal's interest was piqued.

"I assume reasoning with him is out of the question?" he asked.

There was a general bobbing of heads and murmuring of agreement.

"Don't you understand?" asked Russell. "We can't go back."

"Don't see that you have much of an alternative," Mal said, "unless you want to relocate to the Governess's compound."

Agate made a face. "No way."

"She helped us, it's true," Eli said, nodding to the Governess herself, who sat in the corner, quietly observing. "And we're all grateful to you for that, ma'am. But the compound ain't our home."

"I won't pretend to understand, but know that the compound is open to you if you need it," offered the Governess, her tone heavy with sweetness in the way of Kaylee's protein frosting—chock full of sugar, but still gritty underneath.

"So, you can't go back to town, you can't stay here... What's the plan?" Mal turned his gaze on Agate, who shifted uncomfortably in her seat. "First thing you need to know 'bout being a captain is, it's your job to figure out what's next."

There were a few moments of silence as Agate stared back. Then she said, "We leave. That's what's next."

"We... leave?" Julian repeated, exchanging curious looks with their fellow Bromans. "There isn't exactly anywhere else on Brome for us to go."

"Then we leave Brome," Agate said. "This is a spaceship,

right? So we find another moon, another planet. We don't have to stay on Brome."

"Oh, honey." Dina reached for her daughter and squeezed her shoulder gently. "That's not a real solution."

"What else can we do?" Agate's eyes shimmered with tears. "Horne isn't gonna stop, so we have to go."

Dina pushed Agate's hair back from her face and wiped her cheek with a thumb. "Us leaving isn't gonna stop Horne. He'll keep on hurtin' folks whether we're here or not. Someone's gotta stand up to him, so it might as well be us. And I don't know about you, but I don't back down from a fight."

"I'm no coward!" Agate stood to her full height, a measly five feet, and stared her mother down. "None of us are."

"Then it's decided—we ain't runnin' away. Not from Horne." Dina looked over at Mal. "Don't suppose you're feelin' inclined to help us with that?"

Mal shrugged. "Ain't good business to leave a job half done, especially when there's coin on the line." It was true that *Serenity* was hurting for cash. He couldn't very well tell his crew they'd be eating bromegrass for the foreseeable future and expect to go without mutiny. Jayne, at the very least, would have something to say about that—so it was a good thing he wasn't there. "Then again, it ain't good business to treat your workers like trash."

"Does that mean you're with us?" Tuan asked hopefully.

"Well, I'm certainly not against you." Mal surveyed them all carefully, taking stock of the chaotic medley of fear and determination in their faces. "But we'll need to be smart about this. We can't just waltz into town, shoot some guns, and expect to make headway."

"We can't?" asked Dina and Agate at the same time.

Eli put his head in his hands. Mal wanted to do the same.

"You mentioned Horne's got enforcers," he said instead.

"Something tells me they wouldn't take too kindly to a show of violence. Besides, with or without Horne, you've got Blue Sun to contend with. We'll need some kind of leverage, I should think."

The others eyed him with varying levels of trepidation. "So, a peaceful approach is what you're suggesting?" asked Julian.

"Shepherd." Mal's gaze flicked to Book, who was still avoiding eye contact. "You know Horne best. What do you think? Will he see reason?"

Book didn't reply right away. He set down the sponge and dried his hands on a towel before turning to face them all.

"When I knew him, Lyle was less a man of reason and more a man of feeling. You'll be better off appealing to his sense of humanity, and if that fails, appeal to his purse." Book's expression turned sour for a second. "Then again," he added, "it's been decades, and a lot can change with time. If I've learned anything today, it's that Lyle Horne is as much a stranger to me as I am to him, I'm afraid."

Mal nodded. As he'd suspected, the Shepherd remained cagey about his past relationship with Horne. It would be easier if Book would just be straight with him, tell Mal about whatever secrets he was clinging to—but then, he supposed they all had secrets, and Mal's weren't available for trade even if the Shepherd's were.

"So we make it unprofitable to treat you like dirt," Mal said.

"How?" Julian asked. "He controls our jobs, our pay, damn near our whole town. We control nothing."

"That's not true," said Shepherd Book, stepping forward with a solemn expression. "He doesn't control *you*."

Before the others could say much of anything in response, there was a loud crash from the direction of the bridge as Wash and Zoë came barreling down the hallway toward them.

"Bad news, Captain," Wash said. "Couldn't find that bottle anywhere."

Mal rolled his eyes. As if they'd spent any time actually looking for it. He made it a rule not to get involved in his crew's personal lives, but if he knew one thing about Wash and Zoë, it was that they'd take every advantage of alone time they could get.

"Is there any good news?" Mal asked as Zoë came to her husband's side wearing a mirthful grin.

"Depends how you define good," she said.

"As in something that will make *me* happy?"

"That's a tall order, sir."

"I'm not exactly in the mood, Zoë."

"We found the geese." Zoë exchanged a glance with Wash, whose eyes were wide with guilt. "They may have taken to nesting on the bridge."

"Well, get them *off* the bridge."

"Easier said than done, Mal." Wash deflated a bit. "They're crafty, they're cunning, and they're organized."

"They're gorram birds, Wash." But Mal's mind slipped over something Wash had said. *They're organized.*

"It's true," Zoë said. "I may have fought in the war, but I'd take a legion of Alliance soldiers over a flock of geese any day."

"I'm not a weakling, you know. One, I could take." Wash flexed unimpressively. "But all of them at once? I wouldn't stand a chance."

"That's how we do it," Mal murmured, eyes glazing over as his brain began to spin.

"Nah, Mal, I was just saying, there's too many of them." Wash's words sounded far away, as though coming from another room.

"No, not the geese. Horne." Mal ran a hand through his hair as the pieces fell into place. "When it's just a few of you, he can make an example of you—scare the others. But if you all stand together, there's nothing he can do. If you don't work, he can't profit. It's as simple as that."

It really was so simple. It was one of the strange universal laws of labor that those who made all the money did none of the work. The workers always outnumbered the bosses, too. And yet time and time again, those at the top got everything they wanted by exploiting the workers. Horne was just one man, and if he wanted to keep his position, he needed to listen to them. It was time to remind Horne of that salient detail.

The others exchanged tentative glances. Finally, Eli spoke up.

"What's to stop him from going to Blue Sun and getting new workers sent in?" he asked.

"Or moving the refinery off Brome entirely?" Julian added.

"Or just throwing a grenade at us and watching the chaos unfold?" Dina's eyes went wide, halfway between dread and desire.

It was a fair assumption Horne would try all three.

"We're not gonna let him," Mal said, shifting his attention to the corner of the dining area. "Are we, Governess?"

The Governess, who had been sitting silently all this time, holding fast to a chipped ceramic mug of tea, jumped ever so slightly at being addressed. "I'm not sure I can be of help, Captain. I don't have much of a relationship with Horne."

"It's not Horne I need you to have a relationship with." Mal turned to face her fully. "Excuse me for saying it so plainly, but we ain't got time to beat around the bush. You understand the language of money. And if we can't get through to Horne, I'm thinkin' we may need to take things a bit further up, talk to Blue Sun direct. They won't be bothered with me, I reckon, but *you*...?" He tilted his head, an unasked question in his eyes.

The Governess surveyed him warily. When she finally spoke, her tone was clipped like she wished she could say something entirely different. "I suppose so. I can't guarantee they'll listen to me, but I can try."

"That's all we ask. As for the rest..." Mal turned his gaze on Shepherd Book. "Well, we've got leverage."

25

Lyle Horne was a bad influence. It had been a long time since Jayne had had this many drinks before noon. Well, not that long. Since Higgins' Moon, at least. He didn't make a habit of it these days. He needed his mind—or at least his shooting arm—sharp. Alcohol made for drifting aim, and he couldn't go putting a bullet in the wrong target.

The good news was that Jayne wasn't likely to need to discharge his weapon any time soon. Then again, maybe that was bad news. After several hours of sitting in the mostly empty tavern and exchanging tales with Horne, he was itching for a little action.

"Never thought I'd end up here," Horne was saying, fingers loose around the handle of his mug. Liquid sloshed over the side as he gestured animatedly. "And I never thought it'd be because of a real job. Thought I'd be running cons and robbin' folks forever, but now look at me! All respectable."

Jayne didn't think Horne looked all that respectable, but he wasn't about to say so. Truth was, most people looked like trouble to Jayne. That was how he liked it, though. Too many fancy folks about and he started to feel out of place. Inara was all right—it didn't hurt that she was nice to look at, of course—but the doctor and his sister were a stretch too far. It didn't matter if River was easy on the eyes; she wasn't easy on the brain.

Horne, though… Jayne could tell he wasn't that sort. There was a roughness to him that the upper crust didn't carry. It was in the slant of his shoulders, the curl of his lip, the trailing Gs missing from his verbs. Horne was just like him. Whether that was a good thing or not, Jayne hadn't decided yet.

"Suppose that's the real con, ain't it?" Horne asked with a coy lilt to his words. "Makin' the big wigs believe I'm worthy of it all." He spread his arms wide, a blistering grin on his face.

Jayne didn't think Brome was all that special. If Horne was worthy of this scrap of nowhere with more grass than people, well, then that didn't make him much more impressive than anyone else. And he was just drunk enough to say as much.

"So you got yourself a little barren moon, is that it?" Jayne tossed the last of his drink back and set his mug down with a *thunk*. He'd had enough now he no longer cared that it tasted like dirt. "Don't see how that's much to brag about."

Horne let out a long laugh from deep in his belly. "Course you don't," he said finally, wiping his cheeks. "Brome is a shithole, you got that right. Nothing here but grass as far as the eye can see."

Jayne might've argued they also had dirt, if he was feeling charitable, but he wasn't. He was feeling a mite queasy from all the drink on an empty stomach, though.

"Truth is, the operation we got here couldn't work somewhere with more. The minute you give folks another option, they'll take it. Best they don't have too much choice in the matter."

"Makes sense," Jayne said. He'd seen that sort of logic work before in places he never wanted to see again—Higgins' Moon, Whitefall, Silverhold. Not a one of them offered anything but misery. "Still, seems awful depressin' out here. The drinks aren't even good."

Horne made a face, wrinkling his nose. "That's why I don't spend much time in town. Got much nicer digs back at the refinery. Better drinks, too."

Now that got Jayne's attention. "Then why are we dallying around with this *xióng māo niào*?"

Horne stood up, his chair sliding back with a loud screech, and threw a few coins down on the table. "Good point."

It was a short walk from the tavern to the refinery. They made their way through town just as folks were starting to wake. From the way Zoë and the others described their first foray into town, he half expected someone to leap out of the tall grass to stab them or something. At the very least, he thought they'd get some odd looks. Instead, they got nothing at all. Not a soul looked their way. Folks in the crowd stared determinedly ahead, as if afraid to look at Horne directly, like he was one of their suns, shining just a little too bright.

The refinery came into view behind a thick patch of bromegrass. It was a massive warehouse with tall distillation columns, shining silver in the light of Kalidasa and Penglai. The people heading that way filed in through a door out front, but Horne didn't stop to join the queue. Instead, he beckoned Jayne around the back, produced a key card, and led him through a door Jayne hadn't seen until Horne had opened it.

"Perks of being the boss," Horne said, flashing the key card and a devilish grin.

"Mr. Horne, good morning," said a man in a tight-fitting brown jumpsuit with circles beneath his eyes. He held out a mug of steaming coffee. "Night shift went smooth. No absences, save for the missing folks. Did you want a full report or—"

"Do I look like I want a full report, Gray?" Horne said, gesturing to Jayne.

"Uh, no sir." Gray's gaze flicked from Horne to Jayne and

back again. "I'll just, uh… I got your messages here and a few deliveries." He indicated a couple of crates and handed over a device with a screen displaying the Blue Sun logo.

"That'll be all." Horne waved him off with a dismissive hand, then bent to pick up one of the crates.

"You need help with those?" Jayne offered, surprised at his own generosity. He wasn't keen on doing more work than he had to most of the time, so he didn't make a habit of doing things for others unless there was something in it for him. Today, though, he felt more than a little useless, and lifting a crate for Horne wasn't all that much of an imposition. Besides, it wasn't like it required him to use his bad eye. He was plenty capable.

"Nah, I got 'em." Horne brushed him off. "Take this though, will you? I ain't a juggler." He handed over a small pile of things—the device with the Blue Sun logo, the key card, and the coffee mug.

Jayne took them, glancing down at the screen. It was full of little letters he couldn't properly see, not with his eye patched up, but it looked to be some kind of Cortex device.

"Follow me," Horne said, and with a grunt he lifted the crates and set off down the hall.

Horne's office was a square room with no windows but plenty of light. An imposing desk and a stocked bar flanked the room, and there were a couple of armchairs against the far wall. It was decorated with pretty-looking paintings of landscapes—not on Brome—and ceramic plates with gold filigree. What really caught Jayne's eye, though, was the artillery. On one wall, half a dozen guns were on display, and not pansy-ass pistols: a Colt, a rifle, a derringer, a double-barreled shotgun. Horne even had a few grenades mounted on the wall, each in a glass case. All in all, the office was plenty bigger than Jayne's bunk, but he wasn't sure he preferred it.

"Mighty fine arsenal there," Jayne said.

"My pride and joy." Horne gave him a wide grin, his eyes dancing as his gaze swept over the collection. "Some of those are one of a kind, you know."

Jayne did know. His fingers itched to hold one of them, to feel the tension of the trigger. "You got any rounds for 'em?"

"Course I do. Keep 'em loaded at all times, just in case."

Jayne wrinkled his nose. "Ain't that a pain in the ass with them all behind glass?"

"Nah. They open with just a swipe of my key card." Horne set the crates down and gestured to the armchairs. "Take a load off. Don't have many visitors this way. Nice to get some use out of the furniture. Now, what're you drinkin'?"

"Same as you," Jayne said, not altogether sure what beverages Horne did and didn't have on hand and not wanting to offend. He glanced over at the bar cart to see a dozen or so bottles of liquid—some clear, some amber. A few used glasses sat on a tray awaiting cleaning. There was a sugar rim with a red stain and an olive or two beginning to collect mold. "Whiskey, if you've got it."

"If I've got it?" Horne popped the cork of a bottle and poured Jayne a double in a clean glass. "Here, I'll trade you," he said, offering him the glass in exchange for the coffee cup Jayne still carried.

Jayne took a sip, wishing he'd thought to eat something before leaving *Serenity*. Had he known exactly how much alcohol Horne was planning to ply him with, he might have prepared better.

"Now, do you see?" Horne said, gesturing around. "I ain't doin' all this for the pretty view. Blue Sun could send me to the most monkey's-ass planet, and I wouldn't even blink. The money's damn good, and the office sure doesn't hurt."

Jayne nodded, but the motion made him feel sick, so he stopped quick. "Money's that good?" he asked. "Didn't think a foreman's salary would be all that."

"Oh, it ain't the foreman's salary that pays for all this. I got myself a little side hustle."

"Oh, yeah?" The words felt heavy on his tongue, like he was weighed down by much more than just the Cortex device. "Didn't think there were many opportunities for that sort of work out here."

"Oh, there ain't." Horne didn't elaborate. He just plucked another clean glass from the bar and busied himself with pouring himself a drink from a different bottle—maybe vodka or gin, from the look of it.

Jayne swallowed thickly. His mouth tasted ashy. It occurred to him—the thought feather-light like it barely mattered—that this was not how he normally felt when he'd been at the bottle too long. Somewhere in the recesses of his mind, the pieces gathered, ready to be put together by a sturdier brain.

He glanced down, trying to hide his difficulty—he didn't need Horne seeing him sick after only a few drinks—and his gaze snagged on something on the screen. A new message. He couldn't read it with his hand in the way, so he gathered his strength to lift his arm, knocking the key card to the ground as he did.

Text flashed up at him, swimming and swanning before his eyes. He did his best to focus. Between the spots in his vision, Jayne made out a few words:

We need to talk.

The message was signed *Jenessa Leon*.

The name rattled around his skull, familiar and strange all at once.

"You gonna tell me about your side hustle?" Jayne slurred, trying to keep abreast of the conversation while he mentally leafed through all the information he'd heard and dismissed as unimportant in the last twenty-four hours.

"Maybe," Horne said, coming to stand over him. "Not sure if I can trust you yet."

"I'm real trusty," Jayne said, vaguely aware that trusty wasn't the word he'd been trying to say. His gaze flicked over to the bar again, his vision swimming. The different bottles, the dirty glass with red lipstick on the rim, the message from Jenessa Leon… Horne had told them he didn't know the Governess, but the evidence didn't point to that being the truth. "Think it's you who ain't been honest."

"Oh, certainly." Horne's smile was a serrated knife across his face. He lowered his hands onto the arms of Jayne's chair, bracketing him in. "And I'll tell you all in due time. You're going to take a little nap now. Don't be alarmed—I ain't gonna kill you. Just got some business to attend to and I don't need you lookin' over my shoulder, is all. Then, when you wake, we'll have a good long chat about what that captain of yours is plannin'."

If he could, Jayne would've told Horne he had no idea what Mal was planning, or that more than likely neither did Mal, but his lips felt leaden. The last thing he remembered as he slumped off the chair and onto the floor was feeling the edge of the key card between his fingers and pulling it into his pocket.

26

River sometimes wondered what it would feel like to fly. Not on a ship, but with her own body. The rush of wind, the rush of want. How was it different from falling? She wanted to ask someone, but no one could tell her the way she wanted to hear it.

The geese had eyes like stones, polished and round. Were their brains as smooth? Unwrinkled, untroubled? All they knew was eat and sleep and fly and honk. It would be nice to be so simple.

"There you are," said Simon. He came to stand below her on the bridge, looking up at where she clung to the ceiling, gazing at her with a curious smile. "How did you even get up there?"

"I flew," River said. Maybe that wasn't the literal truth, but that was how it felt inside her.

"That your harebrained sister, doc?" the captain's voice floated in from the hallway, his heavy footsteps following. "Best get her out of there. Don't need her riling the geese none."

"River, why don't we go… somewhere else?" Simon suggested without panache.

River sighed and let her legs swing down, releasing her grip when she was more or less vertical.

"*Lāo tiān yé!*" Mal jumped back, hand to his chest. "You'll give a man a heart attack like that."

River's finger found a loose thread on her sweater and twisted it around and around. "Most coronary heart events occur in geriatric patients."

"What's she sayin', Doc?" Mal asked.

"Think she called you old, sir," said Zoë, coming up behind him.

"Me? I'm a fresh-faced son-of-a-gun if ever there was one." The captain pinched his own cheeks, bringing color to his pallid complexion.

Zoë let out a laugh. "I could count the wrinkles, sir."

"You won't if you know what's good for you."

River swayed to the rhythm of their banter. It was soft and warm, like a blanket long loved, frayed in places where it was clutched too hard but still holding together no matter the wear and tear. She longed to wrap herself in it, to feel the fabric on her skin.

A loud honk from the driver's seat made the others jump. River silently agreed—it was rude of them to intrude while the flock was nesting. Her eyes traveled back to the ceiling, where a few other geese nested in the rafters. She could climb back up, blend in with the metal, disappear.

"Let's go, *mèi mèi*." Simon reached for her, his fingers closing around her wrist.

River let out her own honk of displeasure.

There was a flurry of feathers as two of the geese descended to flank her, their heads bobbing and weaving in a hypnotic dance.

Simon stumbled at the sudden assault on his kneecaps. Mal caught him and took a few steps back himself.

"Woah, there," the captain said, putting Simon to rights and eyeing River. "Got yourself a flock."

River looked down. Sure enough, the rest of the geese had joined the other two and were now surrounding her in a protective circle. They chorused together, letting out a harmony of honks.

"River," Simon began, wielding concern on his tongue as he stepped forward. His love for her had always been there, a constant in their chaotic lives, but it wasn't always a boon. Sometimes, when he used it as a shield, seeking to protect her—like he was doing now—he forgot to protect himself too.

He needn't have worried, though. River knew the geese meant her no harm, as if they spoke her own language. They were one, her and the flock, searching only for a place to call home, a place to nest, a place that would love them back.

Without reservation, she held out a hand. The goose closest to her leaned in to her touch. Feather-soft. It was a greeting, a welcome to the fold. Maybe they saw in her a kinship, the same yearning for community, for stability, for a soft landing. She would be one of them if she could, and here was an invitation.

"She's gone and made friends with the geese, then, is that it?" Mal asked gruffly.

"I… suppose so?" Simon looked from her to Mal and back again. "My sister is very… She has a great capacity for empathy, and—"

"Don't need to explain it to me, doc. I've seen what she can do. Just prefer it stays convenient for us. Don't need her forming them into some kind of organized unit—unless it's on our behalf, of course."

"You know I can hear every word you're saying." River rolled her eyes. The way everyone was so keen to talk about her as if she wasn't there was maddening.

"Right. Uh, are you… Are they… Can you tell them to get off the gorram bridge, then?" Mal asked.

"No." River gave him a contemptuous look. "Do I look like I speak goose?"

"If I said yes, would that change anything?"

She sighed, casting her gaze at the geese around her. There were half a dozen in all, crowding around her feet. She felt in them a desire for quiet, for solitude, for a warm place to settle for a nap. She could do with the very same. The soft curtains of Inara's shuttle came to mind.

"Come on," she said. Maybe she couldn't speak goose, but that didn't mean they didn't understand each other.

Taking a hesitant step forward, she carved a path toward the door, shooing at Simon as he tried to go with her. She didn't need his interference. The geese didn't understand he was her brother or that he meant her no harm. They didn't know that he'd saved the goose who was shot down; all they knew was their friend's blood was on his hands.

Miraculously, they followed River as she led them out into the hall.

"Nice work," Mal called after her. "Guess you can speak goose after all."

"I didn't do it for you," she countered. The geese didn't care for him, and she couldn't blame them. The captain was loud and imposing. That was his job, of course, but they didn't have to like it.

"I thought she didn't like geese?" Mal said in a low voice.

"So did I," replied Simon.

They weren't talking to her, of course, but if they had been... Between this and how they handled Jayne before...

What could she say? The geese were beginning to grow on her.

27

"What's the damage?" Mal stood at the center of the bridge with his arms crossed as he surveyed the aftermath. Who would have thought that the most trouble would come not from the ones who'd hijacked his ship, but from the livestock aboard? If he ever got the chance to pay Arvin Helios back for this, he'd take it and then some.

"Can't be entirely sure," said Wash, his hand dancing speedily over the ship's center console like a hummingbird. "They chewed through a few wires at least. Engine's not firing, least not from up here." There was a wet squelching sound and he groaned. "I do believe our passengers mistook the bridge for a latrine as well."

"Can you blame them? Look at the state of this place," said Zoë, indicating the mess covering the console. Toy dinosaurs were strewn everywhere and there was a half-eaten plate of food sitting in a corner.

"I'd clean up, honey, but I'm a little busy trying to figure out if this ship will even fly again," Wash said through his teeth, ducking his head to get a better look at the underside of the console.

"Will she?" Mal asked. Alarm shot through him, but he did his best to tamp it down. He didn't need the others knowing he was rattled. If they saw his composure drop, his nervous energy would spread like a pestilence to the rest of the crew. They could do without the additional distraction.

Wash extracted his head from beneath the console and shrugged. "Can't be sure. I need Kaylee."

"Kaylee!" Mal roared.

"No need to shout, Cap'n," she said from the doorway. She tied the arms of her jumpsuit around her waist and gave Mal's cheek a quick peck as she passed by. "We'll get her squared away. Inara and Book are helpin' the others get settled, so you go on and do your captainy thing."

Mal wasn't sure what his "captainy thing" was, exactly. Under normal circumstances, he might sort cargo or take a nap or converse with another member of the crew while he waited. But he didn't have any cargo to sort—unless he counted the geese, which he decidedly didn't—and he wasn't tired. That left talking, a pastime he'd never developed much fondness for.

"Sir?" Zoë's voice pulled him back to reality like fabric snagging on a nail. She eyed him carefully, awaiting orders.

Mal nodded wearily, buying himself a few extra seconds to decide what, exactly, the next course of action ought to be. "Get the Governess. We may not be skyworthy yet, but we can at least get things ready for her to talk to Blue Sun. See what she needs, and such."

"Got it." Zoë brushed past him, taking to the stairs with a clatter.

Mal followed a few paces behind. The dining area was blessedly empty. He passed through to the cargo bay just in time to see their guests disappearing beyond the infirmary toward the guest quarters. All was handled. So why did it feel like nothing was? The uncomfortable stirring in Mal's stomach was making him queasy. Maybe a little quiet would do him good.

But the cargo bay wasn't quiet. Not entirely.

As Mal stepped out onto the stairs, he heard the sound of muffled crying. At first, he thought it was an errant goose, lost from its flock, but then his gaze fell on a puff of red hair. Agate sat with her legs dangling off the side of the walkway, her head in her hands.

He could have walked away, slunk back up to the dining area, maybe cleaned a few dishes. But something in him felt responsible for her, despite all that had happened.

"Didn't anyone tell you? Captains don't cry," he said.

Agate looked up, cheeks blotchy and eyes rimmed red. "They're all," she sniffed, "mad at me. Even Russell, Lenny, and Bo."

Mal nodded, surmising those were the names of her fellow hijackers. "Sometimes that happens when you're in charge. You make the plans, and if they go awry, then you take the blame."

"S'not fair." She wiped her nose on her sleeve.

"Nope, it ain't," Mal lowered himself down to sit beside her. "There's a lot about this life that ain't fair—but you know that already, don't you? Greedy folks will take what's yours, or take what should be yours, just cause they want to. And the world lets 'em cause they care about profit more than people."

"That's why I want to leave. Just… get off Brome and go somewhere better."

"Ah, kid—"

"I ain't a *kid*," Agate shot back with a glare.

"Sorry, force of habit." Mal put his hands up in surrender. He thought of almost everyone younger than him as a kid. It wasn't so much their age that defined that position in his view but their hope. He'd seen that spark wiped out time and time again in his comrades-in-arms during the war. Agate had that glint in her eyes still, and it pained him to think of it leaving. "Everyone seems young to me these days, especially those not yet carrying the weight of the world. But I can see you carry plenty. Won't happen again."

"Good." Agate crossed her arms, but Mal caught the twitch of her lips as she tried not to smile.

"Truth is, what you said about leaving Brome… There's plenty of other planets out there, but there ain't nowhere better, just different."

"There should be!" She narrowed her eyes at him, as though trying to see through his words to the real truth of it all. "Why aren't there places with more laws? Places that would stop people like Horne?"

Mal let out a long sigh. "I wish it were as simple as all that," he said. "I wish laws were made to protect people like you and me, but more common than not they're just threats that only apply to folks who ain't rich enough to pay the fine. Any law can be broken for a price. You just have to have the coin."

"But what about… what about lawmen? They're supposed stop that sort of thing from happening," she said.

Mal shrugged. "I never met a lawman who didn't use his position to break the laws he was meant to defend," he said. "They might have their uses now and again, on account of the way the 'verse is run, but I wouldn't go puttin' my faith in 'em, is all." He'd faced off against his fair share of authority figures, from officers in the war to men like Dobson, who'd shot Kaylee all those months ago. He supposed to some folks, they were heroes of a sort, but Mal had never seen eye to eye with them, even before he became a smuggler. He recalled the particularly nasty Sheriff Bundy from his home planet, Shadow, and grimaced. "More'n likely, someday you'll leave home. I just don't want you thinkin' the rest of the 'verse is ponies and rainbows."

"Don't like ponies and rainbows," Agate growled, but then her eyes turned up at him, a hopeful glint there amidst the gray. "You really think I'll leave home someday?"

"I know it." Mal set his jaw. "Folks like you and me, we ain't meant to sit still."

"Don't care to be idle." She shrugged a shoulder defensively.

"That's why you launched that plan, right? You saw what was happening and you decided to do somethin'."

Agate nodded.

"Thought so," Mal said. "Yeah, knew I was right about you."

"Right about me?" Agate's shoulders straightened as she looked up at him, a practiced expression of hardened fervor on her face. "Before you go judgin' me, you should know I don't quit. Just cause they're all upset with me, doesn't mean I'm giving up. I can't. I *won't*. If there's a way to fix this, I'll find it. I promise, I'm captain material."

"I know," Mal said. "That's what I was going to say."

"It was?" Her eyes widened, then she recovered herself. "I mean, course it was."

"That's the thing about being a leader, Agate. Even when things go wrong—and they will, trust me on that—you can't give up. Captains, we can't let things get to us, can't get overwhelmed. We have to figure out the next step no matter what. Our crews count on us to be strong."

Agate nodded with renewed vigor. "I can do that. I *will* do that."

"All right. Well, no use wallowin'." Mal clambered to his feet and held out a hand to help her up.

In a show of independence, she didn't take it, pushing herself up on her own. Determination shone from her eyes, but she paused with her hand on the railing, gaze trailing down at the place they'd just been sitting. "I don't know," she began, then looked back at him. "I think you're wrong about one thing."

"What's that?" he asked.

"I think captains should cry a little sometimes."

Mal raised his eyebrows. "You think so? Not worried that'll make the crew think you're weak?"

"Not weak, no." She shook her head, her gaze drifting over Mal's shoulder.

He glanced back to see Inara standing with Zoë and the Governess. For a moment, he locked eyes with Inara, who surveyed him with a curious expression.

"I think if you let people see you cry it just shows them you're a person, too," Agate said. "You *are* a person, right?"

If Mal showed the crew he was worried, they'd worry, too. If he showed them he was lost, they would find themselves floating in a vast sea of nothing. Maybe that would make them resent him, or maybe it would make them love him in ways he couldn't yet fathom. He let his gaze linger on Inara, wondering what she'd think of all this. He held his emotions like a weapon, with the safety on, but hers were like a jewel, polished and worn round her neck for fine occasions. Mal wanted so badly to say yes and mean it, but he settled for the best he could do.

"Come on, *Captain*. We got a plan to make," he said. And the look on her face when he said *we* made him feel like they'd already won.

28

If there was one thing Book would never tire of aboard *Serenity*, it was the gravitas with which Malcolm Reynolds addressed the crew. He had a weight, a confidence that struck home to make all who heard him believe the impossible was possible. There was an art to it, not unlike a preacher at a pulpit, though he imagined the captain wouldn't take kindly to the comparison.

Of course, Book could see through him like an open window, but it didn't lessen the impact.

"If we're to succeed, we need to act like a team, *dǒng ma*?" Mal said, eyeing them each with intensity as his gaze swept them, gathered around the dining table. "I don't want to hear of anyone not pullin' their weight. No slackin' on the job, and no squealin' to Horne about any of this. I ain't in the mood to be stabbed in the back, not by you lot." His eyes fell on Book, a clouded expression on his face.

Book understood the captain's hesitance. He was Horne's old friend, after all. It wouldn't be unreasonable to expect old allegiance to factor in.

"We did the first leg of this job in three groups, and we're gonna keep to that plan," Mal continued.

"Didn't that plan fail?" asked Wash, looking around for backup. "I distinctly remember that plan failing."

"Not in a way that matters," Mal said. "We ended up here through some providence or other, and now we have to move forward."

"I think we all know who's to thank for that," Book said with a meaningful glance at Mal.

"If you're thinkin' I'm about to thank that God of yours for this, think again, preacher."

Book heaved a sigh. It said something, perhaps, that Mal always jumped to conclusions with him about God. True, it was God's hand that guided them, but they still had to choose to walk the path, and Mal didn't need to believe in God for that to be true.

"I meant that Captain Agate was instrumental in helping our crew understand the intricacies of this situation," Book said, gesturing to the girl. "Acknowledging her seems the least you could do."

"Right, well, I was just getting to that." Mal turned to face her.

Agate, who up until now had mirrored Mal's posture down to the placement of her hands on the table, glanced at the captain, a question in her eyes.

There was an almost imperceptible nod from Mal, a gesture that seemed to go unnoticed by most, but Book caught the look of pride in his face. It was a rare joy to see the captain so invested in someone's growth. It wasn't that he was a man of stagnation, exactly, but Book had seen him prioritize survival over all else time and time again. He understood, of course—that was the way life was out here—but surviving was not the same as thriving, and he hoped Agate and the others saw their way to the latter someday.

Agate lit up, turning to address her fellow teenagers. "We're Team Spread-the-Word," she began. "The four of us have gotta find as many folks in town as we can and tell them the plan. We don't want nobody working, and we need everyone to come to the town square bright and early in the morning to show support. Any questions?"

"I've got one," said the one called Russell, raising his hand. "How will Horne know what we're about? Won't he see all of us protesting and just think, ah, what a bunch of good-for-nothings? How will he know what we want from him?"

Agate grinned. "Well, we're gonna spell it out from him real nice. Put it on signs and whatnot. We'll tell people to write down what they're mad about, and we'll make some, too. We need Horne to know exactly what we want him to do, elsewise he might think we're disorganized."

"Aren't we, though? Disorganized?" Wash muttered under his breath.

Mal shot him a dangerous look. "Yeah, but we don't need him knowin' that."

"What about the rest of us?" Zoë asked.

"Glad you asked." Mal turned to face the Governess. "The second prong of our attack comes from you, Governess. We'll need you to get in touch with the folks at Blue Sun, make an appeal to them on behalf of the people here on Brome."

She nodded carefully. "I'll certainly try." There was a measured quality to her posture. Book could tell when someone was uncomfortable, and the Governess was a fish out of water here.

"Only one problem there, Mal," said Wash held up a hand, mimicking the children's motion, although not waiting to be called on. "We can't wave anyone off Brome. The Cortex is still wobbly."

"Brome's infrastructure isn't built for signaling off-world, I'm afraid," said the Governess. "I have equipment back at my compound that allows for a farther reach."

"Then that's where you'll go."

"I'll go with her," Inara said. "I may not have any personal connections at Blue Sun, but the Guild likely does."

"Good thinking," Mal replied, a strained expression on his face. "Could be it makes a difference. Besides, there's no need to put you in the fray with the rest of us."

It was a source of curiosity for Book, the pull and push between Mal and Inara. They were far from lovers, and yet they danced around their attraction like it was a maypole, tension high. Book, who had given up such things as romantic love and carnal pursuits—if it could be considered a sacrifice at all, for to him it was nothing compared to a life of good works—did not fully comprehend it, but he observed it with interest nonetheless.

"And me. They'll need protection, just in case." Zoë stared Mal down, a challenge in her gaze.

"Need someone to watch my back," Mal said.

Zoë just shrugged. "Maybe you won't. You said so yourself—this might not come to blows at all."

"I wouldn't count on that. Horne sounds like a nasty fella, and if there's to be a fight, I'd rather not rely on Jayne if I can help it. I don't like the thought of goin' into this alone."

"You won't." The words left Book's lips before he'd thought to say them, but he would sooner worship the flying spaghetti monster than let anyone go up against Lyle Horne without him. In some ways, he'd gotten them all into this mess. It was his responsibility to get them out. "I may not have the finesse with artillery of your first mate, but I have something better."

"What's that, preacher? God?" Mal didn't roll his eyes, but his derision was heavily implied.

"No, although now that you mention it..." Book cleared his throat. "What I have is history. I knew him once. Could be that comes in handy if things get interesting."

"Let's hope they don't. Could do with a little languor around here." Mal rapped his knuckles on the table once. "That's all, then. Group A gets the word out about the demonstration, Group B works on Blue Sun, and Group C—that's me and the preacher—head straight to Horne."

"What about the rest of us?" asked Wash. "Not that I'm hankering for a leading role in all this, just wondering if you'll be needing your supporting cast." He indicated himself, Kaylee, and Simon.

"Let's hope we don't, but if it comes to violence, you do your best to help folks as you can. And if that fails, throw a little chaos into the mix. Maybe a few flyovers will calm any bloodthirsty notions among Horne's enforcers." Mal grimaced. "Speaking of bloodthirsty notions, any word from Jayne?"

Wash shook his head. "I tried him again a few minutes ago, but I've got nothing. Either his comm isn't working, he dropped it, or he's passed out in some tavern or other."

"Let's hope it's one of those three options and not somethin' else," Mal said. "Now, let's get a move on."

There was a bustle of chatter and movement as the others got up from the table and began to file out. Mal crossed the dining area, heading for the bridge where his crew gathered, Book following a few paces behind. He never could be sure if Mal considered him only a passenger, or if he ranked among the crew. Perhaps he was a secret third thing for which he did not fully understand the rules.

"Soon as she's skyworthy, we head toward town," Mal said in an undertone. "Not too close, though. We don't want to alert Horne to our presence. Just enough that the others can walk the rest of the way to start talking to folks. We'll move in a mite closer after dark."

"I should have her ready in a few hours," said Kaylee. "Just need to finish cleaning out the wiring. The geese really gummed her up bad, Cap'n."

"Good. Wash, try Jayne again. I don't like that he's gone quiet."

"Really? I usually love it when he stops talking—"

"I mean it, Wash. You check in with him every hour." Mal gripped the other man's shoulder tightly, eyes shining with intensity.

Wash blinked in dismay. "You got it, Mal." He turned to go, but Mal held him back a moment.

"Don't go tellin' him our plans, though. In fact, make it seem like we're run down, delayed."

"We are." Wash shrugged out of Mal's grip and flashed a coy smile that didn't match the concern in his eyes. "But I guess that makes sense."

"There's no telling who has his comm."

As the rest of them dispersed, Mal turned to go and found himself nose to nose with Book.

"You're not really worried the comm has fallen into the wrong hands," Book said in a low voice so only Mal could hear.

"You know that for a fact?"

Mal brushed past him toward the kitchen area, rolling up his sleeves as though about to wash dishes. It had been a long while since Book had seen the captain do chores, and he wouldn't be doing any today. Book had already scrubbed all their plates clean in a meditation of sorts earlier.

Book didn't answer the question, instead barreling on. "You're more concerned he has it and is just ignoring you."

"Jayne ain't stupid." Mal paused and cocked his head in thought. "Well, he ain't stupid enough to do that. Point is, he knows better."

"Maybe so, but you're concerned about more than his well-being."

"And what's that, preacher?"

Book surveyed Mal carefully. It wasn't his business to tell the captain his own thoughts, perhaps, but Book worried that if he didn't, Mal would let them go unexamined.

"You're worried he may turn on you."

"Wouldn't be the first time, now would it?" Mal sighed, shoulders sloping. "Fact is, Shepherd, I ain't half so worried about his loyalties as I am yours."

Book raised his eyebrows, though it wasn't exactly a shock to hear Mal say so. "I'm not planning to betray you, Captain," he said.

"Well, I'd say that's a relief, but it's the spontaneous betrayals that keep me up at night." Mal's gaze swept the kitchen, no doubt finding it spick and span, and then drifted up to Book's face once more. "Good number of months you've been sailin' on my boat, preacher, and I still can't say I know you. How is that?"

Book blinked. "I didn't know you cared to," he said. Mal had never spared him much interest, something Book had written off as a symptom of the captain's aversion to his profession. "Besides, there isn't much to know."

"Now, that I don't believe for a second." Mal took a step closer, then another, until they were a breath apart. "You're so full of secrets, preacher, I might start believin' in miracles if you don't combust sooner or later."

Mal didn't know the half of it. The secrets Book carried… well, he planned to carry them to the grave.

"You can trust me," Book said, doing his best to mean it.

Mal knocked their shoulders on his way to the bridge, shooting him a thin smile as he said, "I really can't."

29

Kaylee didn't like it when *Serenity* was hurting. It felt like a wound in her own body, achy and raw. Trouble was, she couldn't go complaining to Simon about it like it was a fever or a fracture. There wasn't anything the doctor could do for poor old *Serenity*. That was Kaylee's job.

With a flick of her wrist, she tightened the last bolt with the wrench and slid out from under the console.

"All done," she said, looking up at the upside-down faces of Wash, Mal, and Zoë.

"She good to go?" Mal asked.

Kaylee nodded. "I think so."

"Wash, care to fire her up?"

"I thought you'd never ask!" Wash rubbed his hands together and practically danced his way to the pilot's seat.

It took only the press of three buttons, and *Serenity*'s engines whirred to life. Kaylee let out a sigh of relief.

Mal squeezed her shoulder. "Good work, little Kaylee."

It was moments like this that made Kaylee feel all was right with the world. She worried sometimes that she'd been wrong to leave her family behind. Her folks had been good to her, and she loved them something fierce. Most people she knew who left home did it because home wasn't really home, or because they could make a better living somewhere else. That wasn't true for Kaylee. If she'd stayed, she and her pa would've gone into business together doing repairs. It wasn't like she'd be eating like a queen, but the pay working on *Serenity* wasn't exactly steady either. Still, somehow she'd found her way from one loving family to another, and she felt like she was exactly where she was meant to be.

"Suppose this is where I leave you." Zoë bent to kiss Wash on the cheek, her hand trailing the slope of his shoulders. Then she turned to Mal and said, "I'd say don't get into any trouble, but I know better by now."

"Only the good kind," Mal said with a nod. "Keep in touch, *dōng ma*?"

Zoë patted the comm clipped to her vest. "Every hour." And then she was gone, slipping away like a shadow.

The captain frowned after her, his shoulders tense. Wash mirrored his dour expression.

"Well, aren't you two a pair of storm clouds," Kaylee said.

"Could order her to stay back. She'd actually listen to you." Wash drummed his fingers on the steering wheel, like little anxious rumbles of thunder. "Don't see why she needs to go, anyhow."

"I don't like it anymore than you do, but it's what has to be done," Mal said.

"Couldn't you send someone with her to watch her back, at least?"

"Like who, Wash?" Mal swung around to face him, a growl in his throat. "I got no one to spare. We're stretched as thin as we can be as it is. You're just gonna have to trust me."

"Well, what if I don't?" Wash stood up, leveling his blowtorch gaze at the captain.

Mal raised his eyebrows. "Thought you'd got this out of your system. Or wasn't the business with Niska enough for you?"

Wash deflated slightly. "It's just... *Serenity*'s running on empty, Mal, and I gotta worry about someone or I'll go crazy."

Mal's expression softened. "Zoë knows what she's about. You worry about getting us to town in one piece, or worry about the geese gettin' into Jayne's weaponry. Or hell, you can worry about me, if you like. I'm the one who's gotta face Horne with only a preacher for backup."

"Right, cause it'll be a piece of cake sitting here on the ship like a bunch of sitting ducks."

"Uh, I'll just... I'm gonna..." Kaylee motioned toward the exit, but neither of them were paying her any mind. She edged toward the hall and hopped down the steps, their argument fading into the distance behind her.

"They don't even see you. Barely even a thank you. Just a monkey with a wrench to them," she muttered to herself as she passed through the dining area.

"A monkey?"

Kaylee whipped around to see the blue eyes of Simon Tam watching her from the kitchen. He held a couple of unopened cans of rations in his hands.

"Oh, hey there, Simon," she said, tucking her hair behind her ear. A warmth crept up her neck as he looked at her. She knew she had engine grease in her hair and on her hands from her work, and of course she'd been talking to herself. Not exactly the picture she wanted to project to the doctor. "Hungry?"

"No, I—" Simon examined the cans in his hands. "Trying to determine what would make a good meal for a goose. She'll be waking soon and I'm not eager to suffer the same fate as Jayne."

Kaylee sidled over to him, took one of the cans, and read the label. "Well, I don't think electrolytes are what geese crave."

"You know, you're probably right about that." Simon sighed and put the can down. His gaze, weary but bright, rose to meet hers. "You're right about a lot of things, Kaylee."

"That so?"

"It is." He leaned back, propping his elbows up against the counter. "Whoever said you were a monkey with a wrench—"

"Nobody. Nobody said that." Kaylee shook her head furiously, hoping to direct the conversation elsewhere as soon as possible. "It's just, everyone's gearin' up for a showdown and I'm just… here."

"Didn't you just fix the ship? *Serenity* wouldn't run without you."

"Oh, that? It was nothin', really. Just had to unmuck what the geese did." She shrugged. "Anyway, it's already done, so now I've got nothin' to do. Feel useless, is all."

"If you're useless, then so am I." Simon heaved a sigh, looking up at the arched ceiling. "It's strange, isn't it? Our jobs necessitate something going wrong before we can be of any real help. I don't wish anyone on the crew ill—"

Kaylee raised her eyebrows. It hadn't been long since Jayne had had his eye pecked by a goose, and she seemed to remember Simon taking some dark pleasure in that.

"Okay, I don't wish *most* of the crew ill," Simon amended, catching her meaning. "But still, I worry that if there isn't some injury or other to tend to every so often, the captain will decide you've all outgrown my use to you."

"You've got other uses," Kaylee said before she could stop herself. "You're real smart about stuff. Like that job you had us pull on Ariel? That was some crack thievin'. And you're nice to… talk to."

Simon snapped his head to look at her. "Am I?"

Kaylee's eyes traced the curve of his jawline, his exposed neck, the place where his shirt peeked open just a smidge to show off his clavicle. There were lots of things about him that were nice, though she wasn't ready to admit that out loud.

"River tells me I'm an abysmal conversationalist. Absolutely terrible at parties." Simon's face fell, a self-deprecating frown creasing his expression.

Kaylee's stomach twisted. Something about the way he said it made her feel stupid, like she was somehow lesser for not realizing his deficiency. Like, if she was on his level, she'd have noticed—she'd have cared. And the thing was, maybe he was awkward, but she liked that about him. She liked a lot of things about him that weren't traditionally good qualities.

"Well, *I* like talkin' to you," she said as the blush spread into her cheeks.

Simon eyed her carefully, gaze gentle but searching. "Sometimes I… Sometimes I worry I'm a tad uncouth. I'm clumsy with my words, say things the wrong way. I'm so focused on what I'm saying, I forget to consider how I'm saying it."

Kaylee knew exactly what he meant. She'd been on the receiving end of his awkwardness on more than one occasion. And yes, it stung when his insistence on propriety left them in a flirtatious stalemate. One of these days, she was afraid she might get so sick of the song and dance of it all and make a move herself, though she didn't want to. She'd much rather let him take the lead. Whether he would or not was another question altogether.

"I like that you're focused," she said. "Means you care."

"That's a very generous way of putting it."

Kaylee couldn't resist it. She put her hand on her hip and cocked it. "I'm a generous kinda gal."

Simon nodded earnestly. "You really are. The captain should be more grateful for all you do. It's not just anyone who can diagnose a ship."

"Diagnose?" Kaylee's disappointment at Simon's obliviousness was overshadowed by the pleasant feeling that rushed through her at his words. "Like she's a person?"

Simon shrugged. "From the way you talk about *Serenity*, I got the impression your methodology isn't all that dissimilar to mine. We both fix things, and though your medium is metal and mine is flesh and blood, our work has more in common than I first thought. It's impressive."

"Oh." Kaylee couldn't think of what else to say to that. Why was it he could treat her like an equal when it came to their work, but not when it came to their hearts?

"We should do something together," Simon said with a glint of inspiration in his eyes.

Kaylee lit up. "Do you mean like—"

"To help the workers. Maybe they don't need a surgeon or a mechanic, but we're people. We're bodies. We could stand with them."

Kaylee tried not to let the disappointment show on her face. She didn't know why she'd hoped he was going to make some kind of romantic overture. He never had before, so why would he now? It wasn't a bad idea, though, so she put her smile back together and nodded. "You mean instead of sittin' here on the ship?"

"Exactly! We aren't useless just because our particular skillsets aren't needed. We can help." Simon pushed off from the counter, an eager bounce to his stance. "Oh, this will be great, Kaylee!"

She hadn't seen him so excited about something since he got to use the Councilor's equipment to reattach Mal's ear after they'd fought Niska. "I'll tell the captain!"

Kaylee turned toward the bridge, but Simon caught her arm. The touch sent an electric pulse through her, far more powerful than the little shocks of static she got every so often working on the engine.

"Hey," he said, holding her gaze intently. "You're nothing like a monkey with a wrench, all right?"

"I do have a wrench." Kaylee let out a nervous laugh and raised her free hand, still holding the adjustable spanner.

"Well," Simon began, a flush creeping into his cheeks. "You're not a monkey. You're much prettier." He let go of her then, scuttling away in the opposite direction before she could reply.

"What've you got to be smilin' about?" Mal asked a few moments later as he descended the steps to the dining area.

Caught in a moment of dazed bewilderment, Kaylee leaned her head on Mal's shoulder in a side embrace. "I just fixed the ship, Simon thinks I'm pretty, and *Serenity*'s back in the sky. What about that don't warrant a smile?"

Mal patted her arm gently. "You did good today, little Kaylee."

And that combined with Simon's compliment would have buoyed her spirits all night, if not for the waning sound of the engine as *Serenity* plummeted.

30

Flying away from *Serenity* never felt good. Inara wouldn't have guessed it, the day she rented the dingy shuttle with cold, unwelcoming walls from the equally unwelcoming Captain Malcolm Reynolds, that *Serenity* would one day feel like home. Every time she felt the pressure release of the shuttle tearing away from the ship, she felt a little tear in her own heart. Leaving the Firefly—and the people inside it—was getting more and more painful each time, and she dreaded the day it became permanent.

But everybody left one way or another, and she knew she'd have to do the same when the time came. At least for now, it was only temporary.

"Rare to meet a registered Companion this far away from civilization," the Governess said.

She looked like she belonged in Inara's space, seated at the foot of Inara's bed, her dress a compliment to the other fine fabrics hanging from the walls. Despite the excitement of the day, she still looked put-together, her coiffure undisturbed. In another life, another day, another world, she might have been one of Inara's clientele. She was a beautiful woman, though perhaps a decade or so older than Inara. There was a loneliness in her spirit that Inara saw mirrored in herself, the sign of a wayward soul from one world now living in another. It was enough to make her give the Governess a second chance.

"Just as rare to meet a woman like yourself," Inara replied. It was refreshing, if perhaps slightly embarrassing, to be done with all the pretense. She was glad the Governess could see her for who she was rather than who she'd pretended to be. Inara didn't give second chances lightly, but perhaps they both had elements of disguise to shed. The Governess might yet prove to have hidden depths. "It takes a real resilience of spirit to do what you've done, to leave your world behind to try to make a better one out here."

"You left, too. What chased you away?"

"Who says I was running away?" Inara took her eyes off the horizon for a moment to survey the Governess. The older woman's face was hard to read, gaze hooded, mouth relaxed. Perhaps she'd meant nothing by it. "I wanted to go places, see more than the inside of House Madrassa. A transport ship seemed the way to do it. Besides, who wouldn't want to travel with the crew of *Serenity*?" She gestured toward Zoë, who was leaning against the back wall, unsmiling.

"Oh, we're a fun bunch," Zoë said unconvincingly, her fingers drifting to her holstered gun. "Life of the party."

"I'd like to see that." The Governess didn't so much as look at Zoë, gaze intent on Inara, eyes trailing her motions as she began the landing sequence.

As a Companion, Inara wasn't often surprised by her own emotions. Before she could learn to attune herself to others, she'd had to learn herself inside and out. These days, few people had the power to make her feel anything she wasn't prepared for. Mal was among them, but even with him she'd learned to expect the unexpected. But right now, with the Governess's eyes on her, she felt a deep connection with her she hadn't anticipated.

"Perhaps you shall," Inara said. "There will be plenty to celebrate if we all do our jobs well." She hated how much she sounded like Mal in that moment, but the reminder was as much for her own benefit as for the Governess's. It would do them no good to get distracted now. Not when there was work to be done.

They landed outside the compound and filed out quickly, the Governess leading the way. It was dusk now, the sun sinking below the horizon.

Zoë stopped in her tracks, eyes trained on the dome of the compound, where the last vestiges of sunlight dappled the surface.

Inara halted beside her. "It's beautiful, isn't it?" she breathed. "Strange that we've seen this place at sunrise and sunset, but nowhere in between."

The electromagnetic dome lowered as the Governess stepped up to the gate, and any reply Zoë might have summoned would have been swallowed by the sound.

"Please, come in." The Governess beckoned them forward. "My office is at the top."

Inara and Zoë caught up to the Governess and stepped over the threshold, but their host didn't follow. Looking back over her shoulder, Inara traced the Governess's gaze off toward the back of the compound.

"Is everything all right?" she asked.

The Governess blinked and turned back to face them. "Apologies. I'll join you in a moment. I need to change a few settings on the control panel." She pointed in the direction she'd been looking. "We have to be conservative in our use of power in a place like this, and contacting people off-world requires an extra boost."

"I'll come with," Zoë said, tapping the headlight she wore. "Might be you need a light to see by."

Inara read the tension in Zoë's shoulders, the way her body

faced the Governess but her feet pointed away. Something was amiss with her, something Inara couldn't discern.

She half expected the Governess to refuse, but the older woman smiled graciously and said, "That's kind of you. Thank you." She turned to go, beckoning Zoë to follow, but the other woman hung back until the Governess was out of earshot.

"You're a smart woman, Inara," Zoë murmured.

"I'm— Well, thank you." Inara smiled despite herself. Though she'd known Zoë as long as she had the rest of the crew, their paths didn't cross as often as she would have liked. The first mate was warm of heart and her laughter was like a cold drink on a hot day. The time she and Inara spent together was almost always in a group, with Mal and Wash in the dining area, or sometimes with Kaylee for a bit of a feminine reprieve. Inara had always thought highly of Zoë, and while she had no reason to believe the feeling wasn't mutual, still it was nice to hear it once in a while. "Any particular reason for the observation?"

"Just a reminder." Zoë undid the strap on her holster. "In case you forgot." Then she slipped away after the Governess.

Inara climbed the stairs alone, lingering as she went to observe the fine craftsmanship of the handrail. There were framed watercolors with gold stenciling of women's faces spaced evenly along the walls, delicate pieces that made Inara pause to admire each one. The Governess had excellent taste in art, though Inara wondered if perhaps the coin spent on such decorations might have been put to better use—then felt the sting of her hypocrisy. She spent her wages on more than just necessities, after all, but it still struck her as odd that a woman so dedicated to helping others had decorated the place so lavishly.

When she reached the top floor, she stepped into the Governess's office. Here, the walls were covered with printed news clippings announcing various charitable works and a series of nearly identical photographs of the Governess shaking hands with people Inara didn't know. On a large desk in the center were three large screens—all dark, but with a light blinking beneath each one, indicating a power source or an alert of some kind, perhaps. There wasn't much to do but wait for the Governess and Zoë to return, so she entered the room and made for the chair in the center.

As she sat down, a mechanical voice sounded: "Governess, you have one new message."

Inara leapt from the chair, looking around for the source of the voice. There was only the blinking light. Cautiously, she approached it.

"Governess, you have one new message," the voice repeated.

Surely there was an off button somewhere. With a careful hand, Inara felt along the bottom of the screen, searching for a control panel. Thinking that maybe it was a touch-screen like hers, she swiped a finger across it.

"Playing message," said the voice.

"Oh, no," Inara muttered. How would she explain this to the Governess? She'd not been intending to pry—though maybe she should have. The moment the message began to play, she recognized the voice immediately.

"Got your wave," came the voice of Lyle Horne. "Fear we may have a situation on our hands after all. Shouldn't have brought outsiders into this, but… well, you know I couldn't resist. Not with *him* bein' among their crew. Anyhow, I'm holding the big one for questioning. Might be he'll be sympathetic to our efforts or at least to our coin. Join me when you can. We may need to make an escape real quick like if things take a turn."

Horne was going to be a problem, and so, it seemed, was the Governess.

There was the sound of footsteps behind Inara and she turned, eyes wide. "Zoë, I don't think—"

But it wasn't Zoë standing behind her. "I so wish you hadn't heard that," said the Governess, reaching for Inara's arm.

A sharp stabbing pain flashed in Inara's bicep for just a moment and she looked down, already woozy. The last thing she remembered thinking before darkness claimed her was that if she'd had been as smart as Zoë had said she was, she would've seen this coming.

31

Jayne's eyes blinked open to a blurry scene. Above him, a face swam in and out of focus.

"There you are, Mr. Cobb. Good of you to come back now." Horne.

Jayne was on the floor, an imprint of the carpet pressed into the side of his face.

"You drugged me," Jayne said through his teeth, the words strangely gelatinous on his tongue.

"I'd apologize, but I think we'd both know I'd be lyin'." Horne reached a hand down to help Jayne up to a seated position. "Plus, you needed the beauty rest." He indicated Jayne's eye and grimaced.

"I ain't about to thank you," Jayne said. He glanced down at his hands and flexed them. "You didn't tie me up."

"That, I hope, you *will* thank me for." Horne sat back in a chair opposite Jayne and surveyed him. "See, I needed you to take a little nap while I sorted out some details, but I'm not convinced we're enemies, you and I."

"Been wonderin' that my own self," Jayne muttered.

It was true—he'd seen more of himself in Horne than he'd thought he would. Horne was a man who knew how to get what he wanted. Jayne might've been the same if what he wanted was as simple as it used to be.

Money. That was what mattered to folks like Horne, to folks like Jayne. Money was all there was that mattered in the gorram 'verse. He couldn't send things like Kaylee's smile or Mal's approval or Wash's laughter home to his ma.

"You gonna offer me a deal?" he asked, getting to his feet and shakily sitting in his vacated chair. He subtly checked his pocket. The key card was still there. Horne had no idea. Good. He had options.

"I might," Horne said, lifting his chin. "You seem an enterprisin' young man who likes to know when his next paycheck's coming."

"I surely do."

"Then we have that in common." Horne leaned back, eyeing Jayne with interest. "What would you say to a steadier line of work, one where you always know you'll get paid on time, and you might get to fire one of these?" He indicated the guns on the wall.

Jayne's gaze flicked to the weaponry, tidily sitting in rows of glass cases, and raised an eyebrow. "I'd say I'm interested. What'd you have in mind?"

"Well, let's start with getting your pain-in-the-ass captain off my moon."

"You want me to… fight Mal?"

Horne cocked his head, a knowing smile on his lips. "Don't tell me you haven't thought about it before."

Jayne almost laughed. "Oh, I've thought about it. Just never thought I could win."

"That so?" Horne gave him a quizzical look. "I'd wager even with your eye like that, you're evenly matched."

It wasn't that he was weaker than Mal—Jayne was bigger and stronger, and he was fairly sure he could take the captain in a fight. But Mal… Mal was better. There was a level of loyalty, of determination, of having something worth protecting that fueled Mal, and no matter how long Jayne sailed with him, he couldn't seem to tap into that same ferocity of spirit.

"Come on, you must be a decent shot to carry a weapon like yours." Horne looked at Jayne's sidearm, a LeMat percussion revolver Jayne had christened Boo, and the antler-handled knife at his waist.

"You didn't disarm me."

"Hoping I won't need to."

Jayne nodded. "Say I was to turncoat and work with you. What's our play?"

Horne reached into his pocket and pulled out Jayne's comm. "Seems your captain is awfully eager to check in with you."

Jayne made a grab for the comm, instinct driving him.

"Ah, patience." Horne held up a finger. "We'll need to discuss what you're plannin' to say. See, I want him to come here, and to bring that beautiful bastard callin' himself a Shepherd with him. Been far too long, and we're overdue some closure."

"Patience ain't exactly my cup of tea," Jayne grumbled.

"I was never much good with that myself, you know. Told myself patience was an older man's game. Well, I'm an older man now, and I've waited a long, long time for my day to shine."

Jayne wasn't sure he'd ever shine—not like Inara's fine jewels or Kaylee's toolbox or Mal's moral compass. He was a rusty nail among the righteous. Might as well act like one.

He let a grin play across his face as he held his hand out for the comm. "You play at patience, Horne, but Mal ain't accustomed to waiting. You let me talk to him. I know exactly what to say."

32

"That's not a good sound," Wash muttered.

"Wash!" Mal roared over the sound of the dying engine. He and Kaylee came barreling onto the bridge. "Tell me that's just some kind of Broman bug in my engine or somethin'. In and out, no fuss."

"I could, but I don't make a habit of lying to you, Mal." Wash held tight to the steering wheel as he eased *Serenity* through her descent.

"Well? What's the problem?"

Wash heaved a sigh. "I don't know. I'm a little busy at the moment."

"Well, get un-busy. One moment my spaceship's in the sky, the next, not so much." Mal's words had an acidic tone, the one he adopted when he was frustrated. "Now would be good."

"Do you want to crash?" Wash snapped, turning to face the captain. "Do you?"

"Well, no—"

"Then maybe you should let me steer!" He turned his eyes back toward the window and hit a few buttons on the console. "And hold onto something. This isn't gonna be pretty."

"Kaylee—"

"I didn't do nothin', Cap'n. Promise." Kaylee's voice was small and wounded.

Wash didn't like it when Kaylee got the blame for things going wrong. It was always her responsibility, but it was rarely her fault. Just because she was the one who could fix it didn't mean it was on her to be prepared for every possible catastrophe. Mal usually understood that.

"Less talking, more… not talking!" Wash shouted as he gripped the steering wheel even tighter. "I need to concentrate, I need to—" That was when the ground caught up to them.

The only thing Wash was better at than flying was crashing. It was the first lesson of flight school—how to land in an emergency. There was no point getting off the ground if you couldn't find your way back to it when you needed to. He knew gravity like he knew tropical shirts or ill-timed jokes or how to treat his wife like a gorram queen. They were all inexorably part of his DNA.

So he knew, even with the jarring impact, that *Serenity* was still in one piece. Because of course she was. He knew what he was doing.

"Okay!" His voice hadn't yet returned to a normal register, so he shouted—unnecessarily, as the sound of the engines had completely died. He pried his fingers from the steering wheel, easing the tension from his arms. "Okay," he repeated in a more normal tone. "You can start talking again now."

"What in the gorram blazing hells happened?" Mal demanded. His expression was firm, but there was a tremor in his voice. "This shouldn't have happened, right? You fixed her, didn't you?" He turned his gaze on Kaylee, who shrank before him.

"I… I thought I did. I *know* I did." She shook her head, gaining confidence. "*Serenity* told me she was good to go, Cap'n, I swear. Would've told you elsewise if it weren't the case."

"Well, something went wrong, and you're gonna find out what. I ain't in the mood for things to be anything less than shiny, *dǒng ma*?"

It was a scolding she didn't deserve. Wash sighed heavily. "Mal," he began.

"I ain't talkin' to you," Mal snapped back.

"If wishes made it so..." murmured Wash. He wasn't in the mood either, and two could play that game. "But you're in my cockpit yelling at the one person who might be able to fix things around here. Maybe you should stop with the shouting and start with the letting her work?"

Mal let out a long breath, closed his eyes, and turned toward Wash. With a sharp gesture, Mal pressed the tip of his finger into Wash's sternum and said, "It's my cockpit, on my ship. You just happen to fly it."

There was a joke to be made about the cockpit measuring contest they'd found themselves in, but for once in his life Wash recognized now was not the time. Instead, he gave Mal a tight-lipped smile and said, "Well right now, I just happen to be the guy telling you it's not Kaylee's fault."

"How do you figure?"

Wash pointed to a red flashing light on the center console. "Cause we're out of fuel. *Serenity*'s empty. No amount of tinkering from Kaylee can get her back in the air."

Mal's shoulders slumped. "Well, I suppose it was bound to happen sooner or later."

"Sooner. Decidedly sooner," Wash muttered.

"Guess we'll be hoofin' it the rest of the way to town?" Kaylee asked.

"You guess right."

Wash checked the map on the Cortex. "Looks like we're only a few miles out. Won't be too far."

"Go tell the others." Mal nodded to Kaylee. "We've got a bit of a hike ahead of us. Make sure folks bring enough water. Don't need anyone fallin' behind due to dehydration."

"Maybe this is better?" Kaylee suggested. "Gives us an element of stealth."

"You always find the bright side, don't ya, little Kaylee?" Mal said as he followed her out the door.

Wash leaned back in his chair, taking a moment to let the adrenaline run its course. Tension was wound deep in his shoulders and hands from the crash. *Serenity* was likely feeling it too, having just weathered a less-than-ideal landing for the second time in one day. What they both needed was rest. A little peace and quiet.

"Captain, you there?"

Wash leapt from his chair, bashing his knee painfully on the underside of the console. *"Gū yáng zhōng de gū yáng!"* he exclaimed, hopping over to the side to hit the button in the center. "Jayne? About time."

"Sorry 'bout that. In a bit of a situation."

"I'll get Mal."

"No need, heard your monkey racket." Mal ducked back inside. "You got Jayne?" he asked Wash.

"He's in a bit of a situation," Wash repeated, indicating the speaker.

"You almost done with the job there, Captain? Could use a pickup." Jayne's voice sounded strange, oddly formal.

"We're closin' in. What's the problem?" Mal exchanged a glance with Wash, a warning in his gaze.

Wash didn't need to be told what Mal meant. He might not have the same apparently psychic link Mal and Zoë had, but he understood the captain well enough most of the time. He'd let Mal do the talking.

"Too much to drink. It's been hours, I think."

Alarm shone in Mal's eyes now, but he cocked his head in thought at Jayne's words. "Not like you to let a little liquor knock you down, Jayne."

Wash thought it was exactly like Jayne, actually, but now wasn't the time.

"Not just liquor. Horne got me with somethin' extra. Drugged me."

"You in any danger?" Mal asked.

"Nah, don't think so. He just wanted me off his back, is all. Might be he's up to somethin'."

"Might be he is." Mal took a breath. "You keep eyes on him for now, *dǒng ma*? We'll come by to get you in the morning."

"Thanks, Captain."

There was a pause in which Wash wrinkled his face incredulously, an expression matched by Mal. Wash could count on his hands the number of times Jayne had thanked anyone and meant it.

"Strange company for the Shepherd to keep," Jayne said. "Curious to know how a preacher got mixed up with a *hún dàn* like Horne."

"You let me worry about the Shepherd. We'll be by once it's light."

"Yes, sir."

Mal took his finger off the button and Wash let out a stifled laugh. "Okay, that was funnier than the geese."

Mal wasn't laughing, though. "Somethin' ain't right."

"He called you *sir*."

"Hence me sayin' something ain't right." Mal narrowed his eyes. "Did he actually say 'thank you?' "

Wash nodded, wiping his eyes as tears of mirth formed there. "I wish I'd thought to record that. There's no way Zoë will believe me. How many times did he call you Captain? Was it twice?"

"Don't see how it matters." Mal shook his head, a frown line creasing his expression.

"Why aren't you laughing, Mal? This is objectively funny. Funnier than the time he was a hero, funnier than when you tried to duel that ponce from Persephone—"

"I'd thank you not to bring that up," said Mal. "Still hurts."

Wash raised his eyebrows. "Like, from the stabbing, or your pride?"

"Both." Mal shrugged, eyes back on the night sky outside. "And I ain't laughing 'cause I don't think this is just Jayne bein' a hoot."

"Come on, Mal. He was drunk! An inebriated Jayne trying to act sober? That's gotta be in the top ten—"

"*Bì zuǐ*." Mal knocked his knuckles against the console once. "Maybe you're right. Maybe Jayne's just had one too many and we'll all laugh about this tomorrow."

"I'm laughing about it now," Wash muttered.

Mal ignored him. "But more than likely, there's somethin' he ain't tellin' us. Either he can't, or he's decided he won't."

"You think Jayne'll turn on us?" Wash asked, his mouth falling open. He hadn't ever given much consideration to anyone on the crew betraying them. He trusted every single person on *Serenity* implicitly. Well, he trusted them different amounts and in different ways. He trusted Zoë to shoot straight—with both her words and her bullets—he trusted Mal to set their course, and he trusted Kaylee to patch things up if they strayed. He trusted Inara to always keep a level head. He even trusted the newcomers with their wounds—Simon would mend the physical and Shepherd Book the spiritual. River, though… River was in another category altogether. It wasn't that he thought she was going to stab them in the back; it was that he thought she'd forget she was holding the knife when she went in for a hug.

Still, if he'd had any money to spare in that moment, he knew he'd wager it on Jayne being the first to switch sides given the opportunity. He didn't like thinking that way of a man with so very many guns, but Jayne was always the first to suggest violence or veering away from the moral high ground. He'd even mentioned turning Simon and River over to the feds a few too many times to be considered unserious. It wasn't an impossible reality.

"That crossed my mind," Mal said eventually. "But I can't be sure. Seems to me if he were plannin' a little mutiny, he would've put more effort into seeming normal. He wouldn't have called me *sir*, at least. Jayne knows what kind of reception that sort of behavior would get around here."

"What are you saying, then?" Wash asked, turning curious eyes on Mal. It was a strange thing to watch Mal's mind at work. Wash never could quite follow his thought processes, but he knew he'd stand with the captain wherever he ended up.

"I'm sayin' there's a chance Jayne wasn't the only one we were talkin' to."

"Horne? Like he's holding Jayne hostage or something?" Wash's eyes widened and his pulse quickened. What a time for Zoë to be on a babysitting mission. "Do you think it's a trap?"

Mal shrugged. "Can't know for sure unless we walk into it."

33

They left *Serenity* behind just before midnight.

"Ain't exactly a pretty sight," Kaylee muttered as she surveyed *Serenity*, pointing out a significant ding in her hull from the rough landing.

"Yeah, what happened there? Looks like someone crashed your spaceship, Mal," said Wash.

Mal couldn't think about *Serenity*'s condition. Not now. He had more pressing matters.

"We've likely lost the element of surprise, since Jayne knows we're comin'. Horne will have heard one way or another." He addressed the whole group, gaze sweeping over these people, who'd all come together under one goal. Dina, Eli, Tuan, and Julian looked almost as determined as their youthful counterparts. Agate had her hands on her hips and her eyes narrowed. She and her crew would be a formidable force in their efforts. Mal hoped it would pay off. "We'll need to do things quiet-like once we get within a mile or so of town—don't want anyone tipping Horne off. So as soon as I give you the signal, there's no talking, *dōng ma*?"

They all nodded.

"Right. Shepherd, you're with me," Mal said, beckoned over Book, who tucked his chin and took a few paces toward him.

"Don't forget us!" Kaylee piped up.

Mal raised an eyebrow. "I don't got room for no stragglers, little Kaylee."

"Kaylee and I thought we'd lend our aid to the other group," Simon said. "Stand in solidarity with them."

Mal shook his head. "Solidarity's all well and good till one of you gets hurt."

"See, that's the thing, Cap'n, lots of folks *could* get hurt." Kaylee's expression turned cloudy, a somber note wavering in her tone. "It's… it's a risky mission, no matter what. Could be they'll need patchin' up. It's not like we're needed here on *Serenity*…"

"You've got repairs to do, and someone needs to see to River." Mal's chest constricted at the thought of Kaylee joining the workers. It wasn't meant to be a hostile demonstration, but Mal knew how easily something with peaceful intent could turn violent. "No need for you to put yourselves in harm's way."

"Can't do much for *Serenity* in the dark." Kaylee nodded toward the ship, a slight frown creasing her lips. "Besides, can't get her in the air again without fuel anyhow. And Wash can stay with River so she won't be on her lonesome."

"You already asked him?" Mal looked at Wash.

The pilot shrugged. "No, but I don't mind," he said. "If the doc's needed elsewhere, I can watch her… and her flock."

Mal didn't like it, but he wasn't in the habit of doling out orders without reason, so instead he gave a curt nod, and said, "All right, folks, we'd best be off. I meant what I said about no chatter once we get close. Keep your wits about you and stay with the group. Don't need no one wanderin' off into the tall grass." And with that they were off, leaving the shadow of a broken-down *Serenity* behind them. They'd walked only a few hours before the town came into view in the distance. Mal motioned for them to part ways—Kaylee and Simon went with the others, and Mal and Book peeled off to head for the refinery.

Brome was strange at night. Though stars shone in the sky, it was never totally dark. With two suns to contend with, sunset and sunrise weren't so much fixed times of day as they were an ongoing race to the horizon. The moon's orbit and rotation meant it was only without light for a short period this time of year, and the length of a full day was far shorter than on the Core planets where day and night were more standardized. Mal was used to time being a more nebulous thing out in the black, and he and his crew adapted wherever they went. Still, he wished they had more time.

The steel walls of the refinery almost shimmered in the starlight as the group circled around the outskirts of town. Dawn wasn't far off now, but Mal wasn't waiting for the sun to rise.

"Jayne," he hissed into the comm clipped to his suspenders. "Jayne, you read me?"

A few seconds of silence passed, during which Mal and Book exchanged a look of disquiet. If Jayne was sleeping or otherwise indisposed, they'd have to improvise, something Mal wasn't keen on in that particular moment.

Luckily, the sound of static broke the tension, followed by Jayne's voice. "Mal? You close?"

Well, at least he'd stopped calling Mal *sir*. "Not far off. Just need a way in."

"I've got Horne's key card. I can meet you round back."

Mal paused. It was easy. Real easy. They could just grab Jayne and go. But that didn't feel finished. It didn't feel earned.

"He know we're comin'?" he asked.

"I dunno. Seems agitated, though. Might just be the hangover."

"You think Jayne tipped him off?" Book asked in a quiet tone.

"I think someone did." Mal eyed the communicator in his hand, eyes narrowed like if he could glare hard enough, he'd somehow be able to read Jayne's face through it. "Whether it was Jayne or not don't matter to me much in this particular moment. Me and Horne are overdue a face-to-face regardless."

"Are you certain that's wise?" Book asked, his expression unreadable.

"Wisdom ain't got nothing to do with it, Shepherd," Mal said. "Your friend took me for a fool, and I can't let that go unchecked."

"You keep calling him my friend."

"There a problem with that?" Mal hitched his shoulders back, standing tall as he surveyed the Shepherd.

Book looked as unassuming as ever, disarming in the way he regarded Mal—like he saw him in a light no one else did. "Only that you're using it as permission to pass judgement on me for his actions."

"Ain't nobody passin' judgement." Mal shook his head and sighed. "It's complicated, the ties that bind. I understand that more than most. Know a lot of folks from the war I would've taken a bullet for. Still might. Not sure they'd deserve it though." Mal felt a pang of longing for folks who hadn't died but he'd lost all the same. "It's old friends, more than the new ones, who have the potential to hurt us most, no matter how long it's been."

Shepherd Book didn't reply immediately, but as they rounded the corner, closing in on the refinery, he said, "I'd like to hope there will be no hurt at all."

"Not all that realistic of you," Mal grunted.

"I'm a Shepherd, Captain. It isn't my job to be realistic."

Mal eyed the Shepherd carefully. Here was a man who stood for all manner of things Mal didn't agree with—not anymore—

and yet every so often he said something so sensible it shook Mal to his core.

"Well, then. Let's both do our jobs today," he said as they reached the door. He lifted the comm to his mouth once more and held down the button. "Knock knock."

The door creaked open. "Open sesame," said Jayne, who stood on the other side of the door looking no worse for wear than when they'd left him, his eye still bandaged up. He flashed a smile and a flat key card with the Blue Sun logo on it.

"Told ya I'd come through."

"I'd say I never doubted you, but I respect you too much for that kind of falsehood." Mal reached for the card, but Jayne held on to it tightly, so Mal let him keep it. "Now, where's Horne? He owes me one hell of an explanation."

Jayne pointed down the hallway and waved them through the door, taking up the rear. As the door clicked shut behind them, though, a figure emerged from the shadows.

Horne stood a few paces down the hall, outfitted with enough arms to put an octopus to shame. He grinned, and there was the distinct sound of the safety clicking off one of his guns. "I don't owe you a damn thing, Malcolm Reynolds."

34

Zoë didn't take kindly to surprises. Maybe it was on account of the darkness, or maybe she really was that full of herself that she thought the Governess couldn't possibly get the jump on her, a trained soldier. Zoë had assassinated men twice her size and thrice her rank in the war, but apparently all it took to incapacitate her these days was a woman in the dark asking for help reaching the circuit breaker.

She didn't care what Mal said. Next time her gut told her someone was trouble, she wasn't going to mess around, waiting to see if she was right.

With a groan, Zoë righted herself, blinked, and took in her surroundings—a few cots with white linens, some potted ferns, and a central table. If it wasn't the same hut they'd found the others in on their first visit to the compound, it was nearly identical. Swearing under her breath, she jogged over to the door and jiggled the handle. It was locked. Of course it was.

Zoë wasn't the kind of woman who was content to sit idly by while others were up to no good, like the Governess most certainly was. She'd known it from the second she'd first set eyes on her. She knew trouble like she knew the tension on the trigger of her Mare's Leg. The rifle was still strapped to her, too. The Governess hadn't even needed to disarm her. How embarrassing.

With a swift kick, her foot connected with the door in a shower of splinters, creating a hole large enough for her to crawl through. It was darker outside than it had been before. How much time had passed? It might've been only a few minutes, or it might've been hours. Time had thrown Zoë for a loop on Brome, with its strangely short days and nights.

She reached up to turn on her head lamp only to find it was missing. The gorram woman had taken her headlamp, but left her gun. She'd give the Governess one thing: her methods were unexpected.

Zoë assessed the situation as she went—there wasn't time to stop and think about it. Depending on how much time had passed, the Governess might have done all manner of things Zoë couldn't begin to imagine, not knowing her true motive and all.

Inara. She had to find Inara.

Zoë didn't often have occasion to work with the Companion. It wasn't every day Inara got wrapped up in *Serenity*'s illicit business, after all. But that's what made her special to Zoë—Inara was the rare soul aboard *Serenity* who wasn't asking anything of her, whose friendship was a thing to be sought out rather than implied. They didn't have all that much in common, but then, Zoë found, they didn't need to in order to understand one another.

She burst through the doors of the main building without ceremony, rifle first. But there was no one to aim it at down there. Unholstering her sidearm, Zoë made herself one with the shadows as she took the stairs with precise footsteps, rolling on the balls of her feet to cushion the sound. Zoë did her best work in the quiet. In the war, she'd killed more folks who hadn't seen her coming than those who had. Give her a knife and an unsuspecting throat over a grenade launcher any day. She liked her violence quick and to the point.

As she neared the top of the stairs, she felt the faint presence of another soul around the corner. She couldn't explain how she knew, just that there was something to the vibrations in the floor and the weight of the air. It was instinct more than anything else, and Zoë had learned long ago that instincts were sometimes all that stood between a man and his demise—or in this case, a woman.

She hugged the wall, inching forward with minuscule movements. Her breath stilled and she waited a beat. Two. Three.

She swung out, rounding the corner with her forearm ready to block any strike that came her way and her gun at the ready. She'd shoot if she had to. With the Governess on the receiving end of her bullet, she might even enjoy it.

But it wasn't the Governess who barreled into her. It was Inara, eyes wide, jaw set, a reluctant willingness to fight shining in her face.

"Zoë!" Inara cried out in breathless relief. Then her shoulders relaxed and she stepped back into the persona of the composed Companion. "I thought you were the Governess."

"Likewise." Zoë lowered her weapon, but did not holster it. "How long has it been since you've seen her?"

"Couldn't say precisely. She injected me with something. A sleeping agent of some kind, I assume." Inara rubbed the back of her head curiously. "I suspect it wasn't intended to knock me out cold, but I fell, and..." She trailed off, eyes drifting up and to the left, no doubt remembering the last time she'd been knocked unconscious.

Zoë remembered it all too well, the way the crew was taken unawares by that girl. Saffron had been her name, or so she'd said. Zoë remembered her gut had told her not to trust her either. The Governess and Mal's blushing bride had little in common other than a penchant for weaponizing the false assumption that they couldn't fend for themselves. Those were two women Zoë would be glad never to see again.

"Told Mal we couldn't trust her," Zoë grumbled. "But did he listen?"

"Does he ever?" Inara offered her a sympathetic smile. "Still, before she knocked me out, I'm fairly certain I..." She turned back toward the office behind her, eyes skating over the elaborate setup of displays. "Yes, I overheard a message from Horne."

"Let me guess, they're in cahoots?"

Inara nodded, winced, and placed her hand on the wall to steady herself. "Something to that effect, yes. I don't understand, though. Why would they be working together? The Governess's entire enterprise is based on helping the people here escape the severity of his employ."

Zoë brushed past her and made a beeline for the desks. She didn't even bother with the displays, just started pulling open drawers until she found one that was locked. She jiggled the handle, but the drawer wouldn't come loose.

"Cover your ears," she said, and without waiting, she leveled her gun and shot the lock out.

Inside, there were folders upon folders of printed documents, each with a different label. She took a stack and flipped through them: Victoria, Varley, Valentine.

"What are these? Donors?" Zoë asked, not expecting an answer.

Inara flipped through a few as well, reading as she went. "Charity, Conrad, Covenant."

"Wait a damn second." Zoë leafed through a few more. "Barr, Betty, Brome... They're all moons." She looked up at Inara, catching the other woman's curious gaze.

"What does that mean?" Inara asked.

"It means... It means Brome isn't the only place that's been the victim of the Governess's charity. I'd bet all the hair on my head that woman's done this before."

"Done what, exactly?" Inara gestured to the black display screens surrounding them. "Obviously she's up to something nefarious with Lyle Horne, but I don't understand. Why would she ally herself with someone whose entire credo is so antithetical to her mission?"

"Same reason most people do stupid things," Zoë said with a sigh. "Money." She let the folder labeled Brome fall open, revealing what was unmistakably a pile of receipts for sums so large she could hardly grasp them—donations from charitable folks trying to help. It was the kind of money that could have revitalized the whole moon. Instead, the Governess had spent it on a glass castle and her very own moat. "I bet not a soul in town saw a single cent."

"She's a thief!" Inara gasped. "How many moons has she done this on? Someone ought to have noticed by now."

"Not necessarily." Zoë shrugged one shoulder, considering. "How many folks do you know giving this kind of money actually bother to check up on their charitable contributions? Looks like she sends updates to donors in the form of some kind of newsletter, but unless they're willing to fly all the way here to verify, there's no way for them to know she's lying."

"Of course you're right," Inara said with a sigh. "Far too many people actually prefer it that way, giving contributions to salve their consciences for living better than others and doing nothing more. They'd rather give double than actually set foot on a place like Brome."

"Exactly," said Zoë. She closed the folder and piled the others into her arms. "Grab as many of these as you can."

Inara did as she was told, but asked, "What can we possibly do about it? There's no regulatory board this far out to stop her."

"Don't know, but if we need proof, now we have it. Plus..." she paused a moment, then shrugged. "In the event she gets away with it all, I like the idea that we've disrupted her filing system enough to inconvenience her a little."

"A diabolical punishment," Inara said with a smile.

They made short work of her office, taking what they could and moving the rest. Inara stopped Zoë just short of messing with the Cortex displays, reminding her that they might need the Governess's setup to contact Blue Sun later if things got dire. All in all, they spent less than a quarter of an hour there before returning to the ground floor, arms laden with folders.

"Best get these back to *Serenity*," Zoë said, angling toward the front gate. She set the stack of folders down on a side table by the door so she could bump the comm clipped to her vest. "Wash?"

"Zoë? Hope things are going better for you than they are here."

"Can't imagine a scenario where they were, if I'm being honest."

There was a crackle on the other end and Wash's voice sounded somehow closer. "What? Are you all right? Inara?"

"We're fine. A bit banged up, but we'll live. The Governess, though—she's bad news. Been using her charity to con folks out of millions of credits."

"Seems to me if they've got millions of credits, folks might be asking to be conned, sweetie," Wash replied.

Zoë didn't disagree. When folks got so rich that they needed to do a little philanthropy, well... that was a sign they were paid too much. Folks like them didn't care where their money went as long as it was tax deductible.

"We're heading back now. Send us your coordinates and we'll rendezvous—"

"Zoë?" Inara called back to her from the gate. She'd lowered the electromagnetic field ahead of her, but instead of the silver hull of her shuttle through the gap, Zoë saw nothing but grass.

"Scratch that. We need a pickup." Zoë sighed heavily and fell into a chair at the central table. "Guess the Governess steals ships, too."

35

It wasn't often Wash got to play the hero for Zoë. Usually, it was the other way around. Zoë had saved him from bruises and bullets, in addition to his own hubris from time to time, but now he was the one launching the daring rescue—or, at least, the well-timed and efficient if not all that terribly brave rescue.

He just had one problem: he couldn't find River.

The last Wash had seen of her, she'd been curled up on her bed, surrounded by slumbering geese. They'd looked peaceful, all asleep together, though of course Wash knew better. There wasn't anything peaceful about a goose, awake or asleep. Still, River seemed content, so he'd let them be. That had been hours ago, after Mal and the others had marched off into the night. Wash had spent that time dozing intermittently and arranging his dinosaur toys in several tableaux. Perhaps he should've kept better track of his charge.

"River?" he called out as he retraced his steps through every nook and cranny of *Serenity*. She wasn't in the passenger dorm—he'd checked every room just to be sure. The dining area was clear, too. He thought maybe she'd crawled into one of the hideaway spots in the cargo bay, but no dice. At long last, he'd resorted to calling her name like he would a lost pet.

"River!" Her name echoed through the cargo bay. Wash shuddered. "We really are alone out here. Not that that's anything new." He chuckled to himself. "I'm plenty used to it. Staying behind with the ship—that's my job! Don't mind it, though. Best to leave all that dangerous stuff to the experts. Not that Simon and Kaylee are experts… but that's not to say what they're doing will be dangerous."

He winced, uncertain if it was better or worse that River might hear his ramblings. River was a lot smarter and stronger than anyone seemed to give her credit for, and she more than likely already knew the peril her brother was walking into, but on the off chance she didn't, Wash wasn't sure he wanted to be the one to tell her. River could be all sorts of things, but predictable was never one of them. She might do all manner of things if she thought there was something wrong, like lock him in the engine room, or hang from the ceiling, or—

"Aha!" He looked up and immediately deflated. "Don't know what I was expecting…" She wasn't there. She had to be *somewhere* on the ship.

With a sigh, he turned in an undignified twirl, and his foot came down on something hard, then soft. He wrinkled his nose and peered down with one eye open to see the remains of an egg, the shell and runny yellow yolk now coating the bottom of his shoe.

"Well, at least it's not crap," he said to himself. But that particular upside didn't last for long as his gaze followed a path of feathers and, yes, mostly dried goose poop toward the cargo-bay doors.

Wash blinked. *Surely not…*

He jogged over and slammed his fist down to release the doors. There was a hiss, a clink of metal, and then silence.

"River?" Wash yelled out into the night, but he was answered by only silence and a rogue feather to the face as a breeze carried a flurry of them inside.

So, he'd been wrong. River didn't have to be on the ship at all, and neither, it seemed, did the geese.

36

Brome at the crack of dawn was almost pleasant. Well, it was at least less detestable than at full sun, when the heat and dust and grass all mixed in the air to produce a sneeze-worthy concoction. But now, as the suns rose in tandem, the town was bathed in a golden glow the likes of which Simon had never seen before. It made the tall grass look like honey wheat and Kaylee's eyes like the shining depths of nebulas.

"That's a lot of people," Kaylee whispered.

She wasn't wrong. The workers of Brome had come together in a massive crowd. Simon didn't know what he'd expected when the people they'd rescued—or inconvenienced, he couldn't totally be sure—said they'd rally the others, but it had been far fewer than this. He'd thought they'd assemble as a small but mighty force. This was anything but small.

The crowd stretched out before them, filling the town square and spilling into the side streets. People sat atop each other's shoulders, and others even stood on top of roofs to get a better view.

"That can't be safe," Simon muttered.

"Oh, don't be a killjoy!" Kaylee shot her elbow into his ribs, a smile on her lips that made him feel like he was standing just as high. "Look at them all. It's amazing what people can do together, ain't it?"

Simon wanted Kaylee always to feel this awed. Every day of her life, she deserved to see things that made her faith in humanity stronger. So why he didn't say that instead of what came out of his mouth, he'd never really know. "Well, they haven't actually done anything yet, have they?"

Kaylee's smile faltered and she looked away, tearing the shining light of her irises from his view. "I believe in people, Simon," she said with a sharp bite to her words that she seemed to reserve just for him when he said something wrong.

"So do I," he scrambled to say.

"No, you *want* to believe in people, but you're too damn jaded."

"Well, I think I have plenty of reason to be jaded, but I—"

"As if we don't all got reasons." Kaylee rolled her eyes. "The cap'n and Zoë got shot at plenty in the war, but they're still goin'. And before you say it's cause they ain't used to a better life, Inara's been through plenty, too, but you don't see her turning her nose up at everyone in the 'verse who's tryin' to do something big."

"I didn't mean to imply… I don't think that… I didn't have a better life, just a different one, and I—"

Kaylee laughed hollowly. "Spoken like someone who had a better life. But that's beside the point. Your own sister's been through more than you and she's still got faith in people with a lot less reason to."

She had him there. River had been treated abysmally by the very people she'd trusted with her future. They'd promised her an education, to expand the scope of her mind. They'd delivered in a twisted way, but he couldn't begin to imagine the betrayal. Despite it all, she had a capacity for love and trust and hope that evaded him. She was the one they'd cut into, but somehow he was the one they'd broken.

"You're right," he said, eyes clouding. "You're absolutely right."

"Tell me something I don't know already," she chided, but her smile was back. She looped her arm through his and said, "Now, you just watch and see what these folks can do. It'll blow that big surgical brain of yours."

Not one to disobey a pretty girl with stars in her eyes, Simon turned to face forward and watched as Dina climbed atop a stack of crates and waved her arms at the crowd to hush. Surprisingly, they acquiesced rather quickly, and with that, she had their undivided attention.

"We all know why we're here," she said, her voice rising up and over them like a blanket. "Seems Horne's the only one who don't."

There were a few appreciative chuckles from the crowd.

Dina turned around on her makeshift stage to face the refinery behind her, winking silver in the sunlight. "Let's see if you're listenin', boss man! We, the workers, are the sweat and blood of your business. Without us, you're nothin' but an old man with an office. We run your factory, we fill your coffers, but you ain't gonna turn a profit without us. Pay us what we're owed and treat us like we're worth a damn, or we'll spend every waking hour in this square instead of at our posts."

"You tell him, Dina!" shouted someone in the crowd.

"No, no, *we* tell him!" Dina raised her fist and a yell rent the air as a chorus of voices came together as one.

"We're done with Blue Sun!"

Beside Simon, Kaylee joined in, lending her voice to the throng. Simon's stomach twisted in knots, his heart threatening to beat out of his chest, but this was how it was done—this was how change began. He opened his mouth, but before he could shout along with the rest of them, there was the sound of a gun firing—a warning shot—and a dozen armor-clad enforcers waded into the scene.

"Disperse or we will disperse you," one of them shouted through a megaphone, his voice amplified and distorted all at once.

Dina put her hands on her hips and stared them down. "I ain't movin'. Got just as much right to be here as you."

The enforcers either didn't hear her or didn't care. "If you are working first shift, report to your posts. Everyone else, clear the square."

"I'd like to see you make me!" Dina laughed, pitching her head back. "Come on, you want to have this fight? There are more of us than there are of you."

The enforcers stopped a few yards from where Dina stood, conferring with one another.

"Yeah, that's what I thought," Dina began, a smug look on her face.

But the enforcers didn't back off. Instead, one of them reached for his belt and threw something into the crowd that made a loud popping sound. It didn't take long to figure out what it was, as smoke billowed up around them. There was another pop, and another, and more smoke unfurled into the air.

There was a moment of silence as panic gripped the crowd, followed by a scream as Dina dove off her stage. And then there was only chaos.

Bodies jostled them from every side. Simon felt himself pushed and pulled in every direction as smoke began to choke his lungs. His eyes stung and his chest burned. He took an elbow to the forehead as he twisted, searching for Kaylee beside him.

"Kaylee, we have to run," he said through a thick mouthful of smoke.

She didn't reply.

He reached for her, grasping wildly at thin air. But she wasn't there. He'd lost her to the crowd.

Heart racing, Simon pushed against the current.

"Excuse me, pardon me," he muttered as he went, trying his best but failing to evade injury.

By the time he'd reached the edge of the street and climbed up the front stairs of the tavern to get a better look at the crowd, his feet had been thoroughly trampled and his head was pounding.

"Kaylee!" he called again, but it was useless. No one could hear him over the din. He squinted, trying to see through the smoke, looking for a familiar swish of brown hair.

A hand clapped down on his shoulder, and for a breathless moment, Simon thought it was her. If they were reunited, they could get out of there together. But as he turned around, he was met not with a smiling face full of freckles and hope but a visored visage and the blunt end of a rifle.

Pain bloomed across his skull. "Ow!" He staggered back and held up a hand, his vision going bright with the impact. "Hey, wait—I'm just a visitor. I'm looking for my friend."

The enforcer lowered the gun, but didn't raise his visor—probably on account of the smoke still spilling out and making the air nearly unbreathable.

"She's got…" Simon hacked a cough and gestured to his head. "…brown hair."

"That's a lot to go on," said the enforcer with a muffled laugh—he was wearing some kind of cloth over his nose and mouth, by the sound of it. "You're not with the others?"

"Who gives a crap? He's here. Take him down," said another enforcer, looming into view.

"Huh?" Simon blinked rapidly, his eyes beginning to stream.

The first enforcer shook his head and took a step closer. "The protestors, the disruptors. You're not part of this?" He gestured to the smoke-obscured scene behind him.

Simon opened his mouth, but no sound came out. Fear coiled in his stomach at the sight—two men with guns. He'd seen that tableau before. But this time, they weren't after him or River. He could tell them he was just a bystander, he could lie, and maybe he'd get out of this alive, but there were plenty who couldn't. He had the attention of two enforcers. The longer he kept it, the fewer people they could hurt.

"Do you stand with them or not?" the enforcer asked again, drawing even closer so they stood nose-to-nose with only a thin layer of plastic between them.

Straightening up, Simon did his best to fix his gaze on the enforcer who'd asked the question. He smiled despite the pain in his skull and the smoke in his throat. "Proudly," he said, then reached for the rifle and tore it from the man's grip.

"*Zāo gāo!* He's got my gun!"

Simon did indeed have his gun. The only problem was, he didn't know the first thing about using it. He'd be better off brandishing it like a sword than trying to shoot the damn thing, so that was exactly what he did.

He swung up the back end of the rifle, cracking the enforcer's visor in two.

"Hah!" he shouted. "Take that!" He swung again as the enforcer advanced, clocking him right between the eyes.

The enforcer staggered back, and Simon grinned, his adrenaline spiking at this small victory. It was short lived, however, as the second enforcer stepped up to the plate.

"Tā mā de, hún dàn," the enforcer muttered as he advanced.

Simon took another step back, and that was his undoing. The ground came out from under him as he went over the edge of the railing, falling flat on his back in the dirt below the tavern, knocking the wind out of his already struggling lungs. He struggled to right himself, but his vision swam with stars. The last things he saw before everything went dark were the enforcer jumping down toward him and a single rogue feather drifting down from the sky.

37

One way or another, River always had to get things done herself. It had been that way as long as she could remember, ever since they were little. The Tams were a family of high IQ and higher expectations, but they were also a pack of idiots. She'd learned early on that if she wanted something, it was up to her to make it happen. No one was going to do it for her—and why would she want them to? They'd just do it wrong, anyhow.

River had been on her own long before she'd left home. Her parents didn't see her. They saw her test scores and they saw her ambition, but they didn't see her. That's why they hadn't noticed when she'd slipped away, when the Hands of Blue had reached into her brain and taken away the soft edges. It's why they didn't want her back.

But Simon did. Simon was the only one who did. In a world where River was blisteringly alone, Simon came for her anyway. He'd rescued her when he'd had everything to lose, and they'd lost it all together. Now, it was her turn to rescue him.

She'd left *Serenity* while Wash was sleeping, leaning back in his pilot's chair with his mouth open. She'd fought the powerful urge to pinch his nose as he snored, reluctantly deciding that she didn't need him waking up and stopping her. Her mind was made up, and she'd known Wash would try to prevent her if he could, so she wouldn't give him the chance.

Alone was how River was used to operating—not out of choice, but out of necessity. Now, she was flanked by a half a dozen geese. She'd started with eight, but a few hadn't been willing to leave their cozy shelter behind. That was just fine with her.

River moved through the night in hot pursuit. The grass was thick in these parts, and the impulse to stop and graze was strong among her friends. There would be time for that later, she told them. She was a different kind of shepherd, coaxing her flock along with her.

By the time they arrived in town, the rally had already begun. She scanned the crowd for the familiar squeeze of home. River was never at her best in large groups. The sound of so many people, the bodies, the brains, the building tension in the air—it was all too much.

"Simon?" she called as she tried to maneuver between the workers, but there was a rush of fear and everything got loud. "Simon, Simon, Simon." River's breaths became hollow and her voice went concave. She rolled her brother's name into her fists as they curled inward. The rest of her body followed suit.

River made herself small. It was how she dealt with the pain of the world. When things got too loud, inside or out, she tucked herself into a corner until it all stopped spinning. But here in the open, there were no corners, no alcoves, no secret hidden spots. She was in the world and the world was in her.

A wail burst from her throat. At first, she didn't know it was her own. She wasn't a girl, she was a goose, angry and hungry and scared. Soft feathers closed in around her. Bodies pressed against her sides and beaks were tucked into the hollow of her neck.

She was not alone.

River rose from her place on the ground, renewed in her focus. She had to find Simon.

But first, she found Kaylee.

She spotted her hair first. Kaylee sometimes wore it up in little buns that reminded River of cupcakes, but today it was down and wild, sticking to her face and neck. She had a bump forming just above her eye and she was gripping her shoulder like it was dislocated. She staggered to a stop across the street from River, leaning against a post and breathing heavily.

"Kaylee!" The name broke from River's throat, more honk than anything else. She dashed toward her, weaving through the crowd as it began to disperse near the edges.

"Ri-River?" Kaylee gasped. Her eyes were distant, her voice cracking.

Kaylee looked at her like she was a mirage. River sometimes imagined she was—when everyone talked about her instead of to her, or when she wove through the ship unseen. She could go days without speaking to anyone, and on those days she wondered if anyone would hear her if she screamed.

Now, it didn't matter much if she was real or not. What mattered was that Kaylee's lungs were constricting from the smoke and her head was pounding and her heart was racing. River cupped her friend's cheek in her hand and leaned in close.

"It's going to be okay, *mèi mèi*," she whispered, words her brother said to her often. It was all the emotional comfort she could give Kaylee.

Physically, though, River knew what to do. She tore off the hem of her skirt and wrapped the cloth around Kaylee's nose and mouth, tying it behind her head. It was the best she could do to keep out the smoke billowing up from the square.

"I'm so dizzy," Kaylee said, the words like sand falling through her fingers. "My shoulder—I think it's dislocated."

"Simon will fix you," River said as gently as she could.

Kaylee started to shake her head, then closed her eyes as she pitched from the movement. "Got separated in the crowd. I don't know where he is."

"We have to find him."

River knew plenty about the human body, about muscles and bones and veins and arteries. She could probably put Kaylee back together if she tried, but Kaylee wasn't a jumble of puzzle pieces that needed to be put to rights; she was a girl. Just like River. What she needed was a doctor. Who she needed was Simon.

"Stay here." River tore a second cloth from her skirt and fashioned it into a makeshift mask around her own nose and mouth. Then she pushed ahead against the current into the crowd.

The roar of violence around her was deafening. Intimidation was on the air, electric, suffocating, but River had her geese and they honked beside her, grounding her with their noise. Together, they swept through the square. There were fewer bodies now, but the smoke was thicker. Shadowy figures moved in the distance, but River could barely see.

She didn't need to see.

She closed her eyes and listened to the world.

Panic and fear bled from every corner, a distant wail of anguish and anger and the despairing sliver of remaining hope. There was also brutality and vengeance and the desire to harm. It was almost too much to bear. But there, in the middle of it all, there was a flickering beacon she recognized. It was proud and earnest and determined. That was her brother. That was Simon.

With a strangled yell, River dove for the feeling. She opened her eyes on a hazy scene.

On the tavern porch, a man in armor—an enforcer—was advancing on Simon, who held a rifle in his hands. River would have rolled her eyes had the situation been less dire. Simon barely knew how to fire a gun. Not every soul was meant for violence, though, and she didn't mind that her big brother's wasn't.

River reached, as if in slow motion, toward Simon as he staggered backward, but she wasn't close enough to stop his fall. The ground met him, hard and unforgiving, and the enforcer jumped down beside him. There was an ugliness there, a thrill at the chance to hurt someone. He wouldn't get it. Not if River had something to say about it.

As it turned out, she didn't. The geese beat her to the punch.

With an aggressive honk, one goose broke from their ranks and charged toward the enforcer. The others followed suit. They made quick work of him, pecking and honking at every inch of him.

"Ah! What the hell? Get these gorram things off me!" the enforcer shouted, looking every which way for someone to help. His gaze landed on River.

She approached slowly, tiptoeing barefoot over the dry, cracked ground.

"Don't just stand there! Help!" the enforcer cried over the din of honking.

"You hurt people," River said. Even though there was chaos all around them, her voice carried clearly over it all. "Now, we hurt you."

As if on cue, there was a holler behind her and the revving of several engines. She turned to see what looked to be a Mule, like the one on *Serenity*, only painted green and with several fans attached to it. Riding it were four figures—the young crew who'd taken *Serenity* out from under them with Captain Agate in the lead. They drove with reckless abandon, clearing the smoke to make way for the throng of demonstrators, still together, still strong. They marched forward in the Mule's wake. This time, they wore face coverings. Some had goggles. A few had firearms. They would not be defeated so easily.

River pulled Simon from their path and dragged him back to where she'd left Kaylee. The other girl had sat down, leaning against a nearby building, looking dazed but still conscious.

"You found him," Kaylee murmured. "Looks like he's the one who needs a doctor."

"What he needs is a scolding," River replied, propping him up next to Kaylee. "Shouldn't have tried to fight those men by himself."

A small smile played around Kaylee's lips. "Is that what he did?"

Simon's eyelids fluttered and he groaned. "Ow."

"It was very foolish." River crossed her arms and frowned down at her brother, though a thread of relief pulsed through her chest.

Kaylee looked from River to Simon, scooting closer to allow his head to loll onto her shoulder. "I don't know," she said, pushing his hair back off his forehead. "I think it might've been a little brave."

River turned to give them a moment of privacy. Whatever there was between them, it wasn't hers to share. Geese flew overhead, honking along with the protestors' chants. She couldn't fly along with the geese, so she settled herself a few feet from Simon and Kaylee. After all, they were her flock, too.

38

"Jayne, I'm going to kill you." Mal said it often, but seldom did he really mean it. This was one of the rare exceptions.

"Nobody's killing anybody," Horne replied with a sneer. "Least not yet, anyhow." He motioned with his head, eyes flicking toward Jayne.

"Oh, right, right." Jayne sprang into action, pulling Mal's gun from its holster.

Mal stared daggers at him.

"Why don't you step into my office?" asked Horne. "We can have a friendly little chat."

"Don't know that I've had many friendly encounters that involved so many guns," Mal said. He wasn't too keen on moving further from the exit, but the hallway wasn't exactly advantageous terrain, especially pinned as he was between Jayne and Horne. If it came to a shootout, better it be somewhere he and the preacher could take a little cover. He sighed and gestured forward. "Lead on."

"I hope you know what you're doing," the Shepherd said in an undertone as Horne stepped into a room at the end of the hallway.

"I rarely do," Mal replied, and followed.

Lyle Horne's office wasn't special, but that wasn't a surprise; neither was the man. Mal immediately made note of the large desk to the right and the bar cart to the left. The desk would make better cover, but a glass bottle could be a weapon if it came to that.

Mal slung his thumbs through the loops on his suspenders. "Right. Speak your piece, Horne."

"So impatient, Captain Reynolds. There's no need to rush. Let's take our time. Care for a drink?" Horne gestured to the bar cart.

"Lyle, please," Shepherd Book said, grit in his tone. "We deserve some answers, don't you think?"

Mal tried to read Book's gaze. There was a depth there, an intensity he couldn't parse, but that was how it often was between folks who went back as far as Horne and Book. Trust built roads beneath the surface, secret tunnels for communicating without words. He had that with Zoë. Sometimes he thought he had it with Inara, too. It was confounding, and a little disarming, to see one of his crew so in sync with someone who'd tried to fool them all.

Lyle's lips turned up in a smile, though he didn't look in the least bit happy. "What you deserve is a good smackin', *Derrial* Book. I hired you for a job. That job didn't get done. So how abouts we turn things around? Seems to me I'm the one who deserves some answers."

"You hired us to fetch the missing folks from the Governess's compound," Mal said evenly. "They're back here in town with their families. That's a job well done in my eyes."

"You best get your eyes checked, then. Seem to recall specifying you were to bring those folks to me." Horne narrowed his eyes. "Instead, you let them loose and they're terrorizing my guards in the square."

Mal made an involuntary sound that was halfway between a whine and a scoff. "Would we call that terrorizing?" He exchanged a glance with Book. "Folks havin' a little gathering in the square to air their grievances ain't anything to worry about, unless..." Mal gave a little performative gasp. "Oh, I'm sorry, did you do something to aggrieve them?"

"You lost the moral high ground the second you docked their pay, Lyle." Book shook his head, a devastating look of disappointment in his eyes. "What are you even doing? They're your workers. Treat them with a little respect."

Horne raised an eyebrow. "The man I knew wouldn't balk at screwin' somebody for a pile of cash."

"Not people like them," Book said through gritted teeth. "We never took from people like them. We *were* people like them, Lyle. The man I knew wouldn't abuse his power like this."

"The man you knew?" Lyle let out a laugh like a bark. "Oh, my dear friend, the man you knew, you let him die."

"We remember that day very differently, I see." Book frowned, a pained expression crossing his face. "I thought you'd think twice before working for Blue Sun after that."

Mal's gaze flicked between them. He expected to see tension on Horne's face, but instead the man was relaxed, almost casual.

"Started off thinkin' that way myself," the foreman said. "After the fall, I was in a bad state. Would've been a goner, but Blue Sun got me medical. Must've seen the fightin' spirit in me. They knew I could be an asset. They made me an offer, gave me a job."

"And you didn't take the opportunity to hit them back with all you had?" Book asked. To his credit, he surveyed Horne with a great deal more calm than Mal could have boasted if he'd been in the other man's shoes.

"Thought about it. Won't lie." Horne sighed, perhaps wistful for the path not taken. "But that would've been one job, one payday."

"So you settled for a salary." Book said the last word with a derision Mal hadn't known the preacher held for honest work.

"A salary and more."

"You're skimming off the top?" Book asked. Mal couldn't be sure, but he thought he detected a hint of curiosity there.

"The big folks at Blue Sun don't care. They don't hardly notice. Funny how when you're used to something runnin' smooth, it takes a while before you notice it ain't."

"So you… what? Pay your workers next to nothing and take what's left over for yourself?" Book practically spat the words. "Despicable."

"Oh, you think too small." Horne's eyes lit up with greed.

Book's hands curled into fists. "You've changed, old friend."

Mal could see things were heading south. He should've known they would the second he realized Book and Horne knew each other. Book might be high and holy now, but it didn't take a genius to know he hadn't always been. There were all kinds of should'ves in Mal's rearview, though, and there wasn't anything he could do about them just now.

"I ain't here to rehash your history. I'm here to get paid." Mal held out a hand stiffly. "So kiss and make up on your own timetable, but get me my coin and I'll be on my way."

Horne scoffed. "If you think I'm paying you after you incited a rebellion—"

"Who said anything about incitin'?" Mal asked, turning to Book for confirmation. "Did I imply we incited anything? It ain't our fault if your workers are so dissatisfied with your leadership that they decided to do something about it. I don't know what you think we could possibly—"

"See, the thing is, I don't *think* it's your fault. I *know* it is." Horne's lips twitched in a suppressed smile.

Mal glanced at Jayne.

The burly man looked back and gave a shrug. "Weren't me, Mal, I swear."

Mal already knew it wasn't Jayne. Even if he was a traitor, Jayne hadn't known their plans. He hadn't known anything worth a damn, and Mal had kept it that way on purpose. Jayne could be blamed for a whole host of things, but this wasn't one of them.

Cheating his gaze over to Book, Mal's mouth dropped open. He really hadn't expected it to be the Shepherd. For all his caution, there was a part of him deep down that was sure Book would come out on their side. He might hem and haw a bit over his old friend, but he knew what was right. More than that, he *cared* about what was right. But maybe that was all a show, a lie even Mal hadn't truly seen coming. But when he looked back at Horne, the other man wasn't looking at either of Mal's compatriots. He was looking past them all to the hallway beyond.

The Governess stood in the doorway, not a hair out of place. "They've taken the square. I suggest we move."

Mal's stomach seemed to drop right out from under him. "You!" He pointed at the Governess, then turned his finger on Horne. "And you!"

"We." Horne nodded. "See, that's the beauty of our operation. Why take from one end of things when you can take from both?"

"I still don't get it." Jayne shrugged. "You did that whole song and dance about not knowin' each other, but here you are in cahoots. What's the point?"

"Let me guess," Book began, eyes narrowed into slits as he stared Horne down. "Not only are you garnishing your employees' wages, you're also using them to con money out of the Governess's potential donors. The charity, the people in distress—it's all a performance for their benefit."

"Well, not the people in distress. They really don't got much goin' for 'em," Horne said.

"No thanks to you," Mal cut in. "So, what's the deal? You rile folks up to give her somethin' to fundraise about?"

"People like to know their money is going to a good cause," the Governess said, voice eerily calm. "I show them a world in desperate need of help, they send me the credits. Pity is a powerful tool. Guilt maybe more so. And truly, the more money someone has, the less likely they are to check that it's going where they intended. It's simple, when you think about it."

"Not simple enough," Jayne grumbled.

"Do you really expect me to believe *you* have a problem with *my* enterprise?" the Governess asked, blinking at them in disbelief. "I didn't think you'd take umbrage with taking money from those who already have too much."

"It ain't the takin' from the rich so much as the not givin' to the poor," said Mal, his eyes narrowing. His hypocrisy wasn't lost on him. Mal had engaged in his fair share of trickery over the years. Such was the life of a smuggler, after all. But even Mal hadn't been able to stomach stealing from those in need—not when they'd done the train job, and not now. The Governess's scam was designed to cheat folks out of money they needed, money meant for them.

Mal had failed to see past the soft-skinned, well-dressed woman of means the Governess projected, and now he wondered if there was more to her, a rough edge under her glittering façade that he wasn't refined enough to see. It didn't matter, though. Scum came in all shapes and sizes, as did their bank accounts. "You're both the worst kind of *bù huǐ hèn de pō fu* there is—that ain't in question. What I want to know is why. If you're workin' together, what was the point of sendin' us on that wild-goose chase?"

Jayne flinched beside him at the mention of geese. Mal almost wished Wash was there to appreciate his turn of phrase.

"Had to get you out of the way somehow," said Horne. "When I heard you were pokin' around town, I had a mind to take my enforcers with me and send you on your merry way. But then..." Horne's gaze drifted over to Book.

"But then you realized I was with them and you decided to have some fun." Book's voice was icier than a winter on St. Albans.

"Fun ain't the word I'd choose." Horne chewed his lip, surveying Book with a stare Mal couldn't read. "Had to get you out of the way for a spell, figure out what sort of man you turned out to be. See if I could trust you."

"Suppose I'm a disappointment to you, then," Book said in a whisper.

"What the hell kind of *chuī niú* is going on here? Someone better explain this whole thing to me, and fast." Mal pointed at Horne, then at Book. "I'm not messin' around. If there's somethin' about your past I need to know, now's the time."

Horne sighed heavily. "I'm not inclined to explain myself to you, Captain Reynolds."

"Then why are we still talkin'?"

"We ain't." Horne withdrew his gun, cocked it, and aimed it at Book.

Mal dove to the right, taking the Shepherd down with him just as Horne pulled the trigger. No bullet left the chamber. There was a dull click instead, and Horne looked down at his gun with a frown, giving Mal just enough time to drag Book around the back of the desk. He reached for his holster, remembering only as his fingers closed around air that Jayne had his gun.

Horne reached for another weapon before Mal could make an alternate plan. He checked it for ammo and let out an exasperated huff and let it drop onto the desk with a heavy *thunk*. "*Zāo gāo!* How in the hell?" He reached for another, with the same results.

"Funny how when you're used to something runnin' smooth it takes a while before you notice it ain't," Jayne said, repeating Horne's words back to him. He reached for his pocket and withdrew a simple key card and held it up between two fingers. "You're so busy stealin' from everyone else, I figured somebody should do it to you. You got all those fancy guns, but they ain't all that effective without ammunition."

"Well, ain't that a mighty fine metaphor," Mal said from behind the desk. Relief flooded his limbs. He'd never been gladder to be wrong about Jayne.

"I'm smarter than I look, Mal!"

"You'd have to be," Mal said with a smile the other man couldn't see. Rising from behind the desk, Mal fixed Horne with a glare. "Now, Mr. Horne, I think it may be we ain't so evenly matched anymore, so how about you and your friend do exactly as I say—"

Mal didn't have time to extrapolate on what exactly that was. Horne's guns might have been neutralized by Jayne's rare but admirable forethought, but they weren't the only heat he was packing. The foreman took out a small, round device that Mal had seen in the war time and time again. He didn't need to wait for it to go off to know what it was.

"Grenade!" he yelled.

He dropped to the floor behind the desk once more. Just in time, too. The blast sent him sprawling across the Shepherd, who was already on the floor. His ears rang and his stomach lurched. He knew this disorientation intimately. The war had left him with more wounds on the inside than the outside. The sound of the explosion shook loose every repressed memory of heavy fire he had, pain and fear and rage and dread all pooling together in his chest. All his muscles went taut and the sound of his blood rushing filled his ears. His vision went fuzzy and then it went white.

Mal couldn't be sure how much time passed before he felt the Shepherd shaking him gently. His mouth was moving, but all Mal could hear was ringing, too loud for him to focus his thoughts. He squeezed his eyes shut, then opened them again as Book hauled him to his feet. There was a layer of smoke heavy in the air and Jayne lay on the ground, out cold with a little trickle of blood running down his temple.

"Lucky that was just a smoke bomb," Mal said, bending over to check Jayne's pulse, which was as strong as ever. He looked up, taking in the situation. Horne and the Governess were gone, but the office door hung open, swinging in their wake. "What do you say, Shepherd? Should we cut our losses?"

It didn't feel good to lose, but as Mal well knew, there were times to fight and there were times to flee. Horne had obviously decided this was the latter. If he and the Governess left Brome behind, at least they'd be gone.

Book stood resolute, staring out the door into the hallway. He didn't so much as glance at Mal as he said, "Not today," and took off at a run.

So, a fight it was. Mal retrieved his gun from Jayne's still body before following in the preacher's wake.

39

Book ran with everything he had. His legs and lungs burned with the effort, but he didn't care. He'd let Lyle Horne go once. He wouldn't do it again.

He burst through the door and light flooded his vision, sending him staggering into the dusty Brome morning. The suns had risen in the time they'd been inside, and Book wasn't accustomed to the brightness. Still, he heard the engine start and the familiar sound of a shuttle taking off. He also heard a familiar anguished yell.

"*Bèn tiān shēng de yī duī ròu!*" The colorful language came from a few yards off as Horne slowed his jog to make a rude gesture at the departing shuttle.

"You used to have better taste in partners," Book shouted. The Governess, for all that she might have been clever and poised, was just another thief in fine clothing. Book hadn't been anything special back when he'd run with Lyle, but he'd at least been more honest, and a lot more loyal. The Governess hadn't even been willing to wait long enough for Lyle to hop aboard. Book would never have left Lyle behind—not if he'd known Lyle was still alive. "She's a coward, Lyle. Not like you."

Lyle took one look at him and bolted.

"Well, a little like you," Book muttered before following the trail of dust Lyle left in his wake. He put a hand over his nose and mouth to keep from inhaling too much of it, but nothing short of death itself was going to stop him from pursuing this to its natural end.

After a quarter mile or so, Book finally caught his quarry. Lyle was wheezing, hands on his knees. He stood at the edge of a precipice, a crumbling cliffside looking down into a ravine.

"A familiar tableau," Book said, approaching cautiously. Jayne had disabled Lyle's guns, but Book couldn't be sure he didn't have any other weapons. Besides, he wasn't keen to fight this man he'd once called friend. "You saved my life once. Do you remember?"

Book remembered. The relief at having found someone to call friend, to call family… it haunted him like a ghost. Lyle had been his savior long before God ever was. It was a desperate, dutiful sort of reverence he'd had for Lyle Horne, for his violence, for his vengeance. He'd felt he owed Lyle a debt, the kind he couldn't repay with good works and prayer. Somewhere beneath all the thieving and the lying, Book needed to know if the man he'd known was still there.

"Do I remember?" Lyle coughed, a laugh layered somewhere in the sound. "You were such an idiot. Fresher than a green tomato. Would've been easy to squash you. Maybe I should've."

"But you didn't. You were a good man, Lyle. You were a good *friend.* What happened?"

"I fell," Lyle said. His shoulders tensed and he raised his chin, still looking out at the vista. "You let me fall."

Book wished Lyle would turn around and look at him. He wanted to reach out and grab his arm, force Lyle to see all that was in Book's eyes—the hurt, but also the hope. Book couldn't do it. Only Lyle could choose to change course.

"After you fall, there are only two options." Book clenched his fists, ready if he needed to be. "You can stay on the ground, or you can get back up."

"You learn that from your big book, *preacher*?"

"No," Book said quietly. There was an anger boiling beneath the surface, but something else as well, something he hadn't felt since… well, since Valentine. It took him a moment to identify it as something in the realm of grief. Lyle had died in front of him, having fallen from a height Book didn't think he could come back from. Book had grieved the life lost that night. He'd never thought he'd have to grieve Lyle all over again, standing before him with a beating heart. "I learned it from you."

"Yeah, right. Don't be such a sap," Lyle scoffed, but his voice wavered ever so slightly, like maybe he, too, felt a heaviness in his throat, an ache carried with him for all their decades apart.

"If you think you're the only one who fell that night, think again." Book could feel them now: the tears waiting in the wings. "It was the lowest I'd ever felt, the night you died."

Lyle hitched his shoulders. "Yeah, but you've felt lower since. You can't tell me I was the worst thing that ever happened to you and think I'll believe it."

"No, you're right." Book almost laughed. Back then, losing Lyle had felt like the fabric of reality was coming undone around him. He'd weathered plenty of hardship in his youth before Lyle, and a great deal more after. He carried the harsh bruises of the life he'd left behind with him always, but it was a different kind of pain. His father's rages had left him bloodied, and his time in the war had left him hollow. Lyle had left him aching, like a muscle he'd neglected to use. But it was all of it survivable, and he knew exactly who he had to thank for that. "You were not the worst thing to happen to me." That distinction belonged to one man and one man only: himself. "As a matter of fact, sometimes I think you were the best."

"How's that, now?" Lyle turned around at that, gaze strangely soft.

Book let his lips curve, the smile he'd been holding back finally taking flight. "You taught me that no matter how low I felt, I could and would survive." He took a step toward Lyle, then another and another, each movement a reaction to the quiet pain in Lyle's eyes. If he could ease that a little, he would. If he could hold out a hand and lead Lyle's lost soul toward a path to forgiveness, toward redemption, he would never stop reaching. "So can you, Lyle. No matter what you've done—"

"Easy for you to say, *man of the cloth*. You're a gorram Shepherd now. Your sins ain't at my level."

"My sins are deeper and darker than you can begin to fathom, Lyle. If I could crawl my way back into the light, so can you."

Lyle's eyes flickered with something sharp, something pained, as Book drew closer. A few more steps and Book would be able to touch him.

"You really think so, Hevans?" Lyle asked, his voice a mere murmur.

Maybe it was the way Lyle said his name that sent him the rest of the way. Shepherd Book wasn't supposed to want things—not for himself. He was a humble servant of a mighty God. He was meant to put aside selfish notions and do what was right. But in that moment, he wasn't Shepherd Book anymore. He was Henry Evans, unspoiled and full of hope. He held out his hand, forgiveness at his fingertips.

Lyle met it with a knife.

Pain lanced across Book's palm as the blade cut into his skin. He'd been so focused on Lyle's face, on his eyes, he'd failed to notice the weapon. Lyle must have snuck it from his pocket while Book was distracted.

"You're still so naive," Lyle said as he grabbed Book's arms and wrestled him into a headlock. "You think I want to come into the light with you? Take up the cloth and preach by your side?" Pained laughter broke from Lyle's lungs. "I ain't like you, Hevans. I wasn't made for redemption."

"That isn't true," Book began to argue, but Lyle pressed down on his windpipe, putting an end to his words.

"No, I'm talkin' now. Just 'cause you did a big transformation don't mean I want one. I like how I am. There's a reason I haven't changed, and it ain't cause no one came along with an offer like yours. I've always been like this, and I don't see that stoppin' just cause you finally showed up."

"You weren't always," Book managed to say from beneath Lyle's arm, each breath becoming more of a delicacy by the second. The knife wrapped in Lyle's closed fist was pointed away from him now, and he clawed at Lyle's arm, hoping for reprieve, but to no avail. Strange how even now, with the other man trying to squeeze the life from him, all Book could think was that at another time, he'd thought he would never touch Lyle Horne again, and it had almost broken him. Ironic, perhaps, that the opposite was what might actually break him in the end. "You were good."

"No, I wasn't," Lyle spat. "I was always greedy, and I was always selfish, and I was always gonna get my way. You were just a partner, Hevans. You let me fall, but let me tell you, if our roles were reversed, I wouldn't have thought twice about lettin' go."

"But… trust…" Book stammered. He needed to know, all those times Lyle had asked if he trusted him, if any of it had really meant anything. But even more than that, he needed Lyle to keep talking.

"Trust ain't a two-way street, Hevans. Long as you trusted me, it didn't matter if I trusted you."

"I don't believe you," Book said, inching his fingers up Lyle's arm—closer to the blade with every word. None of it made sense. Not a gorram word. Book knew what they'd had, and the way

Lyle described it was nothing more than a revisionist history colored by pain and doubt and loss. Yes, things had been hard, and yes, there'd been plenty of times they'd done wrong, but at the core of it all there had always been the two of them, the bond they had. That had been real.

"Maybe I'm a liar. Maybe I've always been one." Lyle cleared his throat, arm loosening slightly. "Come on, Hevans. It'll be easier for you to face losing me a second time if you believe what we had was never all that special in the first place."

"Maybe so," Book said, fingers meeting steel. "But I've never been about finding the easy way out." He pulled with all his might and the knife came loose, slicing Lyle's forearm as it went skittering across the ground toward the cliff's edge.

"Gorram it!" Lyle shouted, releasing Book just long enough for him to duck out of Lyle's grip. "No, wait—"

They both dove for the knife in a confusion of fingers and elbows and dust. Book could taste iron on the air, felt the pressure of dirt beneath his fingers. Lyle thrust his knee into Book's chest, but Book had weathered worse beatings by better men. He scrambled to his feet and pulled the knife from the dirt before leveling it at Lyle.

Fear did not become Lyle Horne. His eyes danced a jagged jive, searching for help that would not come. Dust caked his shirt and forearms, and there was blood in his beard. By all accounts, he was a bigger man than Book, but in that moment, Book felt as though he towered over him.

"You… ain't gonna kill me," Lyle said, voice high and willowy. "You're a preacher."

"Is that what you think, Lyle? You think I'm too *good* to have blood on my hands?" Book took a step toward him, forcing Lyle back toward the cliff edge. "I've killed bigger men than you, *better* men than you. I've killed more men than you can count."

"Now ain't the time to go pokin' fun at my lack of book learnin'." Lyle tried on a weak smile, leaning forward even as his feet took him back. "Come on, Hevans. This ain't you."

Book's gaze was cold and stony. "You don't know me, Lyle. You don't know all I've done."

"But you… you said, when you fell, you got back up." Lyle's words overlapped as he rushed them out. The heel of his right foot lowered down on the edge of the ravine. Dirt crumbled under his weight and he wobbled, barely managing to stay upright. "You won't," he said with more force, like he wasn't trying to convince himself at all, but Book. "Because you're better than me. You did what I can't. Don't go ruinin' that over little old me."

Book's heart seemed to buckle in his chest. This was the Lyle he knew, self-deprecating and charming. It was the Lyle who'd saved him, the Lyle who'd convinced him time and time again to join his capers, the Lyle who'd earned his trust. This was the Lyle he'd missed all those years, the Lyle he'd do almost anything to get back.

Book's hand wavered, the knife slipping from his fingers.

"That's right," Lyle said in a soothing tone. "You're not gonna kill me."

The knife fell, but in the moment of freefall, somewhere behind Book there was the sound of a gun cocking.

"He ain't gonna kill you," said Malcolm Reynolds. "But I sure as hell will."

40

Mal liked to let people fight their own battles. People needed that, the catharsis of it. For some folks it was an important step toward healing. For others, it was just a much-needed rush of adrenaline. Mal had fought enough battles for a lifetime. He would just as soon sit this one out, if not for the rising suspicion that, unlike the rest of them, the thing Shepherd Book needed most of all was to put down the knife and let someone else do the dirty work.

"You all right, preacher? Been a while since I've seen blood on your hands," Mal said, holding his gun steady.

In fact, the last time Shepherd Book had wielded a weapon with any violence in mind, it had been on Mal's behalf. Mal wouldn't be quick to forget Shepherd Book hadn't wavered when it came time to rescue him from Niska. Conventional wisdom told him that his preacher friend had faced off against many a scoundrel in his day, whether he'd tell Mal about it or not, but maybe Lyle Horne didn't need to be one of them.

Book lowered his arm shakily and muttered, "My cross to bear."

"You and I disagree on a great many things, so pardon me for sayin' so, but I don't think your God would take too kindly to you assumin' responsibility for another man's sins," said Mal as he took a few steps forward, careful not to let his gun arm waver.

"Didn't think I'd see the day you'd be the one preaching to me, Captain."

"Ain't gonna lie, Shepherd, it's a mite uncomfortable."

"For me as well."

Truth be told, Mal knew plenty more about God than Shepherd Book gave him credit for. He'd long put to rest any notions of religiosity for himself. After the war, he'd shed the cross he wore around his neck. There was plenty from the war he'd take with him always—his uniform, for one. Once a Browncoat, always a Browncoat. The same could not be said of his faith.

As Mal drew closer, Horne raised his hands in surrender. "Don't suppose if I said 'don't shoot' you'd oblige?"

"That depends on a whole host of things, Horne, none of which I think you're gonna care for all that much." Mal continued to advance, and Horne's complexion grew paler with each step. "Honestly, it'd be much easier to put you down at this point. Book might've been willing to rehabilitate you, but me? I've got more bullets than I've got patience."

"I'll admit, I screwed you pretty bad, but I think we can agree I could've done worse."

"If your argument is 'I didn't treat you as badly as I treated some other folk', I think you're beyond rehabilitation. Besides which, I'm fairly confident one way or another I ain't ever gonna see you again. But it ain't me I'm worried about." Mal lowered his voice. He wasn't at shouting range anymore, and it made the whole situation a touch more dramatic than was strictly necessary. "You don't paint a very compelling picture as to why I should let you live, Horne."

"I'll do anything—whatever you like." Horne's voice took on a desperate tone as his gaze shifted from Mal to Book and back again. "You want me to join the clergy? I'll do it."

"Don't reckon they'd take you," Mal said. "Think the prerequisite there is, you gotta believe in God, and you don't strike me as the type."

Horne let out a sigh like a faulty engine, half groan, half splutter. "I've had about enough of this."

"See, Horne, I'm the one who decides when enough is enough on account of I'm the one holding the gun and you're the one up against a mighty steep cliff there."

"What's your price?" Horne growled. "We all got one, somethin' we want so bad we'd do anything for it. If it's in my power to give, I'll trade you. My life for your dream. So, what's your price, Malcolm Reynolds?"

Mal paused a moment to consider. There was plenty he wanted—fuel and cash to keep *Serenity* running, a solid lead on a new job, the Alliance to leave them well enough alone, a few moments of quiet sitting beside Inara with their arms close enough to touch—but none of it was something Lyle Horne could give him.

"Mal…" Book murmured, a warning in his tone.

A smile bit at the corner of Horne's mouth as he glanced between them. "I could tell you the truth. You must be curious, right?"

At first, Mal didn't understand his meaning, but as Horne's gaze traveled over to Book, his eyes seemed to catch fire, bright and blistering.

"He hasn't told you who he really is, that much is plain. Got you calling him all sorts of things that ain't his real name. Shepherd, preacher, Derrial. What kind of name is that, anyhow? Who'd you steal it from, huh?"

"Mal…" Book said his name again, harsher, sharper. He didn't say anything else, though, so Mal let Horne keep talking.

"I could tell you all of it, every second of our history. Must be troublin', not knowin' so much about someone on your crew."

The thing was, Mal had spent plenty of time wondering about Book's past. Horne was right about that much. To Mal, his crew was his family. He didn't always like them, but he would always fight for them. They were all essential. Zoë was like a limb to him—he didn't know if he'd stay upright without her—and Wash was the breath in his lungs. Kaylee had carved herself a nest in his heart, with Inara just beside her, and even Jayne was like a scar he'd suffered and grown to appreciate. Simon and River were newer additions, it was true, but they'd found their places within *Serenity*. Mal would take a bullet for every last one of them. He liked to think the feeling was mutual.

And then there was Book, who raised more questions than he answered. In so many ways, he was a strange reflection of Mal's own self. Sometimes, Mal thought Book was his penance for leaving his faith behind. On quiet nights, his thoughts found their way to wondering if it wasn't some twisted trick of fate to land him in such close quarters with a man who, from what Mal could gather, had found his way to God through the same sort of hardships that had made Mal stray. It plagued him, the question of why, like if Mal just knew the path Book had walked, the answer would soothe the hollow place inside himself.

"Makes you question things, don't it?" Horne said, his smile growing wider, like he knew he'd won. "Like if he'll turn on you. Hard to trust someone whose name you don't even know."

Mal lowered his gun, and the relief on Horne's face bled like a stomach wound. "You know, Horne, I've been betrayed a bit too often for my taste, but knowin' their name's never been the problem."

He shot one last glance at Book, finding in his eyes the permission he didn't need but sought all the same. And with that, Mal kicked out, his foot connecting with Horne's sternum. Horne teetered on the edge of the cliff for just a moment, his eyes flashing to where Book stood just beside Mal. His lips moved in a whispered plea—"Heaven," Mal thought he heard him say.

"Nah," Mal muttered as he leaned over the cliff to watch Horne's descent. "I think you're probably goin' to Hell."

41

When Jayne woke, it was to a disgruntled Wash barging into the room yelling, "Horney, I'm home!"

"Told you he wouldn't be here," said Zoë, leaning against the door frame.

"Huh?" Jayne said. Bewildered didn't even begin to cover it.

"Waste of a good joke." Wash sighed, then turned his attention to Jayne. "What happened to you?"

What had happened to him? Jayne pushed himself up from the floor. Every muscle in his body cried out in protest as the memory of how he'd gotten there came back to him. Horne and the drugged drink, waking up alone in the dark, tampering with Horne's weaponry, and then double-crossing him—or was it triple-crossing? Jayne had never been an ace with mathematics. The last thing he remembered was a blast that sent him back into the wall and a cloud of smoke. It was damn near heroic, all he'd done... if he put the right spin on it, anyhow. Still, he'd been out cold in the past twenty-four hours more times than he cared to admit to Wash, so instead he just blinked and said, "Grenade."

"I'd say you need to see the doc, but he's not in a state to look after patients." Zoë uncrossed her arms and entered the room, taking in the scene. "You been through his stuff yet?"

"Took the ammo from his guns," Jayne said through a groan as he propped himself up against the wall. He reached into a pocket and pulled out a few bullets. "Bet there's more worth takin'."

"I meant his papers, Jayne. His documents," Zoë said with an eye roll.

"What're those worth, do you think?" Jayne asked.

Zoë just sighed and crossed over to the desk with Wash in tow behind her.

Eventually, Jayne dragged himself to his feet with a groan.

"Which was worse, the grenade or the goose?" Wash asked.

Jayne wanted to smack the mirth from his eyes. "It'll be me, if you don't stop pokin' fun," he said. "You seen Mal around?" He had a vague memory of the captain standing over him in the foggy haze of grenade smoke, but he wasn't around anymore.

"Nope," said Wash. "Just got here. Kaylee's outside with Simon and River, though, if you're looking for company." He jabbed a thumb toward the door.

Jayne grimaced. "Just wanna lay down in my bunk, get some shuteye."

"Your bunk's a pretty long hike from here. *Serenity* broke down a ways out of town."

At this point, Jayne just wanted to be away from Wash and Zoë and their talky mouths and looky eyes, so he just shrugged and ducked through the door. He regretted it as soon as he stepped outside into the sun. Whoever decided there should be planets with two suns deserved a black eye. Maybe someday Jayne could be the one to give it to them.

"Well, look who finally woke up!" Mal's voice was loud and belligerent in his ears. "How's the head?"

"It's all right," Jayne muttered, turning toward the sound. "Had hangovers that felt worse than this."

"Remind me never to go up against you in a drinking competition," Mal said with a grin that didn't quite match the moment as he strode toward Jayne. He looked none the worse for wear, though the Shepherd, walking behind him, looked more disheveled. Book had dusty circles on his knees and a bruise beginning to form around his neck. Jayne's pulse leapt as he realized he'd missed the preacher in action. A right shame. He would've liked to have seen it.

"You look… happy," Jayne grumbled.

"Ain't a man allowed to vanquish his enemies and smile about it?" asked Mal.

Jayne narrowed his eyes. "You're never happy."

Mal let out a mild gasp. "Now, that's just not true." He glanced at Book for confirmation.

"I do wonder if you'd benefit from a little more joy in your life, Captain," Book said. "There is much to be discovered about oneself from enjoying things."

"I'm a grown man," grumbled Mal. "I got no need for self-discovery, preacher."

Book placed a hand on Mal's shoulder. "I'm older than you, son. We are all of us on a path of discovery until our last breath." Then he nodded to Jayne and continued to walk past them.

Jayne stopped near the edge of the building, where Kaylee sat with River and an unconscious Simon. For a moment he watched them, and felt a pang of absurd jealousy. No one had crowded around him to tend his wounds while he was knocked out. Then, he remembered that was exactly how he liked it. No one needed to see him when he was down.

"So," Mal said, his voice lower than it had been before. "I see we find ourselves on familiar ground again."

"I, uh…" Jayne looked down and scuffed his boot in the loose dirt. "Seems pretty normal to me. Bit dry."

Mal let out an exasperated sigh.

"But uh... you meant with the stabbin' you in the back, right?" Jayne couldn't bring himself to look Mal in the face.

After the last time Jayne had done something like this, Mal had almost shot him out of the airlock. Jayne had reckoned selling out the Tams would earn him a mighty reward—their heads were worth a pretty penny, not to mention that he didn't much care for either of them. As it turned out, Jayne's opinion of them didn't matter much when Mal counted them as crew. He hadn't anticipated Mal's anger to be so fierce, but the real surprise of it all had been how much Jayne had cared.

Belonging wasn't something Jayne had ever been good at. He hadn't much seen the point in it when he never stayed put for long. The last time Jayne had felt at home was back on Sycorax with his family, but by the time he'd reached adulthood, he'd felt a mite too antsy to stay put. From there, he'd gone through partners and crews like his machine gun, Lux, went through bullets. He stayed as long as it was lucrative, then left when it wasn't. He'd never felt the need to linger overlong.

The minute Mal's staticky voice had started yelling at him over the comm through the cargo-bay doors, Jayne had realized *Serenity* was different. No one had cared enough over the years to scold him like that, not since his ma. It was rotten to be on the receiving end of Mal's wrath, but the longer Jayne sat with it, the better it felt. Because it didn't just mean Mal was mad at him, it meant he saw something in Jayne worth keeping him around for, even after what he'd done.

Jayne knew he was out of chances. But he couldn't just let Mal leave him on Brome, partly because nobody ever came to Brome, so he'd be stuck there for ages, but mostly because he couldn't let go without a fight.

"I'm sorry, Mal, I just—"

"It was quick thinking, takin' his ammo. Quicker thinkin' than I tend to give you credit for." Mal tucked his chin in a half-nod of appreciation. "You were in a tricky spot, I know. Didn't leave you much choice but to weigh your options."

"I didn't do much weighing'," Jayne said with a shake of his head, ready to defend himself, but Mal didn't give him a chance.

"Don't sell yourself short, Jayne. That head of yours ain't as empty as it looks." Before Jayne could figure out if that was an insult or not, Mal clapped him on the shoulder and said, "What'd he offer you, then? Couldn't have been good, else you wouldn't have turned on him, right?"

Jayne shied away from the touch instinctively. "Didn't offer me nothin'."

Mal surveyed him with a sharp look. "I don't believe that for a minute. Come on. What was it? Money not good enough?"

Jayne swallowed, locking eyes with Mal. It wasn't the quality of Horne's offer that had prompted his decision but the quality of what he'd be leaving behind. Horne had offered him more cash than he'd seen in a while, and at a reliable rate, but Jayne knew there were things in this world more valuable than coin. It was stupid of him, probably, turning down an offer that good—but maybe he had to be a little stupid if he wanted to be a little good.

"Wasn't what I wanted," Jayne said at last. "Besides, I got something better." From the depths of his pockets, Jayne withdrew a grenade just like the one Horne had set off.

"I don't know why I expected anything else," Mal said. "Help yourself to the rest of his collection. He won't be needing it." He gave Jayne an affectionate shove with his shoulder before walking away toward the others. Then he paused and called behind him, "Good work today, Jayne."

Jayne would never tell Mal, but there was nothing in Horne's collection worth so much to him as those words. Still, all those guns were worth something, so he tossed the grenade, catching it in his other hand and pocketing it, before heading back inside to loot the place proper.

42

They partied long into the night. Kaylee hadn't seen a celebration like this since they'd run those bandits off on Triumph and the settlers had foisted a wife on Mal. None of them were getting married tonight, though. At least, not with the quality of the beverages.

"It tastes like if Mother Nature burped in your mouth," said Wash, sticking his tongue out in disgust.

Zoë raised her eyebrows silently.

"What?" Wash emptied the liquid in a patch of nearby bromegrass. "Don't tell me you like it."

"Just reckoning with the fact that my husband has a more intimate relationship with Mother Nature than I thought."

"Is intimate the word we'd use?" Wash said, furrowing his brow, but Zoë just collected him in her arms with laughter on her lips as she kissed him.

Kaylee grinned. This was the part she liked best—not watching other people get kissed, but the feeling of her family around her, relaxing into the sweet embrace of victory. She turned away from the happy couple, swinging her legs over the side of the tavern porch, and took a triumphant swig from her drink. She regretted it immediately and gagged.

"Grass as an ingredient really leaves something to be desired, doesn't it?"

She spun around to see the source of the question was Simon. He looked a mite peaky but otherwise as normal as a person could be, standing there with one hand behind his back as if he was about to bow.

"I've tasted worse. Probably." Despite the filmy residue on her tongue, Kaylee flashed him a smile. "You feeling better?"

"I *was*…" Simon indicated her mug as he sat beside her.

"Oh, come on. Can't let a little thing like a bad drink spoil things." She elbowed him lightly in the ribs, the touch sending an electric zing up her arm.

Simon, who was usually all worry and coiled tension, looked at her with a quiet warmth in his gaze. "You are always so…" His voice trailed off, but he didn't look away.

"Yeah? What am I always?" Kaylee asked, trying not to sound too eager.

"Bright," Simon said finally. "Even when things are at their worst, when it seems like things can't get better, you find a way to hope despite it all. And look at all this—you were right."

"Course I was right, silly!" Kaylee tried to prod him with her elbow again, but he was sitting too far away. She leaned onto her thigh and shifted a little closer. "You make it sound like things were so dire, but we've been through worse, you know."

"I…" Simon cocked his head. "And you're right again. I suppose it's been difficult to get my bearings. It's just that it seems like every time we land, something goes wrong, and I'm waiting for things to feel, well, stable."

Kaylee almost laughed at him, but she swallowed the sound. It wouldn't be fair to make light of it. Not now. "You've been through so much—you and River both. Sometimes I forget that just cause I've been through plenty myself, don't mean everyone's used to that sort of life."

"What sort of life? The one where the captain keeps steering us directly into trouble?"

"That's the one." Kaylee sighed and put her hand on Simon's shoulder. "The thing you gotta know about the captain is even if he's got a clear sky, he's always gonna head for the clouds."

"Of course he is." Simon rolled his eyes. "Can't let anyone have a break, can he?"

"It's not like that. It's just he knows there's folks he can help out there, and most of 'em ain't where the sun's shining. Maybe it's not on purpose or nothin', but… you've been on *Serenity* long enough to know what sort of man he is."

"A masochistic lunatic, that's what." Simon sighed, leaning ever so slightly into Kaylee's touch. "Guess it's good he's got you around. No matter how dark things get, you're still shiny."

Warmth spread through Kaylee's arms and legs all the way to her toes. She tilted her chin. It would be a perfect moment for a kiss.

Of course, perfect moments didn't exist. Not this far out in the black, anyhow.

"Where's River?" she asked.

"With her flock." Simon turned his head toward a tall patch of grass. "Odd how she changed her mind about them so quickly."

Where there'd been warmth a moment ago, a chill raced down Kaylee's spine. She'd seen River change before, quick and striking. Three men dead in seconds. *No power in the 'verse can stop me.* Like it was all a game. Except it wasn't a game.

"Almost like she's a different girl, don't you think?" Kaylee tucked her hair back behind her ear for cover as she gave Simon a sidelong glance, looking for any sign that he saw what she did in his sister.

It wasn't there.

Simon just shrugged. "River is River, no matter what. Besides, it all worked out in the end. She really loves those geese."

"Too bad she has to leave 'em behind."

Simon whipped around to look at her. "What?"

Kaylee fixed him with an acerbic stare. "Geese? On *Serenity*? You can't expect the captain to let her keep 'em. You should've seen what they did to the engine. I'm a good mechanic, Simon, but even I can't keep up with their damage."

"She's not going to take that well, is she?" Simon's eyes looked almost haunted.

"Sure am glad I won't be breakin' the news to her."

"Seriously." There was a pause, a palpable silence in which their words sat thick in the air, before Simon said, "Oh. I suppose *I'm* the one who'll have to tell her."

"You suppose right." Mal's voice came from behind them, making them both jump.

"Captain!" Kaylee twisted around to smile up at him. "You finally made it to the party."

"Ain't no time for parties, little Kaylee. There's work to be done."

"Already? Can't we just..." Simon cast a dubious glance at Kaylee.

She tried to tell him with her eyes that whatever he had in mind, she was in, but he didn't finish his sentence.

"There somethin' wrong with *Serenity*?" she asked after a moment, worry lacing her tone. She'd just finished getting the ship spruced up, but maybe she'd missed something.

"Only that she's still one shuttle short," Mal said curtly. "Wash's scan finally got us a location. Seems the Governess retreated to her compound."

"She's gone home to roost!" Wash shouted from the far side of the porch, where he sat precariously on Zoë's lap. "Just like a goose!"

"That's chickens, honey. Think you've got your birds mixed up," Zoë said.

Mal ignored them both. "Shepherd's volunteered to help me recover it, so we'll take the other shuttle. See if we can't get the drop on her."

"What do you need me for, then?" Kaylee asked, wishing she didn't sound so desperate to be let off the hook. It was just that she and Simon didn't often get the chance to be just the two of them without their respective responsibilities ruining things. But right now, River was occupied, the ship was tidied, and they had unlimited drinks—albeit terrible ones. Couldn't Mal let her have just this one night?

"The good folks of Brome gifted us with a full tank of fuel for *Serenity* as thanks," Mal said. "I want her ready to go by the time we get back."

"Oh… right." Kaylee started to get up, slowly dragging her limbs from the overhang.

"Could be a while, though," Mal said, a smirk flashing across his face so fast she almost missed it. "Might put up a fight." He said it like he hoped she would.

Kaylee didn't usually wish for violence, but part of her was hoping so, too. "You got it, Captain." She gave him a clumsy salute. Then he was gone, into the distance.

She and Simon sat in silence for a while, conversation settling into what was more than a lull.

Eventually, Kaylee sighed and dragged her feet up. "Better get started fuelin' up the ole girl."

"Wait," Simon said, and reached out, fingers closing around her wrist. "I, uh… I got you something."

"Huh?"

Kaylee's eyes shot straight to the place where Simon touched her. Following her gaze, he loosened his grip immediately, fingers nervously twitching away. Kaylee wanted to reach for him, grab his hand and never let go, but Simon was more than a bit like the geese sometimes—he scared easy. Instead, she extended her pinky finger, allowing it graze across the arcing line of his palm. His thumb came down to press lightly against her knuckles. They held their breath as one.

"What… what is it?" Kaylee asked eventually, the words like oil on her tongue, slippery and strange. It was like she'd forgotten what words were, like her lips weren't really for talking anymore.

"Here." Simon reached behind him and held out a wide-brimmed hat made of carefully woven dried grass like the ones they'd seen at the market. "I thought… it would go nicely with your hair."

He let go of her hand, reaching up to brush her hair back before lowering the hat onto her head.

"I was right," he said with a smile.

Kaylee flushed. Maybe perfect moments *could* happen after all.

43

They left for the Governess's compound to the sounds of revelry. Book had gone many years without, between the first and second deaths of Lyle Horne. Laughter had been a rarity during the war, and it had taken him some time to retrain his muscles to the task.

"You befuddle me, Captain," he said once the sounds of the party had waned and silence had reclaimed the small space of the spare shuttle.

Mal sat in the pilot's seat, eyes on the horizon. "Why's that, preacher? Cause I don't have a taste for celebration?"

"That's not what I had in mind, but yes. I find it curious how little a man like you takes time to unwind."

"Prefer to stay wound, if it's all the same to you," said Mal. His fingers danced across the flight console, flicking a switch and pressing a button, before he turned to face Book, his expression unreadable. "Someone's got to."

Book narrowed his eyes and cocked his head. "I once thought that way myself, but no good can come from neglecting to rest."

"The crew needs to rest. I don't." Mal stood and crossed the short distance of the shuttle, his hands restlessly finding their way to his pockets. "Or I can't. Learned that the hard way. Always gotta stay on your toes in this way of life." He heaved a sigh. "War changes you, Shepherd. I don't expect you to understand."

Book did. More than Mal would ever know.

"Well, what I meant to say was, your decision surprised me. Before, with Lyle." The name passed over Book's tongue with neither bumps nor bruises. In times past, it had hurt just to think the name Lyle Horne. Now, he said it with ease. Somehow that was all the more painful.

Mal shrugged, still facing away. "Didn't think you had it in you, bein' a preacher and all," he said. "Killin' ain't your sort of business. Thought I'd take the burden off your hands."

"He may have died by your hand, but I still take responsibility. At least in part." Book bent his head in a silent prayer, for forgiveness—for Mal's actions, for his own thoughts. Killing was not his business, but it used to be, and Book had not forgotten the penance he would forever owe for the lives he'd taken. "But it's not that which surprised me."

"You callin' me predictable, Shepherd?" Mal turned around at last, a coy grin on his lips.

"Not in the slightest." Book returned the smile. "I just thought you'd take his offer."

"What offer is that?"

"The one where he promised to tell you of my history."

"Not much of an offer," Mal said flatly.

Book peered sidelong at him. It wasn't the response he'd expected. "I thought you were curious about me, about my past."

"Oh, don't get me wrong, Shepherd." Mal took a step forward, then another, closing the distance between them. "I'm gonna want that story. The whole thing. Every gory detail."

Book stepped back involuntarily as Mal's imposing stature grew more threatening.

"I've been a captain longer than I was a sergeant, you know. But there's one thing that's stayed true no matter what."

"What's that?" Book asked warily.

"Trust." Mal's gaze turned stony, as though he wore some kind of internal armor against memories of war. "Without it, you've got a bunch of folks with guns and a grudge. With it, you've got yourself a crew."

Book had been afraid of this, ever since he'd seen Lyle's face—weathered and wrinkled by time. There was a part of him that knew then that the jig was up. Mal would demand the truth from him, and Book would have to decide if staying aboard *Serenity* was worth it.

"I trust you," Mal said, each word enunciated with clarity.

They were the words Book most needed to hear, words that came with such heavy history. Mal couldn't have known the meaning they held for Book. He'd said those words so many times. Lyle had asked it of him again and again and again, never once reciprocating. But here was Mal, standing before him with this immeasurable gift: trust.

"Yes, I'm curious. More than curious." Mal pushed past Book and hit a couple of the controls on the console, beginning their descent. "But I don't want anyone spillin' the beans on what I'm sure is a thrilling tale other than you."

"I don't know what to say," Book began. It was a courtesy he hadn't expected. He'd decided long ago to hold on to his stories, to keep them between himself and God. He did not expect many to honor that choice. And maybe Mal wouldn't understand it, but he'd just told Book he would respect it all the same. "Thank you."

The shuttle landed and the door opened with a hiss of released pressure. Mal led the way out, hand on his holster. The other shuttle stood stark against the night, glittering silver under the light of Mal's headlamp, only a dozen or so yards from the white walls of the Governess's compound.

"Well, that was easy," Mal remarked, hand easing off his gun. "Thought recoverin' the shuttle would require more violence."

"Not so fast." Book squinted in the low light. "Angle the light back toward the entrance."

Mal complied, casting a bright beam toward the door of the shuttle.

"No footprints," Book said, pointing, then indicated a large skid mark in the dirt. "Looks like someone may have had a rough landing."

Mal's fingers returned to the grip of his pistol. "She's still inside."

Book nodded gravely.

Mal took careful, quiet steps—the tread of a soldier—up to the shuttle door, unfastening his holster as he went. With quick fingers, he keyed in the passcode, but Book put a hand on his wrist before he could finish.

"We are not the hands of justice," Book said in a hushed tone.

"Didn't see you complainin' when I sent your old friend down that cliff."

"Still, I would ask that you show mercy." Book shrugged. It wasn't that he'd *wanted* Mal to kill Lyle so much as he'd wanted Lyle to stay quiet—an uncomfortable wish, if he examined it too deeply. He would leave contemplating that for a later time when he had time for prayer. "Or if not mercy, perhaps allow God—or karma, if you prefer—to dole out punishment."

Mal rolled his eyes. "Just when I think we're beginning to see eye to eye, you get on that high horse of yours."

"No horses, Captain. Just a hope that we may not need to lead with violence."

Mal stared at him for a beat before hitting the door control.

There was another hiss of releasing pressure, followed by something louder, something stranger. A loud honk followed by another preceded two geese waddling out the door. As they passed, Book thought he spotted a dark stain on one of their beaks. Oil, perhaps. Or blood.

Book exchanged a wary glance with Mal before following him into the shuttle. A light flickered on overhead, revealing Inara's shuttle in disarray. Feathers and goose droppings littered the floor, and a few of the dark wall hangings were torn. Somewhere in the recesses of Book's mind, he recalled seeing only half a dozen geese with River earlier. So, the others had seen fit to take a nap in Inara's shuttle. How distressing it must have been for them to have it commandeered by the Governess.

The woman in question was curled into the fetal position on the bed, her head in her arms. She had shallow wounds up and down her forearms and a jagged tear in her skirt.

"Well, there's that karma you were talkin' about," Mal said with a sigh. He crossed the room so the Governess was between them, then said, "Get up."

The Governess just groaned into her hands.

"I ain't kiddin' around." Mal reached for his gun.

"Perhaps we can help her back to her compound," Book said. "I'm not terribly sure she can walk."

Mal gave him a perplexed look. "You do that, Shepherd. But I ain't about to occupy my gun arm with anything till those walls are between us and her."

Book complied, stepping forward to pry the Governess's arms away from her body gingerly. "There, there," he said. "You're all right."

The Governess looked far from all right, at least in her eyes, which were wide with shock. Mal was being overly cautious; she'd have to be an excellent actress to be faking this sort of distress. But then again, she'd fooled them with her act before. Book eased her forward, bracing her with his arm.

When they reached the walls, the Governess finally spoke in a small voice, sounding not at all like the imposing woman they'd met before. "What am I meant to do?" she asked. "There are no good doctors this far out."

Mal clapped her on the back, perhaps harder than was strictly necessary. "Come on, Governess," he said. "Your wounds are superficial. Splash a little alcohol on 'em and slap on a bandage like the rest of us." Then he reached for her wrist and pressed the underside of her bracelet like she'd done before. The shields came down and the gate opened.

The Governess stood there for a moment, quiet and still, then took a hesitant step forward, staggering down the path alone.

But not for long.

Two geese followed behind, quietly slipping into the shadows of her gigantic, empty estate.

"Wipe that smug look off of your face," Mal said as the gate closed behind her.

Book clasped his hands behind his back. "I don't know what you're talking about."

"The geese? The karma?"

"All part of God's plan."

"You mean to tell me God's a pair of geese, Shepherd?"

Mal glanced at him sardonically as they slowed, closing in on the shuttles. It had been a long time since Book had flown one himself, but muscle memory was a powerful thing. Book's hand closed around the door frame of the spare shuttle, but he glanced over his shoulder at Mal, who headed toward Inara's, a smile tugging at the corner of his lips as he said, "We're all God's creatures, Captain. Even them."

44

Serenity at sunrise was a sight for sore eyes. As Mal circled the shuttle around, he leaned over the flight console to prepare the landing sequence. It was second nature to him after all these years, but he still wasn't used to flying alone.

Inara's shuttle felt empty without her. She'd only been renting it from him for a short time, but no matter that *Serenity* was his ship, Mal felt out of place among all her pretty things. He wasn't sure what it said about him that the goose droppings made him feel just a smidge more at home.

"Welcome back, Captain," said Wash, his voice crackly over the comm.

"Good mornin'." Mal hit the switch that transferred steering control to the shuttle's docking systems.

"Would be a better morning if we weren't awake yet, if you don't mind me saying so," Wash said.

"I do mind, as a matter of fact." Mal got to his feet as the shuttle made contact. "Preacher should be comin' in behind me, then get *Serenity* ready for takeoff. Don't want to stay on this moon any longer than we have to."

Wash didn't respond, presumably because he was guiding

Shepherd Book through the docking process, so Mal stretched his hands above his head and yawned as he made his way to the door. He was sorely in need of a nap, but he wouldn't indulge until they were firmly out of atmo. He wouldn't feel right again until they were surrounded by stars and the dark expanse of space.

With a sigh, Mal leaned on the door frame. It would be good to be back on *Serenity*, good to take flight once again. As the familiar rush of pressure releasing filled his ears, the door slid open, putting him face to face with Inara.

"Ah!" Mal leapt back, startled by how close she'd been.

"Good morning to you as well," she said, stepping forward.

Mal, thinking as quickly as his exhausted brain would let him, looped his arm through hers and spun her in a slow promenade back toward the exit. "No need to go in there just yet." The feathers alone would be enough to justify discounting her rent, not to mention the goose droppings and the Governess's blood on her pretty tapestries.

"It's my shuttle, Mal." Inara's eyes narrowed as she peered at him suspiciously. "What did you do?"

"Me? What did *I* do? Not a thing."

It was no use. She pushed past him, knocking him into the door frame. Physically, he might have fought her off and won, but emotionally he wasn't prepared to deal with the ramifications.

"It's a mess!" Inara's voice went high, then hard. "It's in a shambles!"

"Just needs a good scrub, is all," Mal said. "Bit of tidying."

Inara swept across the room, pulling wall hangings down and balling them up at the foot of the bed. She held up a blood-stained blanket with the tips of her fingers, her nose wrinkling in disgust. "Did you kill someone in my shuttle, Mal?"

"Nah, Shepherd saw that I didn't. Mercy-minded, that one."

Inara dropped the blanket and marched up to Mal, sticking

her finger directly into his sternum. "I cannot believe I let you—"

"Let me what? You're the one who let your shuttle get snatched from under your watchful eye."

They were nose to nose. Mal was suddenly very aware he hadn't brushed his teeth in quite some time.

"If you're implying that this was somehow my fault..." Inara spoke through tight lips, her gaze dangerous.

Mal put his hands up in surrender. "Ain't nobody's fault but the geese."

Inara lowered herself back onto her heels and took a small step back. "I'll expect my rental rate to reflect the damages caused by your line of work."

"You expect it, do you?" Mal knew he should walk away, but he couldn't help himself. He never could with her. "What about the damages caused by *your* line of work?"

Inara reached up toward Mal, her finger lifting his chin ever so slightly. Mal's heart did what it always did when Inara was too close: it tightened painfully and threatened to beat right out of his chest.

"What happens between me and my clients in my shuttle is none of your concern," she said in a low murmur, so quietly he had to bend his head to hear. "But if there are any damages at all, they are performed safely and with consent." And she yanked, pulling down the final tapestry behind him.

"Mal?" Jayne's voice carried up from the cargo bay.

Only too eager to take the opportunity for escape, Mal jabbed a thumb over his shoulder. "Duty calls."

He slipped away as Inara turned back toward the dropping-strewn room and said, "Duty, indeed."

If Mal thought he was leaving for greener pastures, he was dead wrong. Below him in the cargo bay, Simon stood between Jayne and River, that latter of whom was still surrounded by a small flock of geese. Around them, some of the locals were hauling extra barrels of fuel up the ramp and into the bay. Dina, who'd sustained an injury during the protest, sat atop a crate, directing them like a terribly smug conductor.

"Mal, tell 'em the geese ain't welcome." Jayne was a big man, but in that moment, he seemed nothing but a boy, crying for his mama.

"Don't take too kindly to being told what to on my own gorram ship, Jayne." Mal took to the stairs all the same. The last thing he needed was another goose-related incident.

"I ain't flyin' with 'em, Mal. You can't make me."

Mal slowed as he reached the cargo bay and crossed his arms. "You try givin' orders on my boat again and we'll see exactly what I can make you do."

Jayne turned and stomped toward the crew's quarters, dropping a steady stream of profanity as he went.

"I, uh…" Simon began, looking from Jayne's retreating back to Mal. "I'm not so sure the geese are a good idea."

"Me neither. Much as I love to see Jayne have a hissy fit, they ain't suited for travel." Mal eyed the geese, who pecked unconcernedly at the remnants of bromegrass on the floor, then glanced out of the open cargo-bay door. Sunlight filtered in through a heavy curtain of bromegrass, swaying unnaturally in the breezeless morning. "Seems to me they like what Brome has to offer well enough. Might be we leave 'em with the fine folks here." He raised his voice slightly, eyeing the patch of grass outside. "If only there was someone on Brome with the right knowhow and leadership skills to take over their care."

There was a flash of movement from outside as four small figures stumbled out from the grass. Just as Mal suspected, it was the young captain Agate and her cohort.

"We can do it!" shouted Lenny. "We love animals, 'specially Bo." He pointed to the youngest, who'd yet to say a single word in all the time Mal had known them.

Agate smacked Lenny hard on the arm and straightened up. "We'll be commandeering your poultry. You hand them over real slow, now. No funny business."

Mal suppressed a smile. "Well, you got me there. Suppose it's best not to fight you on that. What do you say, River?"

River frowned mightily at him.

"They'll be happier here, River," Simon cooed. "They like the grass and the sun. They'd be miserable staying on the ship."

The girl sighed, her shoulders slumping as she pouted, but then she glanced at the geese as if silently conferring with them, and nodded. She walked them to the edge of the cargo bay in silence, watching them go as they slipped back into the tall grass with Agate and the others. Their adult counterparts weren't far behind, leaving with jolly waves and smiles at the crew.

"All right?" Mal asked when River returned.

River's head bobbed, looking not unlike a goose herself, and said, "Better this way. Now we can all stretch our wings and fly."

Simon coaxed her away toward the guest rooms, leaving Mal with a dreamy-eyed Kaylee wearing a wide-brimmed hat made of straw. She sat atop a metal crate and chewed a long piece of bromegrass as she regarded him.

"You softie," she said.

Mal clutched a hand to his heart. "Kaywinnet Lee Frye, what did I do to deserve that?"

Kaylee giggled. "Don't you think it's funny how you send Jayne to the doghouse over tellin' you what to do, then turn around and ask River her permission?"

"Don't think it's funny at all," Mal said as he watched River go. "Only one of 'em scares me, and it ain't the one with all the grenades."

Kaylee nodded sagely and hopped down from the crate. "We ready for takeoff?"

"Just as soon as you get her closed up."

As the cargo-bay door clicked shut and Kaylee took off toward the engine room, Mal wound his way through the ship. It was oddly quiet for a full house, but he liked it that way. His fingers trailed along the cool metal of the ship's interior, tracing familiar patterns in her halls. It was good to be home.

"There he is," Zoë said as he stepped onto the bridge. She stood beside her husband, who was sitting in the pilot's seat, arranging his toy dinosaurs in order from smallest to largest. "Everyone safe and sound?"

"As much as ever. Governess got banged up by the geese, though."

Zoë grimaced. "Can't say I'm sorry to hear that."

"Made a real mess of Inara's shuttle, too, so don't bring it up it around her."

"Noted, sir."

Mal put a hand on Wash's shoulder. "Why don't you two get some rest? I'll take it from here."

Wash turned to look at him with exhaustion-rimmed eyes. "You sure about that? I can get her into atmo first, set up autopilot."

"I flew her just fine before you got here, Wash. I think I can handle takeoff."

Wash shrugged and relinquished the chair.

"Come on, you. Bedtime," Zoë murmured. She took Wash's hand and led him away. Her soft, reassuring tone drifted back as they made their way toward their bunk: "Oh, honey, I'm sure the captain didn't mean it. You fly much better than him."

Suppressing a chuckle, Mal turned his attention to the central console. He flicked three switches and let the whir of the engine fill his ears as *Serenity* lifted off the ground. It was exhilarating, the moment they went from standing still to flying. It was unlike anything else in the 'verse, and Mal didn't think he'd ever get tired of it. He had everything he needed out in the black, right here on *Serenity*. He had a crew he trusted, a ship he loved, and the wide expanse of the 'verse at his fingertips.

As they broke atmo, Mal changed *Serenity*'s protocols over to autopilot, keying in a destination in the Georgia system, where there was a black market off the beaten path that he knew Arvin Helios frequented. He'd pay the man a visit, and maybe a bit more if he was feeling vengeful. This was all his fault, after all. But even the thought of Arvin Helios couldn't spoil Mal's mood.

With a sleepy yawn, Mal put his feet up on the dash and leaned back to look at the stars and bask in the peaceful quiet of his ship. He pictured in his mind's eye the whole of *Serenity* and his crew making a home there. Wash and Zoë, so full of a love they would not have found without her. Jayne, likely sulking on his lonesome as he cleaned and categorized his new weaponry. Kaylee on the opposite end of the ship, being lulled to sleep by the sound of the engine. Simon and River, as strange as they were essential, a pair who'd found refuge where they'd thought none existed. Shepherd Book, the unlikeliest of allies Mal could have imagined. And Inara, one he only dared to think of in the dark quiet of moments like this one. It all felt as warm as a mug of hot cider by the fire, wrapped up in worn flannel, cozy and familiar. Mal relaxed into the feeling, relinquishing the last hold he had on wakefulness.

From somewhere in the bowels of *Serenity* came the unmistakable sound of a distressed, lonesome honk.

ACKNOWLEDGEMENTS

In early March of 2023 in the elevator at Emerald City Comic Con, I said: "I would love to write a *Firefly* novel." Exactly 12 hours later, I got an email with the opportunity to do just that. To say this has been a dream come true would be an understatement. *Firefly* was the show that started it all for me. It made me love sci fi, it opened me up to the fandom experience, and it taught me how to mourn a beautiful story cut short by circumstances. To pen an adventure for *Serenity* and its crew has been an honor and a pleasure.

Enormous thanks to the team that made this happen: Saba Sulaiman, my wonderful agent whose all-caps level excitement for this project almost eclipsed my own; Fenton Coulthurst, my editor who did not once balk at my excessive use of avian puns; Daquan Cadogan, who welcomed me to the project and remained a steady support throughout; Hannah Scudamore, Charlotte Kelly, and Katharine Carroll, my publicity and marketing team who have boundless patience; Natasha MacKenzie, cover designer extraordinaire; typesetter Charlie Mann; and proofreader Cat Camacho.

No acknowledgements for this book could be complete without a shout out to M.K. England, author of *Firefly: What Makes Us Mighty*. They have been the most steadfast friend and colleague throughout the writing of this book, and they were the first audience for most of the jokes that made it to the page. Their advice as a veteran writer for *Firefly* has been invaluable, and their friendship and camaraderie a true balm to the soul in this industry.

I would also like to thank Michelle Mohrweis, RoAnna Sylver, Kat Hillis, Linsey Miller, Maya Gittelman, Rebecca Kim Wells, Eric Smith, Becca Podos, and Jen DeLuca who have all supported the writing of this book in countless ways. I feel lucky to be in a community with you.

Gratitude to Juliet Kiester—you brought this show and its fandom into my life, for which I am forever grateful. I hope it finds you, wherever you are these days. And to the other Browncoats who've filled my life with joy over the years: Amelia Burke-Holt, Faye Jones, Claire Murphy, Amy Snodgrass, and everyone else who tolerated my fandom shenanigans back in the day. Who knew eventually I'd get paid for it?

Thanks to my family: Mom and Dad, who put up with years of out-of-context quotes in my teenage years and rarely complained, and made it possible for me to do my dream job now; Colleen who has lived through the writing of this book with me and still manages to be unyieldingly enthusiastic about it; Jane (the cat they call Jane) who has suffered greatly for my art and Petra who has never suffered in her life; Captain KP Hob who joined our little crew smack dab in the middle of it all; and Tess, whose last days were spent at my side while I wrote this book—I will love and miss you always.

Lastly, to all the Browncoats out there still breathing life into the 'verse: it's been over twenty years, and we're still flying. It's not much, but it's enough.

ABOUT THE AUTHOR

Rosiee Thor began her career as a storyteller by demanding to tell her mother bedtime stories instead of the other way around. She spent her childhood reading by flashlight in the closet until she came out as queer. She lives in Oregon and is the author of Young Adult novels *Tarnished Are The Stars* and *Fire Becomes Her*, and the picture book *The Meaning of Pride*. Follow her online at rosieethor.com and on X @RosieeThor.